Paradise Earth

Paradise Earth

Amy Barker

Stormbird Press

Stormbird Press is an imprint
of Wild Migration Limited.

PO Box 73, Parndana, South Australia.
www.stormbirdpress.com

Cover Júlia Both
Typeset by Stormbird Press and Deepak Gupta
with Antique Olive and Kazimir.

National Library of Australia and State Library of South Australia
Legal Deposit

Barker, Amy, 1978–Author
Paradise Earth
ISBN- 978-1-925856-21-7 (hbk)
ISBN- 978-1-925856-22-4 (pbk)
ISBN- 978-1-925856-23-1 (ebk)

This project has been assisted by the Australian Government through the Australia Council, its arts funding and advisory body.

The publishing industry pulps millions of books every year when new titles fail to meet inflated sales projections—ploys designed to saturate the market, crowding out other books.

This unacceptable practice creates tragic levels of waste. Paper degrading in landfill releases methane—a greenhouse gas emission 23 times more potent than carbon dioxide.

Stormbird Press prints our books 'on demand', and from sustainable forestry sources, to conserve Earth's precious, finite resources.

We believe every printed book should find a home that treasures it.

In memory of my father, Glenn Barker,
and Rebekah Barker, 'a special mother'.

This book is dedicated to the residents of
Tasman Peninsula, both past and present.

Evil is unspectacular and always human,
And shares our bed and eats at our own table,
And we are introduced to Goodness every day,
Even in drawing-rooms among a crowd of faults.

—W.H. Auden, "Herman Melville".

Chapter 1
Ruth

For the Term of His Natural Life remains, to this day, Seamus's favourite novel. That it was inspired by the true story of a cannibal killer convict from Northern Ireland is a strange source of pride for him. 'Sent to Australia, never to be seen again!' he declares whenever the chance arises. In his imagination, transportation to a penal colony was a fate worse than death. In reality, though, there was an afterlife, a hell in paradise: Port Arthur.

The discovery that the Historic Site is located on the same peninsula as an international residency program—offering gifted and talented artists such as himself time and space to work within a unique geographic setting away from the humdrum of everyday life—was all the motivation Seamus needed to formulate a rationale for his visit. So the fact that Ruth grew up here is not even the attraction, although convenience dictates that she be his local guide. The striking natural rock formations of the southeast corner of Tasmania have inspired his new painting series about psychic projection of trauma on landscape and drawn him to Tasman Peninsula.

Arriving late, they have seen only highlights of the

hundred acre site but no ruin can eclipse the convict church. Built on high unconsecrated ground, its outer walls and lesser spires alone remain, the fifty-foot-high belfry spire long gone, no roof over the heads of one thousand restless souls. In the flogging yard where a convict could receive up to one hundred lashes with the cat o' nine tails, leaving *their back like bullocks' liver and shoes full of blood,* Seamus reminded everyone within earshot, 'Fecking hell, even the Romans only scourged Christ thirty-nine times'. They have missed out on a cruise around Mason Cove, which would have taken them up close to the Boys' Prison, Point Puer, and the Isle of the Dead, the convict cemetery flung out in the sea like the penal colony's ectopic organ.

First, a shadow falls over Ruth, and then she feels Seamus's weight on the opposite end of the wooden bench on which she sits. Without turning her face to him, she points across the water of the Cove where at the base of a grassy hill stand the iconic ruins of the Penitentiary that once housed five hundred men. From the outside, the original structure is still discernible, its lime wash layers visible as mottled ochre over its underfired red bricks. As well as various modern conservation efforts, the building fabric of the four-storey, sixteen-bay granary and flour mill has been commingled with that of the penitentiary conversion, which saw the top level of windows bricked in and metal bars added to the rest.

"I remember coming here on school excursions," Ruth tells him. "We'd run around those ruins pretending we were convicts, stand with our backs pressed against the crumbling walls, stretching our arms up above our heads as if our hands were in shackles. We let our heads flop to the side and poked out our tongues, like it was all some big joke. No respect at all for the suffering that transformed the place."

"You were kids," says Seamus, sliding across the bench towards her. "Sure, that's what kids do."

The wind blows his split ends against her earlobe and cheekbone nearest him. Though Seamus hated it, people often commented on his Christ-like appearance. Ruth sees him rather as the bushranger type with his sideburns twin silver bridges connecting the dark wavy hair that falls carelessly down his shoulders with his contrasting copper beard.

"I remember the Maze breakout in '83," he says. "At the time it was the best craic we'd ever had in Lisburn. We were all up on the wall looking for escaped IRA men."

"The wall?" Ruth unfolds her arms and takes hold of the edge of the seat either side of her tightly pressed knees. "What wall?"

"The wall outside my nan's house that overlooks the River Lagan," he replies. "Some of the IRA men took hostages in the Old Warren housing estate. We never had a chance of seeing any but that can't be explained to kids. As a child you expect uniforms with arrows on, and them all to be carrying chains with a big ball on the end. To me and my friends we didn't understand Catholic or Protestant terrorist, we were just told they were bad men."

"How did it end, the siege?"

"Most were caught," he says. "One made it to Amsterdam only to be apprehended about ten years later."

Without warning a whirlwind descends. Two young girls rush past the bench with their ponytails, identical shades of blonde, flying like comet trails behind their heads. In matching parkas—the younger girl's light blue, the older girl's red, both hoods trimmed with white faux fur—they can only be sisters. Together they stop at a small monument, a single bronze leaf perched atop a short stone pillar, just metres from where Ruth and Seamus sit. Judging from the location, this is in remembrance of the coach driver.

"Look," the girl in the red parka says, pointing it out to her little sister. "It's a leaf."

As beside her Seamus pays little attention, Ruth's heart rate escalates, so convinced is she that however unwittingly, the children are about to desecrate the memorial. The little girl, never taking her eyes from the leaf, circles the pillar once, a white feather pinched between two fingers—halts.

Leaning over the monument, she brushes the feather across the bronze leaf as gently as if it were a newborn's face. Ruth takes a deep breath and exhales. The sisters continue on their way, followed at a short distance by a woman Ruth's age, who must be their mother, and an older couple who, Ruth surmises, are the grandparents.

The girl in the blue parka chases her big sister with the feather, trying to tickle her with it.

"Mum!" the big sister screams. "Tell Carly not to touch me with the feather. They have diseases!"

"Not this one," Carly calls back, running on ahead over the bridge, towards the Penitentiary, with her feather held high in the air.

"Come on," Ruth whispers to Seamus as she rises from the bench. "Let's follow them."

Inside the Penitentiary, it becomes immediately apparent to Ruth that the ruin is infested with the past like toxic black mould. History, a living organism, releases spores that feed on its decaying matter. This colony branches out across the remnants of internal cell walls, the shelving and the bolt fixings for sack hammocks. It threads over the foul air egress vents in the rear wall and through the rubble debris piled up in corners. Its roots travel deep, right to the bloody Indigenous land beneath the foundation stones. Unsuspecting tourists risk exposure simply by breathing in the air as they access the ruin via its purpose-built walkways. When they pause in the interpretive areas to read about the past, they are unwittingly ingesting it.

"Not real big, are they?" a woman in front of Ruth remarks of the cells to her male companion.

"Can't go far when you're in chains," he replies.

Lions, Ruth recalls. The Commandant used to call the men imprisoned on the ground storey *lions* because they wore leg irons. Together, Ruth stares with the strangers into the closest cell, now just a brick cavern with moss-covered earth, two metres deep and one metre wide.

"Look at the size of them!" the woman exclaims, as the reality sets in. "God."

Shaking their heads in disbelief, the pair move on.

As Ruth climbs to the stabilised second storey, on what is more scaffolding than staircase, a child begins to scream. The sound cuts right through her. In this place, to scream is dangerous for there are too many ghosts to be woken. Within the ruins, scars left where levels were keyed into the brickwork are the only trace of absent floors in the upper storeys. When Ruth finally locates the source of the relentless sound, she is peering down at the little girl, Carly, held like a life-size doll under one of her mother's arms. With a bird's-eye view, Ruth studies her closely. Carly is having difficulty breathing, her eyes are red and watery, her nose is runny with mucus. Ruth determines, as the girl is carried out, that she is definitely suffering a reaction to the Penitentiary's *infestation*.

Outside, Ruth follows Carly who is climbing the hill, having made one of the miraculous recoveries that only a small child can. The blonde head darts like a white rabbit between the Commandant's Office and the Guard Tower, up to the Officers' Quarters and Smith O'Brien's Cottage, reserved for political prisoners. Ruth wonders where the father of the two children is. Are the parents separated? Divorced? Or, did he just choose to stay home this afternoon and watch the football? Only when Ruth comes within a few metres of the family does she realise, this woman, Carly's mother, might be a ghost. Everybody on the Peninsula knew someone involved in the massacre. Most knew several. Beyond the striking physical similarities—the natural butter-blonde hair, milky-white skin, heart-shaped face—the woman is the age her friend would be today, had she survived. These are the children, the children she might have had. A life she might have made for herself. Seventeen years was not long enough, not nearly long enough.

Ruth's old friend is buried in the small, historic Clark Cliffs cemetery, overlooking Norfolk Bay, a ten-minute drive up the road from her parents' house in Nubeena. After the massacre, those who had been involved in the tragedy or directly affected by it found themselves faced with a decision similar to the 'stay or go' predicament in a bushfire. Like Ruth's own family, after her friend's death her family chose to stay. Other locals made the decision to leave early and over the coming year moved to the mainland, or further, some severing all ties to the Peninsula.

In the aftermath, it was those who delayed making their decision until it was too late—like those who find themselves in the firestorm and at the last moment flee from their homes in their cars or on foot—who were ultimately consumed by it.

As the sun slips behind clouds and the Historic Site darkens, an autumnal gust perforates Ruth's lips and then Seamus's hand spoons the small of her back.

"We're losing the light," he warns.

From the Penitentiary, a sealed path along the waterfront leads them, on their way back to the Visitor Centre, directly past what is called simply, Memorial Garden.

At the entrance, Ruth pauses with Seamus, hands held behind their backs, palm in palm, like priests or policemen to scan the information provided. Ruth knows the details by heart. More than two decades ago a young man armed with three high-powered automatic weapons opened fire in a busy café on this very spot and then continued his shooting rampage throughout the grounds of the Historic Site. The gunman was tried and convicted of 35 counts of murder.

"These shootings you had down here happened in '96, straight after Dunblane," says Seamus. "Was this a copycat crime?"

"I don't think so," says Ruth. "I'm really not sure but I don't even remember hearing about Dunblane at the time to be honest."

"I was living in Scotland, studying at the University

of Dundee," says Seamus. "It's not something you easily forget. Those school portraits they showed on the news of the beautiful wee bairns. Even if you weren't directly affected you still felt like your heart had been ripped out. People, complete strangers, cried for days."

Ruth leaves his side.

Where the most lives were lost here, they have built a Pool of Reflection. Inscribed around the stone edges are simple words that acknowledge pain, loss and courage and ask visitors to cherish life as a way to honour the dead. Coins shine up from the bottom of the rectangle of chill, shallow water. Tourists who visit the Port Arthur Historic Site must wander in assuming it's just another ruin. Chancing upon an artificial body of water they feel the irresistible urge to wish, so take a coin from their pocket or their purse and toss it in, unaware that they are asking favours of the dead.

In one corner, a plaque of bronze leaves lies submerged and Ruth does not need to count them to know they number thirty-five—thirty-five fallen. Glancing up, she finds the cross that bears the victims' names: two beams of Huon pine, the horizontal wide and rough-hewn, the vertical cut neat as a fence post, standing in the shadow of the escarpment. At its foot lies a bouquet of white lilies wrapped in brown paper and tied with brown string, the only clue that three days ago was the anniversary of the worst mass murder in post-colonial Australian history.

Ruth interrogates her surroundings, searches for some trace—psychic, spiritual or otherwise—of the violence that occurred. Moments pass and she discovers nothing but the natural beauty of the place. The proliferation of native flora exists in defiant contrast to the manicured lawns and mature English trees that dominate the rest of the landscape. Even when a flock of Green Rosellas fly low overhead, threatening to destroy the tranquillity, their wings merely mimic the sound of rustling leaves. The past, for now at least, is a sleeping dragon.

This was not planned—to return home, to be back at the Site for the first time, so close to the anniversary. The dates of Seamus's wilderness residency were determined by Parks and Wildlife, the Arts funding body, and the Tasmanian seasons, wherein each year winter is born premature. The six weeks from the first of May until mid-June constituted the most extreme of the residencies on offer and the choice to accept was made by the lad who grew up in Northern Ireland.

Seamus's hand falling upon her shoulder startles Ruth and she spins around.

"I'm concerned about ye," he says. "Standing here in a brown study."

"That book of yours," she says, thinking on her feet. "The one with all the photographs of water crystals?"

"*Memories in Water.*"

"Yes." Ruth's gaze sweeps back across the pool. "This reminds me of that."

Seamus tilts his head quizzically. The book was published by a Japanese physicist who carried out experiments on the effect of human thought and emotion on the element of water. Taping typed words to sealed jars of pure water the physicist then took samples from each and studied single frozen droplets under a microscope. Those taken from the jars that displayed 'I love you' or 'Mother Theresa' froze into unique and beautiful crystals, whilst those that were subjected to the words 'I hate you, I want to kill you' or 'Adolf Hitler' froze into amorphous ugly blobs.

"Well," says Ruth, making quick mental calculations, "the Site must get hundreds of thousands of visitors annually, millions since the memorial was opened. I just wonder what thoughts, what emotions, they've left here over the years. If we took a drop out of the pool right now to study it under a microscope, what would we see?"

"Is there something you're not telling me?" he says. "Feels like I'm missing something here. Can ye not give me a clue as to what's really on your mind?"

As Seamus is observing her, he irons out one eyebrow between thumb and fingertips. Is it possible that he senses her deeper connection to this place?

"It just reminded me of your book, that's all. It's silly, I know."

When finally Seamus raises his camera, Ruth is overcome with relief. Two words—the gunman's name, anathema to the Peninsula community—are like stones weighing down her pockets. No, she will not cast them in. Instead, focusing on the very centre of the reflecting pool, Ruth visualises a brilliant, bright hexagonal crystal forming. Within that crystal, an identical crystal forms. Crystals form exponentially, like ripples slowly spreading across the surface of the water, while the centre gradually returns to quietude.

Leaving Seamus's side for the second time, Ruth enters the adjoining structure, a bare room where four stark bluestone walls stand, with paneless windows and doorless frames, beneath the open sky. It is difficult for her to visualise the Broad Arrow Café as it once was, but then that was the point. While the building had not been razed to the ground, the bones had been defleshed to leave a smooth, clean skeleton. You were not supposed to be able to stand and picture a busy lunchtime crowd spilling out onto the verandah—some Tasmanian visitors, others from interstate or abroad—their tables laden with plates of hot food from the bain-marie at the counter, behind which locals were serving. An ordinary Sunday afternoon blown apart by a semi-automatic rifle pulled from a black sports bag.

It happened so suddenly that some died with the cutlery still in their hands.

In the far corner of the room, more flowers have been left, this time a mixed bouquet wrapped in the colourful plastic of a supermarket or convenience store. Against the bouquet rests a card. As Ruth crosses the gravel floor to see what it says, she glances over her shoulder to ensure she is alone. Inside, it reads simply, 'There but for the Grace of God ...'

The words hit too close to home. Written in cursive handwriting, the blue ink has run, the result of tears or more likely rain. Placing the card back exactly as she found it, Ruth flees the building, onto a stretch of grass that used to be the car park for coaches bringing tours to the Site.

It is a race against the setting sun to reach the Tasman National Park before dusk, not only to avoid nocturnal wildlife on the roads but to locate the bothy while there is still daylight to hike by. While Seamus insists on calling their wilderness accommodation *the bothy*, it is simply a disused warden's cabin, without electricity or hot water, at the start of the old walking track to Cape Pillar.

Driving north on the Arthur Highway they pass two victims of roadkill in quick succession. The first is an adolescent Tasmanian devil. The devils scavenge on the roads at night and their young are particularly vulnerable. In the passenger seat, Ruth becomes a vigilant lookout, scouring the roadsides ahead for the slightest movement from the bush, reminding Seamus to slow down. The second is a large male wombat lying on its back with stiff legs in the air. It is total deracination, almost biblical. The way the animal is engorged it appears that all the organs ruptured at once, leaving behind a fur bag of blood about to burst open.

Breaking his silence since leaving the Historic Site, Seamus says, "A wombat, aye? Not how I'd imagined my first encounter. Long before emigratin', I remember hearin' stories from friends who'd been backpacking in Australia 'bout waking up in their tents to find one of those creatures settled on their chest, or rummagin' through their pack searching for a bag of crisps. Ach, what a shame!"

They turn off the highway and onto a wide, corrugated gravel forestry road winding deep into the Fortescue Reserve Forest. The Eucalypts are giants who steadily regard the car as it enters at their toe roots. A passing four-wheel drive washes their Subaru Forester in dust. Such traffic, conspiring with a recent lack of rain, has silvered the roadside foliage.

Beyond a fast flowing creek they enter the Tasman National Park, arriving at Fortescue Bay Camp Ground. Seamus parks in the temporary bay and goes alone to the onsite caretaker's office, a new demountable building, to announce his arrival and collect his Parks Pass.

Leaving the car unlocked, Ruth crosses the day use area and steps out onto a dolerite outcrop between a boat ramp and the beach. Great reams of bull kelp skirt the rocks beneath her feet, glistening like wet black rubber. The water purling on the dolerite is impossibly clear and glassy. Down on the shoreline a pied-oyster catcher traverses the shifting water's edge with the precision of a tightrope walker, its beak a bright orange knitting needle, matching the colour of its eye. It is a tame bay and even with the onset of twilight the colour of the water is turquoise, the sand as white as paper. Here, the Southern Ocean shows a different side of itself. Ruth takes a deep, conscious breath and immediately feels cleansed, clear-headed.

In the distance, beyond the bay, the horizon forms a curve as sharp as one made with a drafting compass. Hidden from view, Canoe Bay lies to the northwest and Bivouac Bay northeast. All three bays flow east back out into the ocean. From Fortescue beach where she stands, the wilderness extends all the way to Cape Hauy, a five-hour return hike. Growing up, Ruth's existence was bounded by the wilderness. From a very early age she was taught it was a realm that was not her own—uncultivated, uninhabited by human beings, a place you don't go if you have no business being there. The hamlet of Stormlea, which was her home, occupied a position at—or on both sides of—a significant boundary and threshold. This is why these temporary residents of Fortescue Bay bush walk, scuba dive and kayak. Otherwise the wilderness is not only natural and free, it becomes dangerous and disordered. The untameable ferocity of this wilderness would cause you to flee in fear.

Only now, being present at the scene, does Ruth's imagination dare face the question of what really happened to the tourist who went missing at the start of the year whilst on the Three Capes Walk. Before this moment, like the majority of people who had been following the story, Ruth has been hoping for a happy ending. Or at least she's been unwilling to entertain the sinister probabilities. In the wilderness the boundary between humankind and the divine is but a membrane and if you do not remain vigilant, penetration can occur without you so much as realising it.

"The warden's got the bothy fire lit," Seamus announces, walking straight out onto the sand in his hiking boots. "Happy days!"

"Where are you going?" Ruth calls after him.

If he has heard her, he shows no sign of it.

The beach is walled in by scrub-covered dunes all the way down to the lagoon. Walking a few paces behind Seamus, Ruth observes the seawater instantly dissolve, with the artful wave of a magician's hand, the shoe prints he leaves in the sand. At Ruth's feet is an almost imperceptible flickering, the fairylike movement of land hoppers.

"What did he say, the warden?" asks Ruth, the missing tourist still on her mind.

"Say about what?"

"I don't know, about anything," she says, defensively. "Did he give instructions?"

"Aye, the official word is to boil the creek water before drinkin', but it'll not kill us. And we've to carry our firewood up from the campsite. There's a single hot shower at the Mills Creek camping ground. Takes coins, like a laundrette. And we're to live in peace with the walkers."

When they step off the beach, veering left onto the shore of the lagoon that flows out into the bay, shearing through the sand like a cleft palate, the atmosphere alters dramatically. An eerie beauty envelops them. The rippling freshwater, murky with tannins, is suggestive. On the opposite bank, a forest of white gums quiver. The scrub at Ruth's back, part of the dune system, although impenetrable has her contemplating what might emerge from it. Ruth detects something from childhood on the air here, a vibration rather than a memory, which heightens her senses, both an allure and a warning simultaneously. This pocket of the National Park is a liminal space and it is not wallabies, pademelons or echidnas you hope to see, but the fabled Tasmanian Tiger.

Turning from the lagoon back towards the Bay, she finds Seamus standing on dolerite boulders below the start of the walking track to Canoe and Bivouac Bays. The stench hits her before the sight, and without immediately realising what she is looking at, Ruth stares into the unseeing black eye of a dead Australian fur seal. Startled, she gasps and covers her face with her hands.

"The waves are not long after washing it up," says Seamus, staring intently at the carcass.

The massive size of the animal, alone, is shocking.

"Come down," says Ruth, pinching her nose.

When a death occurs close to shore, if the deceased isn't consumed by sea life it usually appears on the beach within a few days.

"Aye." Seamus jumps from the rocks. "We're away."

As he leads her by the hand back down the beach, Ruth feels the chill settle on her, bite deep in her nostrils and cling to her skull. Even in this paradise there is death and decay. Just as she feels the darkness begin to fall all around them, Seamus starts to whistle. She recognises the tune as *Stairway to Heaven* and a smile plays at the corners of her mouth—it's the wobble board version.

An anticipated hike through wilderness to reach the bothy turns out to be a short stroll on duckboards. While Seamus is underwhelmed, mumbling into their box of groceries, Ruth is thankful for small blessings as cold sweat films her calves and back beneath the weight of her rucksack.

"So when's the bonnies again?" asks Seamus.

"The what?"

"I asked ye, when is bonfire night down here?"

"Oh, it's the 26th of May," she says. "Empire Day."

"Should be great craic!" says Seamus. "We've bonfire night at home on the eve of the twelfth of July. Usually over the twelfth holidays, like most Catholic families we went across the border. We'd go camping to Donegal, or Salthill Galway or Mosney, an adventure park near Dublin. People became very polarised around that time. About a month before Protestants who would talk to you all year round turned ignorant suddenly and would shun you. One year, back in the eighties, we couldn't afford to go away. It was the height of the troubles and my ma feared being petrol bombed so she had us all in the back room and all of our spare blankets in the bath full of cold water just in case, to quell the flames, ye know? Our neighbours, the Graceys, whose son was in the RUC, they got burnt out, house gutted. I'll not ever forget the fear and confusion. The McVeighs, the Tennysons and McKays, who went to my high school, were all burnt out in one year. Anyway, it's much different now."

A corrugated iron roof of rusty tiger stripes becomes visible, peeking out from the understory of musk and Bedfordia. As they step into a small clearing they are met by the comforting scent of woodsmoke. The bothy is dwarfed by the surrounding trunks of stringybarks. Seamus can barely contain his excitement, striding up and balancing the box on his knee to pull open the door with both hands.

Inside, is a single room of whitewashed wood and grey stone. The exposed rafters overhead are strung with sooty cobwebs. To the right of the front door, within an original fireplace, a small cast iron stove is burning. A rope lined with pegs hangs just below the mantel, upon which rests an empty bottle of Jameson Irish Whiskey with the stub of a dinner candle jammed in its neck. A traditional wooden scrubbing brush takes pride of place beside it.

"We've to do something about that!" Seamus says, nodding at the whiskey bottle.

Ruth knows only too well that if you're Northern Irish your whiskey of choice must be Bushmills. Seamus crouches and opens the stove door, then sitting up close, takes off his shoes and socks.

The opposite side of the room is dominated by a sleeping area where a strange wooden box, like a coffin big enough for two, is raised just high enough off the floor to avoid draughts. In the white paint around this sleeping platform former residents have scratched their names and the dates of their stays. The bothy has been well used by artists over the past few years.

"That creek is loud!" says Ruth.

"No worse than traffic," replies Seamus. "Sure, you'll get used to it."

"Yes, but you mostly work at night, when there's not much traffic."

"That out there, that's a natural sound, meditative. The environment is s'posed to influence the art. That's the point."

"I know, I know." Ruth draws her open cardigan across her midriff.

On the far side of the room beneath a casement window stands a simple kitchen bench. Fixed on the wall beside it is a round red object the size of a large dinner plate. Ruth crosses the bare stone floor, moving around a plank table with four hard-backed chairs tucked neatly underneath, to take a closer look.

It is a *Lucky Star* brand canned pilchards clock and its fishbone-fine hands are about to tell six o'clock.

After a makeshift meal, with full stomachs and cold beers, they sit before the stove fire on their hard-backed chairs. Seamus uses a piece of firewood as a footrest and stares silently into the flames.

"A penny for your thoughts?" Ruth offers.

Shifting his gaze from the fire, he looks at her in surprise, as if until that moment he had forgotten she was sitting beside him. "Ah, I was just thinkin' of home there."

Ruth knows he doesn't mean their home on the mainland. "Me coming home has made you homesick?"

"Aye, a wee bit. Course it has."

"Will you take me to *Norn Iron*?"

"Aye, take ye home to meet my ma."

"I'm serious," she says. "I sometimes try to imagine it, where you grew up."

"Not much to it, you'll be disappointed. Not much in Lisburn. Is a market town, barracks town, backwater dump. But sure I'll bring you around."

"How far did you say it is from Belfast?"

"Eight miles, just. But in terms of things to do and state of mind, about four thousand. If you imagine the difference between Sydney and Alice Springs, it's like that." Seamus kicks his footrest aside. "Besides, now that we're here it's you who's to take me home to the old farm to meet your Johnny."

"Don't call him that to his face," she warns. "Seriously."

"Back at Port Arthur, you avoided my question."

"Question?"

"When I said I was concerned 'bout ye, I could see there was something goin' on in your head. Depressing you, was it, remembering the shootings? Nothing you felt like talkin' about?"

A noisy scratching from the other side of the door interrupts the conversation. Ruth is first to her feet.

"What's that?" hollers Seamus. "That a devil at the door?"

"If it was, you'd know about it," she says. Ruth is only too familiar with the unearthly growls of devils searching for food at night, which was nothing compared to the harsh screeching and blood-curdling screams of a group of devils fighting over a carcass.

"We have a visitor." Ruth crouches down in the doorway, staring into the bold brown eyes of a large black brushtail possum. "The last resident must have been feeding him."

Ruth is forced to block the gap in the doorway with her foot to prevent the animal coming inside. As it tries to scramble past her, its claws scratch right through her sock. Firmly, she pushes it back out and slams the door shut.

"Sure a bit of bread won't do it no harm?"

"Definitely not. No bread!" Ruth stands behind her chair, gripping the sides. "Bread is probably the worst thing you can give wildlife. It makes them sick and bloated. If you insist on feeding them, at least cut up some veggies."

"Give my head peace, wee girl!"

Ruth hasn't meant to snap at Seamus. It's just that when he said the words, 'devil at the door', it triggered a flashbulb memory of the first conversation she had with John after the shootings. When her brother told her about how the authorities had to keep watch over the bodies that could not yet be removed. All night, beneath fluorescent work lights and wearing white forensic coveralls and face masks, they patrolled to keep at bay the Tasmanian devils that might be attracted by the carnage. With a shuddering breath, Ruth raises her shoulders up to her ears and then drops them back, casts the image off as if it was a shrug she'd been wearing.

Once they retire to the sleeping platform, Seamus is snoring obnoxiously in no time. Ruth rolls him onto his side and then blows out the last candle. Knowing that the absence of light is absolute, that she cannot simply reach over to switch on a bedside lamp, that there is no possibility of instantaneous night to day, the darkness cradles her in its vast arms.

At last, she lets go.

The next morning, Ruth wakes to birdsong, and beneath it, the sound of Agnes Creek. For a moment she misperceives she is still in a city. Then reality descends. Tasman Peninsula braces her in its primeval rock. Beside her, Seamus is sleeping soundly, his snores barely audible. As she rises with the creased face and stiff body of one who has spent the night on a friend's couch, Ruth carries the aching cold in her phalanges. The pictures on the Arts Council website had shown the bothy after a heavy snow dump, thick horns of ice grown over the eaves like curled fingernails on an interned corpse. Staring through the window she sighs briefly at the sunshine before she starts to build the stove fire on top of last night's ashes. Ruth is curious about recent news despite Seamus's insistence that for the duration of the residency they simply let it go on without them, secluded in their Elysium. While Seamus sleeps in she sits at the plank table and reads. Open before her is a copy of *The Mercury* from last week, reclaimed from the woodpile. A news story causes her to groan. A Tasmanian man broke a six-month-old baby's leg after the baby kicked him in the testicles, the Supreme Court heard. In separate incidents the baby suffered a broken left femur, broken ribs and two broken tibias, a bruise to the left cheek and a haemorrhage to the left eye. In an all too familiar refrain, it was submitted that the man had endured a traumatic childhood and adolescence and was repeatedly physically abused. Less than two years earlier he had been jailed for a month for starving a dog to death in the yard of his house. Ruth can't help but pause to wonder about that baby's future. Already so damaged, so broken before it has even taken its first steps on this earth. Innocence thrown mercilessly into the most vicious of cycles like some diabolical machine, cogs interlocking and revolving, attacking its victims like rows of shark teeth. Would history repeat? It seems more than likely. The weight of it lands on her chest. Instinctively she raises her arms in support, as if it was the infant resting on her breast. Seeing her empty palms held up below her face she feels completely foolish and is glad that Seamus isn't awake to witness it.

While she reads, the sunlight lengthens. Eventually, becoming protective, Ruth rises from her chair to fetch a beach towel and standing on her tiptoes attempts to fashion a makeshift curtain across the window.

Behind her, Seamus's voice booms from the sleeping platform, "What's wrong with light?"

Startled, she drops the towel in the sink and spins around. "Nothing. I just thought you might be hungover."

"I ain't hurtin' that bad."

Without saying more he gets up and shuffles outside to the toilet.

In his absence, the hands of the Lucky Pilchard clock tick obnoxiously. To muffle the sound, Ruth begins to scrunch up pages of the newspaper and pitch them into the dying stove fire.

When Seamus comes back inside he is muttering. "Gotta, gonna shake it off. Gotta, gonna shake it off."

Ruth asks, "Everything OK?"

"Aye, I'd a disturbing dream last night."

"Really? What was it about?"

Seamus pushes the hair back from his shoulders. Ruth strikes a match and, with it pinched between her fingers, waits.

"If I tell ye," says Seamus, "ye'll think I'm mad."

"I already think you're mad." Ruth flicks the lit match

into the stove and takes a seat at the table. "Tell me."

They look at one another, forming a tacit agreement.

"Go on then," she insists.

"Ach." Seamus begins preparing tea at the bench. "I dreamed I was a second world war soldier returning home onboard a ship with all my comrades. We were having a great time celebrating getting home. As we came into the docks we realised there were only a few people there, one of them was my wife but she looked straight through me without expression."

Anticipating what is to come, Ruth's skin breaks out in goosebumps.

"There were men going 'round the docks handing out little yellow pieces of paper to everyone. I felt so angry that no one was paying attention to me that I pushed him away and threw his paper to the ground. Some others took the paper and they walked off together towards ..." Seamus stares past her and through the window.

"Towards what?"

"Jesus, it's a cliché." Again he hesitates. "A light, they walked towards a light, and as I looked away I noticed the wives and partners had gone and there was a large funeral procession taking place. It was for us. So we boarded the ship again and headed off for another war."

Ruth rubs her forearms briskly with her hands.

"So these yellow pieces of paper, what do you think they mean?" she asks. "The telegrams, the ones they sent to the families during the war, weren't they yellow?"

"Don't ask me," says Seamus. "I don't want to think about it. It's disturbed me enough."

"Don't you want to know though?" says Ruth. "We should find out."

Seamus shakes his head. "I told ye, I just want to forget 'bout it now."

Ruth watches Seamus bring the tea to the table and then she asks, "What did she look like, your wife in the dream?"

"I honestly don't know." Seamus sits down in the chair opposite her. "You know those dreams where you can't see people clearly or make out faces but yet you know who they are?"

"I think so," she says. "Like when you try to read in a dream and it's like being dyslexic?"

"Dead on, love."

Of the many small towns on Tasman Peninsula, the largest is Nubeena. Ruth's old school is still there. Closer to the wilderness, but not yet on its doorstep, is the hamlet of Highcroft. Here, Ruth and Seamus encounter the vestiges of the Peninsula's apple industry, a scattering of orchards like crumbs thrown to the birds. The sight causes an aching in her chest.

"Some of these trees are over a hundred years old," she tells Seamus, nodding from the moving car towards the pruned rows, each trunk and its branches resembling a skeleton umbrella blown inside out.

Of course, few survive to be centenarians. Bushfire is a constant threat as well as the codling moth, its little wing mirrors enclosed in deadly gold rings like the tips of hollow point bullets. It is trauma though, the wounding, mortal wounds—heart rot is the silent killer. For many, it is a slow death. A wound to the bark lets in the disease and it spreads, softening the wood inside, weakening the structure until finally the very heart decays. By the time fungus is visible, either hard leathery conks or soft mushrooms, the individual is already at high risk of breakage or fatal fall.

"Democrats they're called," says Ruth. "Those apple trees."

"Never heard of a *Democrat* apple," replies Seamus. "They still produce 'em?"

Ruth raps her knuckle on the passenger side window beside her face and whispers, "Democrats."

Leaving Highcroft, Ruth sees the first of the logging gates. No 'Keep Out' sign, just a generic warning in whitewashed steel. Throughout Stormlea, pine forests have been grafted onto the native landscape where the old wood forests have been cut down. The wage payout for planting and tending the pines in those early seasons went into the pockets of her father and other locals. While the pine forests serve a purpose, in this landscape they remain as conspicuous as the face of a burn survivor in a public place. Otherwise, the hamlet is accented in yellow; it is the colour Ruth associates with childhood. Not just the reigning daffodils, it is the hay bales piled high around farm structures, daisies dotting the paddocks while fireweed groundsel brightens the roadsides. Even the silence is golden. Raised here, Ruth had not perceived how precious it truly was, the Stormlea silence, didn't appreciate its power to settle her mind, regulate her heartbeat, and induce deep, untroubled sleep.

On the final hill before home, the rocky, single lane dirt road is profound. The eucalypts crowd in so that only dappled sunlight descends through their crowns to illuminate the way ahead. Below the road, on the left-hand side, Cripps Creek runs concealed. On the right the earth rises up forming forested hills beyond which are cleared paddocks. Finally the bracken fern begins to advance, scratching the car doors as scrub scrapes the undercarriage, forcing Seamus to drive at a snail's pace.

From the gate of Rare Bird Farm is a view of dairy cows on the hill, the farmhouse and beyond it, over a thin belt of preserved wilderness, Maingon Bay flowing out into the Tasman Sea.

Seamus turns off the engine but it continues to tick slowly as it cools. Just beyond the front fence, the name of the farm is burned into a shingle, which hangs by rusted chains from the arms of a vintage wheelbarrow. While Seamus gets out of the car and takes some shots of the sign and the farm from the road, she searches in her pack for a muesli bar. They say you shouldn't eat when stressed or anxious but since she gave up smoking food is her only remedy besides beer. Ruth flips down the sun visor to watch herself in the mirror, breathing through her nose as the snack quickly disappears into her mouth. It is a fact that she has gained an extra stone in the months since she quit and she just knows that her brother will notice. To make matters worse she is wearing double denim, a mid blue jacket and mum jeans, with a green t-shirt. *Blue and green should never be seen without a colour in between.* John had bullied her about her weight even before she reached puberty and began to develop a womanly shape. Looking back, she was never fat, only softer and with slightly more flesh on her bones than the skinny adolescent boy John was. It would have been impossible to become overweight fed on their meagre rations whilst also performing their scheduled chores. The most popular girl in her class, right the way through school, was on the plump side, but with her blonde hair and blue eyes, still the benchmark for female beauty. It wasn't until those last years of school that Ruth's unusually long, dark eyelashes drew compliments from the other girls. Like so much else in life, what at first seemed a curse over time turned out to be a blessing. And as for the most popular girl, it would prove true that the biggest stars have the shortest lives.

Ruth recalls the time a new student, a tall brunette called Rachel or maybe Renee, told her that she had been chosen from their school photo that year by her older sister as the prettiest girl in the class. The student was as surprised as Ruth, "I expected her to say *you know who* but she said you have such beautiful black little eyes".

Ruth took little notice of class photo day as their family never bought the ten-dollar prints, in their austere existence that would have been considered *extravagant*. She never stopped to consider the reality that she would still appear in the photo albums of other students.

As Seamus is wrestling with the gate latch her brother's voice bellows down the drive, startling them both. "Oi! What are you doing?"

Next a pack of barking dogs descends the drive, an unfamiliar German Shepherd and Boxer among them, with the pack leader charging behind. Seamus takes a step back from the gate as John puts his thumb and forefinger in his mouth to whistle. Ruth watches through the insect spattered windscreen with her hands in her lap. When the dogs are brought under control John addresses Seamus. "I'm the landowner. What do you want?"

"You are John, of course," says Seamus, extending his hand over the gate. "In the flesh."

John's eyes narrow on Seamus, still not having

noticed her in the car. The folded brim of his black beanie sits half an inch above the tops of his ears, the domed crown collapsed like a failed soufflé.

"Do you not recognise your Ruth?" asks Seamus. "Parked there in the sun?"

They sip tea to fill the uncomfortable silence; it is the silence of estrangement. Opposite Ruth, John sits with his mug sheltered by his hands, forearms resting on the tabletop. Lesion-like bruises extend over his right arm, from wrist to elbow. The colours appear different, darker the deeper they go in the skin. From a brownish red near the surface they turn to purple, almost black, where the blood vessels in the hypodermis have broken, blood leaking into the surrounding tissue.

"Are you OK?" she asks, indicating his injuries with a tilt of her head.

"Just bushwhacked, it's nothing," he replies curtly.

Ruth takes a sip of her tea to wet her throat then says, "And Rusty?"

"Yeah Rusty, he's had his birthday," says John. "You know, you sent him that *It* tunes voucher, or ..."

"Yes, an iTunes voucher."

Just through the archway dividing the dining room from the kitchen, John's shotgun rests on the benchtop. In this house it was a common enough site, nothing to raise an eyebrow at, but having brought her partner here Ruth is more than self-conscious about its presence, she is downright upset with John. Ruth is afraid that at the first sign of confrontation, the precise moment her voice should rise instead it will fall. When that happens, trying to speak is like breathing with a collapsed lung.

It isn't the time, she tells herself, to bring it up. It is a relief to hold her tongue. Steam eddies off the surface of her tea like wrestling spirits, the victors dispersing their opponents up into air beneath her face.

Now, John sits with one hand resting on his thigh beneath the table, slowly wiping it on his pant leg each time he takes a sip. Finally his palms come together and fall between his knees.

"About before, Seamus," he says. "I didn't mean to bite your head off. I thought the new resident greenies were back. They've had the farm under surveillance for months."

"No bother, John," replies Seamus. "You'd not get many visitors, I imagine, living this far out."

"Perennial university students," says John, "with nothing better to do with their time than cause aggravation for those of us who just want to work and feed our families. They launch unwarranted attacks under the banner of this Peninsula Vegan Network. 'PVN' they call themselves."

Being raised on a farm, Ruth accepted at an early age that the animals around her would eventually end up on her plate. Or someone else's. As a child she adopted the rationale that farm animals wouldn't exist at all if they weren't bred for food and the most you can hope for is that they have a happy life. From what she understands of their lifestyle, vegans made it difficult for themselves.

"New residents from where?" she asks, as unexpectedly her stomach rumbles at full volume.

John seems paranoid, like their father on one of his rants about the environmentalists in the good old days of Australian Newsprint Mills. John's forehead is reflective with an oil-less shine as if he had scrubbed it with a bar of Sunlight soap. Old habits die hard.

"It's not just the mainland they come from now," says John. "What I want to know is where they get their sense of superiority, this sure knowledge that they can manage our affairs better than we, in our Tasmanian simplicity, can. Attitudes better left on the other side."

"Aye, sounds like you had good reason to give these people a warning, a stern reprimand, John," says Seamus. "I'd kill someone if they hurt my family. It's the nature of communities in Ulster. We're prepared to take arms to defend ourselves. That's just part of the culture." Then he adds cheerfully, "By the way, this is a great cuppa. I went clean mad when I first emigrated, trying to find a decent tea. There's one back home called *Barry's Tea* and damned if I could find it anywhere in Sydney."

"I saw on the news you lot have started blowing each other up again over there, Seamus," says John. "Which side are you on then, the ones who are doing the blowing up or the ones getting blown up?"

Ruth is speechless. What the hell kind of question is that? John is a shit-stirrer and always has been. Ruth glances sideways at Seamus but he doesn't miss a beat, his silver sideburns brushed horizontally straight beyond his cheekbones, set in place by creek water residue. In his eyes there is a sudden bloodshot, like a red sock washed with the whites.

"I don't know if you're religious yourself John, nor do I care," he says, "but where I'm from there are thousands who will happily kill you depending on your denomination. Not religion but how you worship Christ. Anyone I speak to from abroad, John, I always say it's a beautiful people but don't tar us all with the same brush. Not all Catholics are republicans, not all republicans are in the IRA, not all unionists are sectarians and not all are Orangemen. Too much one or the other syndrome at home."

"You're Catholic though," says Ruth.

"Culturally, yes. A believer in Christ, no," says Seamus. "I love the concept of a religion and all the imagery that goes with it but I doubt I believe so much in the concept of heaven and hell anymore."

John leans back in his chair, apparently giving up.

Without warning, Ruth burps, releasing a foul smell around the table. Quickly she covers her mouth with her hand.

"Jesus, what have you been feeding her Seamus, rotten eggs?"

"My ma always told me that you know a girl's in love when she starts burpin' and fartin' in front of ye."

"That's disgusting," says Ruth.

As Seamus winks at her, she manages to keep a straight face. It's last night's beer that has caused her sulphur burp. Ruth seizes the opportunity, pushing her chair away from the table, scraping its legs across the floorboards.

"Anyway, we can't stay," she says. "We just stopped in on our way to Remarkable Cave."

"I'm taking pictures of all the rock formations in the area," Seamus tells John.

"Right, she told me about it. Congratulations on your Parks residency," says John. "I hear they're competitive."

"Cheers, John," says Seamus. "Thank you very much."

"We've had more than our fair share of *troubles* down here, you should feel right at home."

Through her teeth Ruth hisses. Saliva bubbles up inside her mouth but her lodged tongue refuses to speak.

"Just jokin'." John smacks the tabletop with an open palm. "You're gonna have a blast."

Chapter 2
John

The sky can tell you a lot, it is true. Right now, with this mid-level storm cloud, the sun is only visible in impressionistic watercolour through the blue grey bands of altostratus. A drop of rain hits the tip of John's nose, another landing on the cheek beneath his right eye. The cloud it fell from has already dropped from alto to nimbus. Ruth and her Irish van Gogh are bound to be given the royal treatment by the sea swell at Remarkable Cave this afternoon. Turning his back on the weather, John relocates indoors.

Standing alone in the kitchen, observing the dining room where only moments ago he had been engaged in conversation with his visitors, it is as if John can detect a faint echo. John noticed that Ruth looked at Seamus when he was speaking. Helen never gave John that. So it is real love between these two.

So what?

When Ruth asked about Rusty, John almost let slip about the shotgun he bought him for his birthday. The break-open single shot isn't only practical, it is trendy too, a gift that will keep Rusty in the field until he outgrows it in a few years' time. Although it is exciting news in their world he held back. Some subjects are dangerous, not to be broached with impunity, and unfortunately private gun ownership is now one of them.

To the naked eye, the room is empty. So quiet that the tinkling of his keys sounds like wind chimes. To some other sense, the space is still inhabited. John believes in ghosts. Hauntings. Living on the Peninsula how could you not?

Half the house and the land were left to Ruth in their father's will but John bought her out years ago and she spent her money on whatever she chose, imagining she got the better end of the deal. So this house is his and her presence here evokes certain memories, vibrations that make him feel ill at ease, the skeleton of the house struck like bone chimes.

It won't do, this. Not another night sat before the television with nothing but his shotgun laid across his knees for company and comfort. With deliberate weight in each step, he heads to the telephone table in the hallway and in the dim light calls up to the pig farm to speak to Helen. It takes some time for her to come to the phone. John taps his foot on the floorboards, the smell of good smoke wafting from the stove fire. They both have mobile phones but depending on where each of them is on their respective farms, and the time of day, the coverage can't always be relied upon. Landlines might have gone out of fashion in the cities but not here. When she answers, Helen is breathless and John cannot muster the energy to put on a performance, can barely keep the hostility towards his ex-de facto from his voice. So he keeps the conversation brief, merely requesting Rusty stay the night so that they can submit the online application for his minor's permit, and then hangs up without saying goodbye. Rusty has been accompanying him on duck hunts for the past two years, since he turned twelve. Only permitted to fire his weapon on the range, the boy was stuck watching from the shore and plucking the feathers from other hunters' birds, sharing the meat of their kills. John feels for him and shares his frustration. It is time he became his own man. Since the boy could walk and talk, John has been watching him closely with the sustained observation of a guardian. Rusty has what you might call a *sensitive streak*. To start with, there is the hair. Something about mothers, they always have a sentimental attachment to a child's hair. For daughters sure, long hair on a girl is natural, it is best practise, but on an adolescent male? John has put his foot down and prevented the pair of them growing it past the earlobes, below the eyebrows in front, or past the collar in back, but sometimes he feels like that little Dutch boy with his thumb stuck in the dam wall. Also, Rusty is the type who listens through closed doors and peers in windows. It is the sum of all these apparently small things, rather than any single one, that worries John.

John rattles the kettle. Satisfied there is sufficient water for one he places it on the hotplate. They could last a century, even longer, these cast iron wood-burning stoves. He puts two teabags in his cup and listens to the water hum. Winter is well underway, May not June in southern Tasmania. The kettle begins to scream. Too hastily he pours the boiled water, a splash scalding his knuckle. With the back of a teaspoon he takes his annoyance out on the teabags.

Unsurprisingly, neither he nor Ruth mentioned

the anniversary, even though she would have been as aware of it as him. Not that he ever speaks of it directly. You don't look it in the eye. While for him it is a time for solitary and simple contemplation, for others it is a time for family gatherings, fellowship and remembrance. For anyone, it can change with every passing year. Around the anniversary something is different. For John, it begins weeks before. Feelings and thoughts unbidden, as beyond his control as the weather. The whole thing almost seems unreal now and this year he had run his fingers over the gouge in the front door of the farmhouse to prove it to himself.

Not even Ruth knows that he was on *the list*. Probably she's not even aware there was a list. That was never made public. The official thirty-year moratorium on the case continues to provide him with some relief. The news and the internet might be full of discussion about Port Arthur but at least the government sanctioned silence remains in place. It allows him to take his mind off those things and keep to his usual routine. It helps him keep going with a sense of normalcy in a time when he's especially vulnerable to onslaughts of memory. John has found that sticking to his normal daily routine as much as possible at this time of year, while avoiding exposure to other locals who also have intimate knowledge of events, keeps him grounded and functional.

With every changing year there is one constant: John has never been back to the Historic Site. It costs nothing to visit the memorial garden there. The staff do not question your connection, if any, to the massacre. Simply wave you through. It has always felt wrong to him though, to set foot there, an insult to the dead and their loved ones who visit the spot. To stay away has seemed the best thing to do, and still does. Why anyone would want to go back to Port Arthur is beyond him. John is certain the entire place is haunted. It has been a cursed place since convict times. Now it is just an evil place. A stain on the Peninsula. An open wound, still, in many ways. Christ, even that bloody halfwit could see it. About the only thing he said that made any sort of sense after the shootings was that a lot of violence has happened at Port Arthur, that it must be the most violent place in Australia and that's why he chose it. John completely avoids Port Arthur, driving the longer way around Nubeena Ring Road up through Premaydena and Koonya. Although it is inconvenient, he uses the route to get to Fortescue Bay and Cape Hauy to fish. Only twice has he ever taken the road through Port Arthur in more than two decades. Once because of major roadworks in town. Another time to avoid a large grass fire at Premaydena.

John does not notice the car pull up and then leave outside, the dogs failing to alert him because they recognise Helen's vehicle. The front door simply opens and a second later the room fills with electric light.

"What are you doing sitting in the dark?" asks Rusty.

John murmurs something about sunset whilst silently reassuring himself that the anniversary has come and gone, just as all the other anniversaries have, and Ruth being back on the Peninsula doesn't change a thing.

"This is from Mum," says Rusty, offering up a Tupperware container. "It's ham and pea soup leftovers from last night."

John is a backseat driver leaning over Rusty's shoulder while he is in front of the PC. Pointing at the screen, placing his hand over Rusty's on the mouse, John issues instructions. In a couple of years it truly will be him teaching his son to drive a car, taking him to get his learner's licence. In the meantime, father and son are engaged in another rite of passage, applying for a minor's permit to use a firearm in the field. John has already written his letters, one as a parent giving Rusty permission to have a minor's permit and a second as a current firearms licence holder stating that he will supervise Rusty in the safe use of a firearm at all times. John just used the letter he wrote two years ago to allow Rusty to shoot on an approved range as a template.

"I don't put down *Rusty*, do I?"

John reads the brightly lit screen.

Are you known or have you ever been known by any other names?

"They mean aliases," says John. "Not nicknames. Tick 'no'. Go to question eleven."

Have you ever needed treatment for or are you being treated for? (Tick applicable box/s).

John gulps. Too quickly the floor of his mouth floods with saliva and he is sure he detects electrolytes hit the taste buds of his clenched tongue. Rusty turns his head, looks up at him, his left leg sliding out from beneath the desk, led by the heel in his sneaker. Of course, John knew these questions were lying in wait for them. At every precarious moment, every fork in the road, of Rusty's adolescence he has taken them into account.

Mental/emotional problems ... Any serious injury?

Rusty is in the habit of calling females his 'girlfriend', girls who, on a good day, might just remember his name. Rusty is also in the habit of getting a black eye or bloodied nose over these girls. The boy already has one cauliflower ear. Quick to throw the first punch, he doesn't squander words, waste conversation, like other boys his age. You can't fault him for that.

"You get up," says John. "I can finish off the rest of this."

Rusty reaches up to pluck an eyelash from John's cheekbone.

"Here," he says, offering it back to him. "Make a wish."

John hesitates, staring wide-eyed at the lash as if it is evidence presented against him. Flaring his nostrils, he blows it from Rusty's fingertip.

"Wait, there's another one," he says. "You're moulting!"

"You have a wire coming out of your ear," John tells Rusty, catching him with headphones plugged into the phone in his pocket.

On Friday afternoon at half past three, John waits for Rusty in the ute parked across the road from the little yellow church on the border of Highcroft and Stormlea. This is the last stop on the route. Here, the bus drops off the youth who live perilously close to the wilderness. The onus is on the parents to ensure their progeny arrive home safely. Usually this is Helen's job but today John plans to take his son along on his fortnightly fox patrol. The red fox has been a pest on the mainland since convict times but it wasn't until the close of last century that one was let loose on the island state. Two years, almost to the day, after Port Arthur. Of course, the city people put their faith in the official eradication program. What they don't understand is that it is near on impossible to detect foxes when they are in low numbers like they are now. They are still here. John and others like him, responsible and informed citizens, remain vigilant. The fox 'escaped' from a container ship two years after Port Arthur, one year after the new Firearms Act was passed. John is no conspiracy nut but the timing gives you pause for thought.

Rusty carries his backpack with a single arm strap across his torso from shoulder to waist. Although it has been the fashion amongst his son's schoolmates all year it still irritates John. There is a reason the bag has twin straps. Despite that A-frame of a torso—when he stands, Rusty drops his shoulders as if he's given up ahead of time, not just a slouch, a real A-frame of an upper body—the boy can climb. Credit where credit is due. Even this though, his flexibility, the fluidity of his movement, it is not just agility, there is gracefulness in it. That says it all, the boy can climb *too well.*

"You'll throw your back out carrying your school bag like that," he warns for the umpteenth time as Rusty gets into the vehicle. "Won't be able to fire your shotgun."

"Dad relax," says Rusty. "There's not even any books in it."

Confounded, John can only start the engine.

"Where does your mother buy these clothes from, anyway?" John asks, tugging at the sleeve of Rusty's long-sleeved t-shirt.

"I buy them," he says. "Online."

"Oh, online is it? Well, that explains it."

At the letterboxes, John keeps the motor idling while Rusty gets out to collect the post. Wild blackberry bushes run riot over the rise behind the assortment of colourful plastic and rusted tin receptacles lined up on a plank propped up by posts. The last of the fruit was picked in the summer to make jam for winter. Only the thorns remain, like concealed razor blades beneath the jacket of faded leaves.

John casts an eye over the envelopes that Rusty returns with. Not much is sent on paper anymore. When it is an option it is John's preference. Too easy for communications to be lost in these virtual boxes and folders. Although, there is the occasional useful bit of technology. Just last Christmas John splashed out on a pair of Uniden handheld dual band VHF/UHF radios. With a range of up to six kilometres and also waterproof for marine use, which means he and Rusty can take them on the duck hunt, he couldn't afford not to have one.

As they begin the final leg to the farm, John asks, "Let me know the minute that minor's permit confirmation email arrives. Call me. You can forward the email to me as well but make sure you call first. Leave a voicemail if I'm in the dairy."

John catches, out of the corner of his eye, Rusty shaking his head with his gaze fixed in the passenger's side wing mirror.

"You see something?" asks John, rubbernecking.

"See what?"

"Get your head on straight, Rusty." John changes gear and accelerates up the last hill. "I swear you're as useless as tits on a bull sometimes."

At Rare Bird Farm, the way to the wilderness has always been this grass lane between electric fence lines, not continuously live. Growing up, that fact was an endless game of dare and deception. Whether it be a fall from a horse, a kick from a dairy cow or countless small electric shocks, physical pain and a tolerance to it was part of life on the farm. It made sense that their father found it necessary to devise what others might consider cruel and unusual forms of corporal punishment. The kneeling on dry rice, or for a lesser offence beans, for instance. That left an impression, in more ways than one. Of course, those days are long gone and it is John's opinion that society is paying the price for it.

"Get some mud on those boots!" he shouts over his shoulder at Rusty.

The wilderness wasn't declared National Park when they were kids. The Regional Forest Agreement didn't come in until 1999. Now there are all sorts of restrictions—no fires, no hunting, no felling or slashing. Technically you are supposed to pay for a bloody Parks Pass to enter it.

John checks the skies, which make him think of Ruth and her Irishman. There is no mobile reception at Fortescue Bay or he'd have messaged her already. A welfare check to ask her about the incident at Remarkable Cave. Not that there is any real call for concern. His sister has enough common sense to stay out of a coastal cave at high tide, a mistake only a tourist would make. Even fifteen centimetres of fast flowing water can knock a person over. You only get a five second warning before the cave is filled to the roof with seawater. The man who almost drowned must be a damn fool. John has no sympathy for him. The paramedics who treated him at the scene should have taken him to the hospital with sirens blazing, if only to impress upon him the seriousness of it all, that he is lucky to be alive.

Rusty comes up alongside him with the packet of ziplock bags. John disapproves of how he is holding it. Like a worried old woman with a purse, both his hands clutch the top and pull the bag into his chest.

"There's nothing in them yet," says John. "Just carry that in one hand by your side and keep your eyes peeled. What we're looking for is tubular ropes. Twisted or not, doesn't matter. That's just an indication of their diet, whether they're eating grass and fruit or meat and organs. Now if you see hair and bone in a scat, collect that too. It's all relevant."

"Mum said that the bushfires wiped the last foxes out," says Rusty.

"What else did your mother say?"

Rusty eyes him suspiciously. "Nothing."

"Come on, don't stop there. What other fairy tales has she been telling you? Jack and the Beanstalk? Harry bloody Potter?"

John's sarcasm is met with an eye roll.

"What we're doing right now is serious, Rusty. The European red fox is the single most devastating threat to our native wildlife. Not to mention the diseases they carry ... distemper, parvo, mange and so on. They're a threat to our livestock, our dogs. Your mother knows a lot about pigs. When it comes to pigs you listen to your mother. When the subject is something more worldly, like this one is, it's me you listen to. Got it?"

"Yeah."

"Rusty, you do realise that Tasmania's native animals haven't adapted since the introduction of the fox? Your teachers haven't taught you this at school?"

"I dunno, Dad. Can we just find the fox shit and take me home? I have a date tonight."

"Scat, Rusty. The term is *scat*. This is conservation science we're conducting here, you can save the toilet humour."

If the boy can't even collect scat, how does he expect to be trusted on his first duck hunt with a firearm?

"So who's the lucky girl then, eh?" asks John.

"It's the same girl ... Claire. Why can't you even remember my girlfriend's name, Dad?"

"Women are tough, son," he says. "They set you up for things."

Despite Rusty's sensitive streak, John sees in his son himself at that age. The only difference being that John was able to admire from afar, knew that sometimes it was the wiser way to love—at a safe distance. The fact that John never called his first love his 'girlfriend' was no reflection on the quality or steadfastness of his feelings for her. John scratches beneath his right eye and sniffs back a swell of memory; it is not the time for such self-indulgent nostalgia.

"You're a good man, Russell. Don't let anyone ever tell you otherwise."

At the end of the lane, beyond the back paddock, they enter the stand of blackwoods. In a few months this canopy will be transformed by clusters of pale-yellow blossoms. If times ever get so tough that bait is a luxury he can't afford, John always has Acacia melanoxylon up his sleeve. It is an old Aboriginal trick; you can use the tree's twigs and bark as a poison to stun or even paralyse fish, so they become easy to collect by hand.

"Should have brought torches," says Rusty.

"Rubbish," says John. "You passed your last eye test. Or are you wearing contacts? Snuck one by me, did ya?"

"Got an A."

"Smart arse."

Machine-like, John wakes at 4:00 am into darkness and biting cold. Rain drizzles beyond the bedroom window. In a flash of dream, he was in an abattoir slaughtering bobby calves, except it wasn't called an abattoir; it was called 'The Veal Factory'. Sitting up, he rubs the back of his neck, noting he is due for a haircut.

John pulls on his coveralls and goes to the bathroom to splash his face at the sink, bracing himself for the shock of the cold water, leaving his eyes wide open and holding onto a warm breath. Resisting the temptation of a hot shower he dries his face on a stiff, scratchy towel. It is only then he remembers that Rusty is in the house. Usually he stays in bed while John goes to do the milking. Upon his return Helen used to have a hot breakfast waiting for the both of them. Although not a regular coffee drinker, this morning John downright craves it. The coffee is instant and comes from a large tin on the open-faced cupboard above the sink. It is something he learned growing up, to buy in bulk. Helen disapproved, stated that such items only reach their expiration date before you have a chance to use them. Best before dates are simply that, 'best before'. That doesn't mean you can't continue using them well past that time. *Waste not want not* is a rule John lives by. So keen is he for the coffee, he fills the rarely used electric kettle and switches it on. While it hums to life he goes to wake the boy.

Standing at the closed door he raps loudly.

"Rusty," he calls, lips close to the wood. "Come out for breakfast, please."

John opens the door wide enough to see that he is rousing in the dimness. Pitiless, he switches on the light.

Back in the kitchen, the water has boiled. John pours it, steaming, directly over the teaspoon and waits a moment to let it draw out a little heat.

"Do you have bacon and eggs?" asks Rusty as he saunters in. "I feel like bacon and eggs for breakfast."

John plucks the hot spoon from the cup and flings it into the sink, producing a sound like a tolling bell. "No, I do not have bacon and eggs. This isn't a café. Now go sit at the table."

The coffee instantly gives John heartburn. The acid in his empty stomach rears up like a flame. Leaving the beverage on the bench, he crouches to take two bowls from the cupboard, his knees cracking in defeat. From the cutlery drawer he takes two spoons. Then he marches back to the table and sets two places. In the pantry is a sack of Weet-Bix containing a wide sieve and a scoop. The only drawback to this particular bulk item is the inevitable mice droppings. John sieves the small dark pellets from the broken wheat biscuits and carries the clean food in a plastic container to the table.

"What's in that?" asks Rusty.

"This is cereal," John informs him. "This milk," says John, as he pours it into their bowls. "Do you know where it comes from?"

"The fridge," is Rusty's quick response. "And meat comes from Woolworths."

"Keep it up," says John. "Quips like that are why you're up this early to help milk the girls today."

John can appreciate Rusty's sarcasm, is even amused

by it, but the boy still needs to get out in the real world and get his hands dirty.

Every day above ground is a good day. Yet, when John is fishing, he wouldn't call the King his Uncle. It is only whilst fishing that he indulges in one of his other pleasures, rolling a few cigarettes in the ute and taking them in his top pocket to the water, sparking up after he has rigged up his rod so the nicotine rush coincides with the first cast.

Even foul weather won't stop him fishing; he has experienced more than his fair share of windy, extreme wave adventures around the Peninsula. Might stop him smoking though if the tobacco ever froze in its pouch in the glove box. A bit of fog like this won't keep him away, that's for sure. It just means he has to take extra care of his situational awareness. On the Peninsula there are only a handful of good spots for angling with a rod or handlining. Carnarvon Bay is top notch and the closest to Rare Bird Farm but John won't fish there. It is a haunted place. Only 2 km from the Port Arthur Historic Site, from its jetty you can see, directly north, Point Puer, the boys' prison, where throwing a bit of bread at another boy could get you three days in the hole. Harsh discipline, even by John's standards. What you have to remember though is that it was run like the military and who today we see as little urchins were actually the *corrupt fraternity of little depraved felons* that George Arthur, Lieutenant Governor of Van Diemen's Land described them as. The cursed bit of land on which the prison ruins stand hooks sharply around to the left and out of sight where off its pointy end is the Isle of the Dead. Anyway, it's not Point Puer but John's own personal feelings about Carnarvon Bay that mean it is off limits, now and always.

Fortescue Bay is the best alternative but his sister and the bog jumper have taken up temporary residence there. At Nubeena or White Beach he is sure to run into other locals and be forced to listen to the same old rigmarole. If he has to hear about someone's 'online' business one more time, he swears he'll commit an act of violence against their PC. Everybody is doing their business online now. Nobody knows who is selling or who is buying. Scary as hell. If it isn't their online business it's their latest arts and craft project or the health problems of their parent at the aged care home. This time of year there are always sightings of the humpback whales migrating north, as well. No, John would rather risk the off spill of tourists from the Blow Hole, go to *Billy Barkers*. Affectionately named after a daring convict, the handkerchief thief Billy Hunt. The convict disguised himself in kangaroo pelts and attempted to hop to freedom, past the guards at the infamous dog line. What Hunt didn't bargain for was that the hungry soldiers would fall for his act and decide to shoot him anyway for a bit of roo stew. Billy raised his hands in the air and received one hundred lashes for his trouble. Poor bugger. *Barkers* is a reference to the dog line near the fishing spot but no doubt about it, Billy was *barking mad*.

Once outside the vehicle, the fog has the effect of fast refrigeration and John's back arches in response. The thick cloud of tiny water droplets suspended in the atmosphere absorbs sound so that his footfall appears light, even loaded up as he is with fishing gear.

Squinting, John can see perhaps a quarter kilometre out into Pirates Bay. There is no horizon just the white blind pulled right the way down to the surface of both earth and sea. John's brown Blundstones are wet to black before he reaches the improvised rock jetty. *Billy Barkers* juts out into Pirates Bay with a ridge flat enough to venture out and set down your tackle box as well as a rise high enough that the dolerite remains dry except in the most wild weather conditions. The surface is cracked and rolling on a left side slope. On a sunny day the chocolate brown looks like a baked, risen sponge cake straight out of a hot oven before it has cooled and settled and the many imperfections been covered by icing. Sloshing waves sing around the crumbled edges, the whitewater frothing against the dark stuff of the Peninsula creating a Guinness-like effect.

John holds his head high as he marches the slippery surface strewn with fish scales and, here and there, pools of congealed blood. It is when he sets down his tackle box and prepares for battle that his thoughts drift recklessly into memory.

In the twilight John spotted him from the woodpile, sitting on a hay bale outside their dairy with the pale hair of a polar bear. A boy, a few years older than him. At his feet was one of the 20L white buckets they used to store cream. John was outraged! The cream was their single luxury. Who was this boy, who did he think he was taking their cream?

Nearby, a man stood with crossed arms talking to John's father in his steel toe white rubber boots. The stranger's hair was peculiar: a prime meridian, his hairline ran from one ear straight up over the top of his head and down to the other ear, leaving the front half of his skull bald. All the while he was talking to John's father he was keeping close watch over the boy who was wearing blue jeans and a tracksuit jumper. Looking up with his striking blue eyes, the boy saw John. As he smiled the boy's eyes squinted. John didn't smile back. Quickly he bent down to pick up some firewood so the boy would not realise he had just been standing watching him the whole time. With as much wood as he could carry, John returned to the house. On the path, he glanced over his shoulder and met the boy's gaze one last time—a near fatal stare.

Lighting his cigarette, about to cast off, John wonders if he would remember this encounter at all if the boy in question had not ended up on the front page of newspapers and television screens around the world. Helen went through an astrology phase, studying birth charts and such nonsense, when Rusty was born. For whatever reason, she did the gunman's astrology. John took notice of one bit, has not been able to forget it, because of how the words were put. As a result of the placement of his sun and moon, something about a bull and a ram combination, what it said was, 'When something tries your patience you become violent without warning' and it finished with the prediction 'At some point in your life you will undoubtedly organise and conduct some significant enterprise and achieve a position of prominence'. You couldn't make it up, that. Eerie is what it is. Downright chilling if you knew him growing up and knew what he went on to do at Port Arthur.

John suspects, though, that he would have remembered his first encounter with the man simply because of who his sister is, the one person he has always thought about, the girl he has dreamed of someday making his wife. There are some people you encounter in life who leave impressions on your soul, like a passer-by's handprints in a fresh cement pour. They remain always, whether you wish them to or not.

The cigarette between John's lips is mostly ash now past the tip of his nose. As his rod gets hit the ash scatters back into his eyes. Quickly he spits the butt onto the rocks and begins to pull the catch in.

Reel, reel, reel, reel!

In a single envelopment, the fog advances on his flank. John's visibility drops so he can see only the rod in front of his face, bending nobly like the neck of an Arabian horse. So John listens, waits for the sound of a wave to bring the fish up. Where is he going to land it? The fog is attempting an encirclement. John steps down onto one of the many rock ledges that surround him. From one he steps blindly to the next, still reeling in the line, until he hears a wave crash and retreat, having offered up the fish for him to drag closer. It's a Striped Trumpeter, a giant too, its head half ripped off, blood pouring out of the flapping gills.

"Obliterated," he grumbles, swinging the rod around to fling the dying fish higher onto the outcrop. Good for nothing now but bait. The fog has performed a feint retreat. John lights a second cigarette and smokes it as he waits for the fish to die so he can change out baits.

As he is leaving *Billy Barkers*, at the last moment something makes John turn left instead of right at the intersection. It has been a week since the tourist nearly drowned at Remarkable Cave and he's not yet gone past the spot. It may be quite some time before he does. It has though been a few months since he saw the *Old Quacker*'s obituary in the Gazette, a few weeks later the realty advertisement for the sale of her property in Doo Town. It'll be the first time in thirty years, perhaps longer, that she won't be leading the charge of gathered protestors at whatever wetlands were open to hunting that season. Nobody could deny she was a good sport, always greeted the duck hunters out on the water at first light. Quakers aren't the problem. Quakers he can live with. John recalls a weekend one year, after packing up camp, he actually stopped to help her broken down on the side of Coles Road leaving Moulting Lagoon. Turned out to be a fault with her car battery, no doubt down to all of the short journeys an old woman makes. That and the winter. John had to explain to her that if she didn't make long journeys very often her battery wouldn't get much of a chance to charge and that she could sort it out by charging it overnight every fortnight.

John is prepared for a sombre drive-by of her holiday shack but instead is confronted by a farce. A pair of hens is running loose on the road outside the house with a young man chasing them. John brakes and puts down the driver's side window but keeps the engine running. As John rests his elbow out the open window, he recognises the hopeless hippy. It's the son. 'Moon' they call him. A horrible name, John has always thought so. He has to laugh, the fellow is sporting bloody mutton chops. Looks like some draft dodger from the Vietnam war era and a typical twentysomething. At the gate, there is the other one, the older sister, standing with a broom on its end like a traffic paddle held in one hand while she holds up the other as a signal for him to stay put. John can't be sure now about the brother, but this one, Marina, she was at Port Arthur the day of the massacre, was there with the *Old Quacker*.

It sent her off the deep end eventually; she went and became a girl pirate. Volunteered with Sea Shepherd as a teenager, still suffering from shock probably. Everyone was in shock for a long while. Looking back, he's not surprised the new gun laws went through. Now that time has passed, when you look back, some things were over-regulated. The sight of the young woman evokes a particular sadness, resonant as she is with the destruction of youth and possibility. That lot ram ships, hurl containers of acid, smoke bombs and hooked flares, point high-powered lasers at other ships, not to mention drag metal-reinforced ropes in the water to damage propellers and rudders. No doubt she sees herself as some great martyr for a cause. If you dare to challenge her she will turn the tables on you and try to shame you for not being a caring person or as noble as her. John knows the type. Victimisation is the other side of the narcissism coin, no matter how high-minded you believe your purpose to be.

As Marina stares down the vehicle, her piercing blue eyes daunt him. The *Old Quacker* had eyes just like that: preternatural. Without her eye patch, you couldn't return her gaze for very long.

John reverses and does a speedy three-point turn. So the children have sold it. Divided up the proceeds from the sale and are back now to pack up the family weekender, the holiday shack. Driving away, he wonders if the new owners will keep the shack's 'Doo' name. Around here, change is considered sacrilege.

It is a comfort to John to have the shotgun lain across his knees as he sits by himself before the television. Not every night, and never while Rusty is around, but on occasion. Tonight, it is the wind that has him ill at ease. The sound started him fretting and this fret soon turned to worry, like a physical pain in his body it warned of danger and urged some kind of action or reaction.

Before the bastard did the shootings at Port Arthur he went after a list of people against whom he held grudges. That morning he came for John. Home alone, John watched him approach on foot up the drive, the sun blinding him. It had been years since *Rubber Lips*—as he was known by the local kids—left the Peninsula. The ice blonde hair was longer, but John recognised him straight off. The whacko was carrying a knife. John panicked, pulled the curtains shut and went to stand in the kitchen while his visitor banged on the door. Eventually he tired of knocking and left his mark. Only after the shootings did John realise what it meant: I'm coming back for you. It was then that he began nursing his gun in the house. It was not because he feared that he would return; the Port Arthur gunman was apprehended the day after the shootings. It simply became a habit. Some people bit their nails, took a drink or smoked—this wasn't any different.

Outside, the wind has quieted. John rises from the armchair, places his gun on the coffee table, and switches off the television. By the lingering glow of coals in the hearth, he makes his way on bare floorboards to the bathroom. In the sink he washes his hands using a bar of Sunlight soap. The cracked skin stings, bleeds some, so he lets the water run it down the drain.

When John turns off the tap, with hands braced on the basin, he looks up at the mirrored doors of the medicine cabinet. A middle-aged man stares back at him. Short brown hair greying at the temples, creases fanned out across his freckled face, skin resembling that of a Nashi pear. Time, of its own accord, has a way of turning regret into guilt. John began to feel the regret long before Port Arthur. The massacre simply calcified it inside him, the memory of what he had done, so that he would carry the guilt always: agonising; intolerable; excruciating; a knife wound. Shameful were his actions, causing untold damage. For though the wrongs we do to others may seem insignificant, we do not know the damage that has already been done them, or will be done them, and so we cannot predict what impact our venial sins will have on the world.

John can't make sense of his own behaviour now, tormenting the brother of the girl you loved. It was just so easy to forget that she was his sister because she was so *normal*. What a difficult time this must be for her each year, when the anniversary rears its ugly head. The heinous actions of her brother dragged out into the light yet again. John's heart goes out to her.

You don't choose your family.

John remembers the times he would telephone the family's holiday home at Carnarvon Bay. If her brother answered, he would fly into a rage when John asked to speak to her. John learned to hang up if *Rubber Lips* answered. Wait. Then call back again. It was jealousy, he realises now. He was jealous that his sister had friends and he didn't. It drove him bloody well crazy. John wonders if she sees him, perhaps writes to him. The good word is that he refuses to see even his own mother now, one of the rare few who had been granted access to him over the decades, a patient in hospital these days, not a prisoner in jail, and fifty-odd years old.

John switches off the light; it doesn't do to think too much.

Chapter 3

Marina

Doo-No-Harm is an original 1930's vertical board shack, bought nameless and lovingly restored and christened by Marina's parents after her younger brother Moon was born. In a tradition dating back to the 1930's, the residents of the seaside village located in Eaglehawk Neck give their places a *Doo* name, the quirkier the better. On Tasman Arch Road, the roof is blown off *Doo-Little* with white curtains still hanging in the windows. Then you pass *Love-Me-Doo, Doo-N-Time, Af-2-Doo, Much-A-Doo, Didgiri-Doo, Just-Doo-It, Doo-F@ckAll, Barba-Doo, Sheil-Doo,* until finally reaching *Doo-No-Harm.* Marina grew up with the view of the sea and Hippolyte Rocks, as well as the Phaedra mythology associated with them. A queen who was so deeply wounded by rejection at the hands of her stepson that she hanged herself, leaving a suicide note to her husband accusing his son of rape. Believing his queen, the king used one of the curses gifted to him by Poseidon to summon a sea monster. Spooked by the monster, Hippolytus's horses galloped his chariot into the coastal rocks. It was a dramatic story and she much preferred it to the one she later learned about her parents' reason for naming her

Marina, meaning 'she of the sea'. Moon, on the other hand, always hated his name growing up. It wasn't until they were both teenagers and he discovered that girls were drawn to it that he changed his mind. The family spent Easters and Christmases here. While not celebrating the Christian festivals they marked them as the secular holidays they have largely become, later the winter and spring school holidays as well as the odd weekend. Marina and her mother stopped coming after the murders.

They never referred to what happened at Port Arthur, if they spoke of it at all, as the *massacre or mass shooting,* like everyone else did. They didn't use any gun-related words. Marina never understood why exactly, except that 'shooter' was a term reserved for the duck hunters their mother combatted each and every year. Even when it came to them, Marina couldn't bring herself to use the word 'shooter' and stuck with 'hunter'.

Right after the murders, at the insistence of one counsellor, Marina wrote down her memories of the day in a journal, while they were still fresh in her mind. For her own protection, she then hid it in the drawer of her writing bureau in her room here, in her home away from home. Marina locked it away, just like she locked away her memories. It was an act of wilful forgetfulness.

Doo-No-Harm remains an architectural beauty, the interior awash with solid Tasmanian Oak, a natural blonde. The crown moulding, dado rails and skirting boards throughout are solid timber. It has the effect of bouncing light around the rooms, the sunlight let in by the glass focus of the renovation. It is time now though to tidy away these rooms before the new owner takes possession of the property. Marina begins to wonder, sitting beside her brother on the front steps beneath his faded Tibetan prayer flags, how does one go about packing up the memories of a lifetime?

As Marina gets up off the front steps to go inside and start dinner she grabs hold of the railing for support. When she lifts her hand she finds three dead ants squashed beneath the heel.

"Ugh," she sighs, holding out her palm for Moon to see. "I suppose they're only ants."

Moon peers over the top of his gunmetal Aviator eyeglasses at her, a corrugated forehead looming, "We're only humans."

Marina almost laughs in her brother's face at the facetiousness of the statement. She is only stopped by his eyes: a pair of hard, grey sepulchre stones.

The chill night air gathers around *Doo-No-Harm*, clinging to its manifold windows. A draught slithers around Marina's bare ankles as she stands at the kitchen bench preparing the evening meal. From the garden basket she takes carrots, capsicum, onion and garlic. From the pantry, a tin of beans and vegetable stock. As she sets a pot of peeled potatoes on top of the stove to boil, adding a large pinch of salt to the water, stray grains escape her fingertips. Taking an extra pinch, she flings it over her left shoulder to ward off evil.

From the table, Moon asks, "Is that my t-shirt?"

"What?"

Marina places a chef's knife sideways on top of a garlic clove and smashes her open hand down onto the heavy blade. Its thin curl of metal flicks up to slice the lower percussion of her hand, narrowly missing the crescent rise of the lunate bone at her wrist. Sweeping the wound up to her mouth she can taste rich iron in her blood. To stop the stinging sensation she bites down on the flesh either side of the cut, her teeth a tourniquet to prevent the pain spreading.

"Did you get it out of the dirty washing?" says Moon.

Marina pulls the outer side of her hand from her mouth. "I thought you were going to put a load on so why didn't you?"

"I'm not your slave," says Moon. "Why should I wash your dirty clothes?"

"Look, it's not your t-shirt, OK? And when I tell you to do something, just do it. Keeps things simple."

Moon returns to reading his phone. Marina has a wry smile on her face. For the pair of them, there is to be no falling back into some brother and sister symbiosis, but rather the heavy, insistent beat of rhythm and blues. Now that she comes to think of it, it could well be his t-shirt. Although Marina is five years older than Moon she shares her brother's slight build as well as his fine angular facial features. Strangers often mistake them for twins. Allowing the vegetables to fry off in olive oil, the scent of the sauté pan fills the kitchen directly.

It was Marina's idea to travel to Moulting Lagoon with the convoy of duck rescuers on the weekend. The plan is for her and Moon to clandestinely enter the sanctuary together before first light, as the rescuers venture out on the water with the hunters, and fulfil their mother's wishes. The funeral home insisted on getting permissions from the Trust of Parks and Reserves, from the local council, consulting the provisions of the *Clean Air Act*, wanting to establish a specific time and place to scatter the ashes to ensure the welfare of the public. It is all just red tape. Most of the land surrounding Moulting Lagoon, listed as a wetland of international importance under the RAMSAR convention, is private property. The northern section, where their mother requested a portion of her ashes be scattered, is a sanctuary wherein shooting is strictly prohibited. It is a pity the water birds are unaware of this demarcation, Marina thinks, rolling her eyes. Anyway, she has changed her mind.

"If we're going to be at Moulting Lagoon this weekend anyway we might as well join the rescuers out on the water," she tells her brother. "I mean, it's what Mum would have wanted, that if she couldn't be there someone else at least would take her place."

Marina glances over her shoulder to catch Moon solemnly setting his phone down on the table.

"You're saying you want to go out on the water with the shooters?"

Marina keeps her back to him.

"Mari?"

Marina spins around. Moon is shaking his head at her, brow furrowed beneath his sparse fringe.

"You can't just remove yourself from what's happened in your life," he says. "I mean, let's get real. Balloons bursting or the sound of a champagne cork popping still scare the life out of you. Don't get me wrong, I'm not saying you can't deal with it, I've seen the way you'll have a bit of a cry and then you get it together but Mari, if party poppers bring back such dreadful feelings and memories for you, what are you going to be like when the shooting kicks off?"

Marina feels the abyss opening up. It's the dark drop of the hanged man, bowels out.

"You don't think I know that? I'm aware of that."

"I know, I know," says Moon, hastily pressing together his hands, palms touching and fingers pointing upwards, thumbs drawn into the chest. "Can we please just at least discuss what to expect–"

"Let's not."

Any further discussion at this point will obfuscate rather than clarify the issue. Marina's mind is made up. And as long as her heart is beating and her lungs breathe air in and out, she will be going out on that water. The fear is something she can deal with later, at the time, when she is pulling on her wetsuit boots and ballistic goggles in the cold and the dark. It belongs there, in that space, and she will not let it in prematurely. So what if she cries? At least she doesn't throw up. In her position a lot of people would throw up. She has a strong stomach. The duck rescue is simply good old fashioned, grass roots, in your face activism. Their parents taught them *civil or uncivil disobedience as long as it doesn't incite violence.* Marina perceives her brother as purely intellectual. From his Quakerism to his animal rights stance he is a mass of fine ideals. Moon is a true devotee–to humanitarianism, to veganism, even to music and art. Only when mastered by a superior will and intelligence such as her own is he actually of any use. Half the time he is off with the fairies. Well he better get ready for the commitment it takes, the forging of armour it takes, because when it comes to social injustice the overwhelming majority just don't give a damn.

Having lost her appetite, Marina watches, ambivalent, the grated carrot soften and bleed out. Although she has not returned to the Port Arthur Historic Site since the murders, she knows by heart the poem in the memorial garden.

May we who come to this garden; Cherish life for the sake of those who died; Cherish compassion for the sake of those who gave aid; Cherish peace for the sake of those in pain.

Life, compassion and peace.

Of the three, Marina knows compassion is the true challenge. In her time as an animal rights activist, it has been proven to her again and again that few understand its true meaning. From the Latin: to suffer with. In her experience, garden variety sympathy is difficult enough to elicit from the average person, let alone the desire to alleviate suffering and the urge to act, which define compassion.

"What about Mum's ashes?" asks Moon.

Surprised by his pragmatism, Marina says, "Don't worry, we'll get to that."

The next day, Marina wakes from a bad dream into the freezing morning with the urge to throw open a window and clear the air, as if she had burnt toast. The nightmares are as frequent as her regular dreams. Then there are the night terrors. Unlike nightmares, your eyes may be wide open but you never wake up during a night terror. Afterwards, you have no recall of specific details.

There are other people who will never experience a night terror, just as there are people who will never experience a tsunami, an earthquake, a bushfire or a massacre–will only see these things in the news. Such is the lottery of life.

Marina wishes that there was no such thing as dreams. If there was an opt out of dreams method, she'd opt out, like she opted out of prayer, and of hope. Dreams are supposed to serve some purpose, god knows Moon could go on and on about it, but as far as she is concerned they are merely disruptions. It is the lack of control in a dream that she dislikes most, the unpredictability. Half the time you don't even know who you are engaging with. A person can start out being someone you know and then turn into a stranger.

This was a disturbing dream. An election was underway, federal or state it wasn't clear. To be eligible to vote each person had to bring along a rabbit. A live rabbit. Not only did Marina not have a rabbit, she objected whole-heartedly to the system and she had argued, until blue in the face, with a polling official. What would happen, she asked, to all of these animals once the election was over? Not every household was set up to keep companion animals. Would they be euthanised? Bred specifically for this event like Thanksgiving turkeys and afterwards cooked up in a stew? Where were voters supposed to source these rabbits? Buy them from pet stores? The demand would outweigh supply and people would certainly turn to trying to trap rabbits in the wild and who knew how they may be harmed in the process.

Marina breathes through the lingering frustration as she rises from bed. It is the emotions evoked in the dream that remain with her. Also, the symbols. Why rabbits, she wonders? For some reason she can't get *Alice in Wonderland* out of her head, the Mad Hatter's tea party. Now she will have to go back and refer to the book as the details are vague in her memory. There was something sinister, she seems to recall, about the character of the March Hare.

On the bookshelf in the study is a battered Wordsworth Classic.

The March Hare will be much the more interesting, and perhaps as this is May it won't be raving mad—at least not so mad as it was in March.

Marina folds down the corner of the page.

Back in the kitchen, with the book tucked under her right armpit, she discovers a handwritten note clipped on the refrigerator door:

Man from Remarkable Cave woke up from coma but severely brain damaged. Can't speak and has to be fed through a tube in his stomach.

Peace.

Marina reads Moon's familiar handwriting a second time, letting the information sink in—but not too deep. When they were driving past Remarkable Cave that day and noticed the commotion, how could she have predicted, even imagined the possibility, that this is how it would turn out? The Peninsula is moody, prone to unusual and rare occurrences. There is no way she could have known what was going on down at the cave. Besides, that kind of an emergency, which involved actual harm, required immediate action.

"Thanks for actually reading it," he says when Marina tells Moon she got his note.

"What's that supposed to mean? Was that a shot at me? What, you're trying to say that I didn't do the noble thing because I didn't stop to help? In case you've forgotten, there were other people everywhere. Someone else had already taken responsibility for the situation, that nurse. You're going to argue that she wasn't more qualified to help? Come off it. We weren't needed."

"When you don't want to know something, you've got a habit of looking the other way." says Moon. "That's all I meant."

"Is that so?"

"You know, when I spoke to her on the phone the nurse told me the whole story. That must be terrible, right? One minute you're on top of the world, the next you'd wish you were never born."

"You always stare into space like that," says Marina. "Let me guess, you're thinking about that nurse? Is that what impresses you, a nurse?"

"You got something against nurses now?"

"You think she'll be hot to go to bed with because nurses have extensive knowledge of how the human body works?"

"Jesus, leave me alone," says Moon. "That's the third time you've mentioned the nurse."

"So what? You haven't answered me."

"I don't know, but I'll be sure to keep you informed."

Marina doesn't even know if her brother has sex. She has her suspicions that he may be asexual. Many times she has tried to get information out of him about who he is sexually attracted to, if anyone, but failed. Yet again, he hasn't taken the bait.

Moon opens the refrigerator door, looks inside and then turns back to her. "I'm sorry, Mari. Why don't we change the subject? Yeah, you think you're being funny but you're not."

"If you're not getting anything out can you please shut the fridge door?"

"You know what I was thinking about? Remember

the time we sailed with Mum and Dad up the D'Entrecasteaux Channel along the Bruny coastline? Dad said it reminded him of the Mediterranean. We both had a turn on the tiller and we moored at Cloudy Bay for lunch. It was a peaceful paradise."

"*Cloudy Bay* was one of the first shore-based whaling stations," she replies. "They slaughtered whales there for their oil and baleen."

"Uh, I don't remember—"

"You know what I remember? I remember when we had to sell *Imago*. That yacht was locally built from all Tasmanian timbers, did you know that? If the new owners have been adding a couple of coats of varnish a year can you imagine how many coats of varnish are on her by now? It's like human beings. Every ten years we become new people, every cell in our body gets replaced by a new one. We're literally not the same person we were ten years ago, let alone over twenty years ago. You don't have to be a *nurse* to know that." Marina flashes her eyes up at him. "It's common knowledge."

Tasman Peninsula hangs by a sandy thread to Forestier Peninsula, even more precariously linked to mainland Tasmania by a swing bridge over Denison Canal. Though it was originally hand dug to allow boats easy access between two bays, this watery divide has inadvertently stopped the spread of the Tasmanian Devil Facial Tumour Disease. The sheer geographical isolation of the twin peninsulas has created a tiny haven for devils. Such are the dual natures of these peninsulas: prisons and paradises.

As they pass Dunalley Beach, Marina notices Moon

closely observing from the passenger's seat the small children playing, while the tide goes out, with plastic buckets and spades on the pale sand. She wonders what he is thinking about. Is he lost in daydreams about their own childhoods again? Visions of paradise? Or is he just thinking about their dead mother, perhaps even feeling her absence? Moon doesn't realise how his rebelliousness hurt their mother. Her brother lacks self-awareness, can't even see himself for what he truly is: the black sheep of the family.

From Dunalley it is a twenty-minute drive along the Arthur Highway to Sorell. Above the main street silver gulls create a latticework of wings. Occasionally, a bird will plummet towards a car or pedestrian.

It is still the same rural shopping town where as children they would come to do their 'big shop', except now both the major supermarket chains are represented. It is 3:00 pm and there is a mass exodus: men with their shirt sleeves rolled up; women in creased pencil skirts; real estate agents and bankers; they are all desperate for their fix from the nearest café. Overhead, a Boeing 747 is descending to Hobart airport.

Dropping Moon off outside the Saint Vincent de Paul thrift store, Marina checks her reflection in the rear-view mirror, rubs a smear of red lipstick off her front teeth with a fingertip.

Inside the supermarket, she finds her eyes are already sensitive to the fluorescence even though she has only been back at *Doo-No-Harm,* with its abundance of natural light, for the briefest time. For a moment she considers going back to the car for her sunglasses.

Instead, she squints as she collects a trolley, the light also exposing the garden dirt deep beneath her fingernails. In the health food aisle, part of an overheard conversation between two shelf stackers makes her feel even more self-conscious, that she might look like some stoned hippy.

"The organic one."

"Tastes like dirt."

"The tree hugger stuff."

"Yeah, we won't put it up front."

In the fruit and vegetable section, rockmelons are stacked in crates like medicine balls and leeks lie top to tail with celery and silver beet.

"Which one should we get?" a mother asks her child, holding up two anti-bacterial cleaners. "Crisp Apple or Lime and Mint?"

"Apple!" comes the reply from the end of the trolley. "Because cider is made from apples and I *love* cider!"

As the woman passes the cleaner to the boy, words in block letters—white on black—walk out in front of Marina like a car swerving into her lane, cutting her off. The bold lettering on the back of a man's t-shirt reads:

... *BUT THERE'S LAUGHTER IN SLAUGHTER.*

Unable to look away, Marina can only see the back of the man's blonde head, the outline of shoulders rolled forward as if he has his hands shoved in front pockets, and the pale calves covered in cactus-like hairs beneath the hem of his shorts. Dressed like that, on a day like this, he can only be a local. As he drifts away, like a reactive predator Marina stalks him, not only to see the front of the novelty t-shirt so she might understand the disturbing punchline she has just read but also to see the face of the man who would wear such a t-shirt.

"I just wish I had a pogo stick so I can go up to the moon," the boy in the trolley tells his mother. "But I am scared of heights because they are not my favourite but I like aeroplanes because they *are* my favourite."

Pity he wasn't outside a moment ago, thinks Marina. The jet plane was so close he could have opened his mouth and caught it.

The slogan leads Marina into the meat section. As the man bends over at the hips to pick up a whole leg of lamb, she manoeuvres past him and then pivots, the trolley swinging around like a regular dance partner. Eyes now level with the man's chest, she reads:

THERE'S NO 'I' IN TEAM ...

So, there's no 'I' in team but there's laughter in slaughter? Is it supposed to be funny? Some kind of sick joke? Just metres from her, the man stands with the shank gripped by one hand and resting on his shoulder, unaware that he has affronted another shopper. Marina is loading a long list of rapid-fire accusations to shoot at him with her verbal machine gun as she raises her eyes to his face and is hit—in the chest and in the gut—by his bullets.

Two bullets of piercing blue.

Immediately her blood runs cold; the past and the present collide. There on the shiny, slippery supermarket floor, Marina suddenly finds herself in the throes of a powerful fear. Hormones released into her bloodstream are priming her body for fight or flight. Faster and faster her heart beats, sending out an SOS message. Marina squeezes her eyes shut to escape the overexposure to fluorescent lighting.

A second later when she opens them, the man in the t-shirt is gone. Spinning around, she casts her sightline to every corner of the supermarket but does not catch him again. Vanished without a trace. The unpleasant cold sensation in her veins plateaus.

Now, this is what is meant by a flashback. Not just a memory but the present violently hijacked by a trauma from the past. Feeling a sudden onset of nausea, she abandons her groceries in the trolley like an absconding honeybee.

Outside, feeling so lightheaded that she is afraid of falling, Marina tucks her hair behind her ears, places both hands on a single bent knee and waits for it to pass. It is a chronic sickness. The sinking nausea is reminiscent of the time she swallowed mothballs as a child and was force-fed charcoal. Whenever it comes on, all she desires is to push what happened far from her mind. Whole days, weeks, even months will pass where she feels nothing; however, like fine weather it cannot last and eventually the storm clouds roll in.

Moon is standing alone outside the op shop where he was given the task of finding them white long-sleeved shirts to wear out on the water. Thin and fidgeting inside his oversized jacket, he attempts to hand brochures to passing strangers. As a woman, perhaps a pensioner, walks by, she offers him a curt smile as she takes one.

He responds with a bowed head and one word, "Peace."

When she looks down and sees that the title is 'Why Vegan?' she stops. Returning to Moon, she hands the brochure back and as she does a flyer slips out of it and to the ground at her feet. Bending to pick it up she says, "I was just going to throw it away so I thought you may as well keep it."

Looking up and down the street, Marina fears for Moon. It is one thing to leaflet outside Flinders Street

Station in Melbourne but this is rural Tasmania for God's sake. Moon is staring down the street, his gaze fixed on the woman he failed to reach. Marina remains unsteady on her feet. For a few moments she watches the flow of pedestrians. The older women, women of her late mother's generation, all carry handbags on the crook of their arms.

"I have to get out of here," she says finally. "Wrap it up."

In the car, on the way back to *Doo-No-Harm*, Moon tells Marina, "I found something weird, in the book I bought from Vinnies." Moon reaches into his bag and pulls out a second-hand hard cover. "It's a postage stamp from Nazi Germany."

Moon holds up the stamp and Marina steals a glance at it. Red soldiers with bayonets are depicted, waves of fire at their backs, a people rising up, some kind of last effort to mobilise young and old to defend the Reich.

"Friends worked with the Nazis in the Hitler years, you know," says Moon. "Helped locate the next of kin of French Jews who left personal effects with them before they were sent to concentration camps in Germany. On the day the train pulled out, loaded with Jews, Friends served them coffee."

Marina's foot squeezes the brake pedal. "What?"

"Did you see something?" Moon, with his hands braced on the dashboard, is peering through the windscreen, searching in front of the car. "Was it wildlife?"

Marina accelerates. "Not at all. I'm just surprised, shocked really, that they allowed that. Seems such a British thing to do. It reminds me of those documentaries about the London bombings in the Second World War. The English would surface from their air raid shelters to have a street cuppa, then stay calm and carry on."

Moon relaxes back in his seat. "You know why they gave them permission, don't you? Because they knew that no Quaker would lie down in front of the train that day, in case they got denied the privilege of serving coffee another time. Friends weren't abolitionists in the Hitler years, they were welfarists."

"Well, we have the benefit of hindsight," says Marina. "At the time, nobody knew what the fates of the Jews on those trains would be. Besides, Friends weren't interested in nationalism or politics. They were only interested in the relief of human suffering. They were willing to work with anyone, apparently even the Nazis."

"Exactly!" says Moon. "Friends and Nazis did work together for humanitarian ends. But like you said, they were only interested in the relief of *human* suffering. Animal Rights is the next great social justice movement and Friends should be at the forefront of that movement, speaking truth to power."

"Quakers are still progressive," says Marina, thinking of their mother. "They oppose blood sports, zoos and circuses, fur, cosmetics testing on animals—"

"I know, I know but they still eat them," says Moon, increasingly agitated. "I mean, how did they transport the Jews to concentration camps? In cattle cars! How can Friends not make the connection? They just refuse to acknowledge their own speciesism."

"Moon, stop!" she orders. "You realise you're preaching to the choir?" In an attempt to divert his attention, Marina reaches up to adjust the rear-view mirror, as she changes the subject. "What's the book from Vinnies that you found the stamp in?"

Moon's gaze is drawn to the movement of her hand. "Oh, Twentieth Century Verse. I think there's an idea for a song there, when I get around to it."

Before she died, their mother told Marina about Moon's 'rants' during silent worship. Now she is witnessing it firsthand. It's not that she can't see why he was provoked to share, stand up and speak his mind, it's that even she respects the fact that you spoke up only once *the Spirit finds you.* Moon was doing this every single meeting! No wonder the other Friends decided that his message, while maybe good for the community, was not beneficial to the meetings. Moon's rebelliousness, like that of an ingrate child, had hurt their mother yet again. Her brother making himself an outcast was one thing; bringing their mother into disrepute or making her an undesirable member of the group by way of her connection to him—that was something else again.

Moon's revelation about Friends serving coffee to the Jews has struck an unexpected chord with Marina though.

Oh, the tea!

That tea at Port Arthur. Cup after cup of tea she and her mother prepared and put into the empty hands of strangers. How could she have forgotten?

That night, Marina experiences a night terror.

Imprisoned in a concentration camp, it is dinnertime. Marina and her mother queue with other Friends, all wearing round red badges on the chest of their pyjama-style uniforms, to select their meal from a type of restaurant, a small café. They wait on a wooden verandah or deck overlooking the rest of the prison to enter a single rectangular grey stone room. The prisoners walk in and then out of an invisible revolving door. Large steel vats of hot water, in which slow cooker containers float, are waiting behind a tall glass front. A Nazi in full SS uniform stands behind the counter serving them. Above him, hangs a sign: 'furnace of Marina'.

When it is her family's turn, they enter and look at the menu written in white chalk on a blackboard high on the wall. Marina realises that the meals are all made from human body parts. Behind the glass, in the vats, are disembodied legs, arms, heads and torsos simmering in a blood broth. Steam sprays out from the surface of the broth in geysers.

Later, they go inside a gas chamber. As they enter, another group of prisoners with yellow triangular badges on their uniforms wave their arms in a slow motion cross in front of their faces, shake their heads from side to side. No sound comes out of their open mouths.

Inside, the gas chamber looks like a large public bathroom. Along each wall are individual toilet cubicles without doors. A shower head faces down over each toilet. When the gas is turned on, Marina stands on her head on top of the toilet seat, balancing like a yogi, and uses her bare feet to smother the shower nozzle.

Limbs thrashing beneath a tangled bed sheet, Marina cries out from her half-sleep.

Chapter 4
Ruth

A cold snap across the island state sees temperatures fall to five degrees Celsius below the May average. As in all freezing conditions it is the extremities, such as the Peninsula, which suffer most. As Ruth turns the key in the ignition her eye is drawn to a deluxe overnight frost, a forest of floor-sweeping shiny gowns, complete with long sparkling opera gloves.

Once the heating is turned on, Ruth plugs her phone into the car stereo and chooses a rock playlist to wake her senses, waiting until she is out of earshot of the warden's demountable before she turns up the volume.

On the way out of Fortescue Reserve, the windscreen continuously mists over, taking only a few minutes to reach total whiteout. The wiper blades restore the spectral forest in an instant. Music is one sound Ruth has sorely missed, something she takes for granted in her other life on the mainland. It is so powerful, music. Not only can it move her emotionally, it can actually move her physically. A melody or a lyric from a chorus can get into her head but when sound waves hit her they quicken her pulse, set her heart racing or just feel like a punch in the gut. The Peninsula has a similar effect on her, the elemental forces of nature in constant battle with the dolerite coast.

Out on the Arthur Highway heading for Stormlea, having psyched herself up sufficiently, Ruth turns off the stereo. Slowly, she allows her thoughts to turn to her planned confrontation with John. In the rear-view mirror she practices hardening her stare. When she told Seamus—busy calculating ratios and scales for his first painting, based on the shots he took at Remarkable Cave—that she was going to see Rusty and Helen she felt guilty for lying to him. Now she also feels guilty she is not visiting her own nephew and his mother, which makes her a neglectful aunt and a bad person.

Even if Seamus is not, Ruth is terribly offended by almost everything John did and said on the day they came to visit the farm. This is one of her delayed reactions. *You've got to live in the present*, Seamus is always telling her. Ruth wishes she could. For Seamus, she really wishes she could. She is an expert at looking back on things and knowing whether or not they were good; she isn't able to know in the moment whether or not she is happy. Even the residency, she's going to look at this experience in posterity. At this very moment she can only think that, yes, it's going to be good when she looks back on it, next year perhaps. That's how she lives; she can't change it; she has tried.

As Ruth takes the driveway up to the house, a small flock of black cockatoos wheel overhead, accompanied by a noise like a toppled champagne tower smashing—at Stormlea, a sure omen of hostile weather.

Ruth peers in the front windows to find the dining room and kitchen empty. The voices of a talkback radio program lead her around the side of the house and then across the yard to the kill shed beside the dairy. Inside, John sits on a stool ramming a rag down the barrel of a rifle with a steel rod, his hands and wrists smeared with oil. The unmistakable scent of solvent instantly conjures up the past, the way only scent can. That little yellow glass bottle of Hoppes No. 9 released a smell like a queer brew of overripe bananas and petrol. Growing up, John practically wore it as cologne and Ruth didn't mind it but now it turns her stomach. For a split second it is her father sitting in there, in that exact spot, on the same stool, a fully-conscious sheep flipped on its back and squeezed between his knees. From outside, perched atop stacked hay bales, Ruth and John would watch through the sliding windows, waiting for the moment the fountain of blood rose dramatically in the air. For some reason, it reminded her of waiting to see the blowhole at Eaglehawk Neck. There was the suspense before the blood sputtered, had a few bursts, and then a vibrant geyser shot up in the air.

Unnoticed, Ruth crosses the shed and switches off the radio. The stool topples over as John jumps up, spilling solvent over the concrete floor.

"It's you," he says under his breath.

Despite a stretching silence, Ruth offers nothing.

"Heard what happened down at Remarkable Cave," says John, finally. "You're OK, I take it?"

The original purpose of Ruth's visit is momentarily set aside as she clamps her hands on her hips. "What's with all the guns?"

John rests the rifle against the wall and takes a fresh rag from the workbench to mop up the spill. "As you can see with your own two eyes I *was* cleaning them, until someone snuck up on me."

John always does this, tries to turn things back on her. Everything somehow ends up being her fault.

Not this time; Ruth stands her ground; the pressure within builds and builds. "What I mean is, why'd you leave the shotgun out on display on the kitchen bench when you knew I was bringing Seamus over? What's wrong with you?"

Is John really going to pretend he's already forgotten what she told him the last time they spoke on the phone? The reason—the only reason—she made the disclosure about Seamus's father, the fact that he'd been murdered by loyalists during the height of the Troubles in Northern Ireland, was to curb the kind of insensitivity John displayed the other day. Her brother is unbelievable sometimes.

"If you're so upset then give me a text next time so I know when to expect you," says John. "Temper tantrums, you haven't changed a bit."

Ruth takes a different tack. "What if Rusty was around? It is so irresponsible, John. Please tell me it wasn't loaded?"

"Of course it was bloody loaded. Come on, you know as well as I do that a gun on a bench is just a tool. It's the person that's the weapon." John rights the stool. "As for your nephew, we ... Rusty's minor's permit is due any day now. There's prime duck hunting at Moulting Lagoon. We're heading up there together. So don't worry about him, he passed his firearms safety course with flying colours. He's a natural."

"That's not the point, John." Ruth's voice rolls over at the revelation, showing its yellow belly.

"What is your point, exactly? Enlighten me. I told you, he's been taught on the range."

Ruth's heart erupts; boiling hot magma rises within her throat; all the words escape like trapped gas. "He's fourteen! He's not even old enough to drive a car. His brain is still forming, John. What *genuine reason* is there for a boy his age to own a gun?"

"Bah! You don't have kids. You don't know what you're talking about," John scoffs. "Anyway, we had them. You're acting like this is all new to you. Has the mainland really changed you that much?"

"You're talking about decades ago," says Ruth. "A lot has happened since then. A lot has changed. Or have you forgotten?"

John looks up, clears his throat.

Then, shaking his head, he says, "Ruth, no one's *forgotten*. We live with it every day. But we don't talk about *that*."

"About what, John? I mean, why would you want your child to be a shooter after everything that happened here? I just don't get it."

"Listen up, mind your friggin' business, keep your trap shut, when it comes to my son. Alright?"

It hurts. Ruth feels her airway closing as the soft tissues of her neck swell. Lifting her chin, she forces herself to go on.

"And what about after the duck hunt?" she says. "He's going to want to show off his gun to his mates. He's going to go out in the bush and who knows what? Boys his age drink, experiment with drugs. Their hormones are raging. They're unpredictable." Ruth shifts her weight onto the opposite leg and swallows. "What does Helen say?"

"*Helen ...*"

The way John vocalises his ex-de facto's name speaks volumes.

"Helen grew up on a farm, she's a primary producer for Christ's sake," he says. "We're not the only good people who own guns, by the way. We agree that there's no place for guns that are nothing but human-killing machines and they've been banned. Besides, there's a combination on the lock box. Rusty doesn't have it."

"Yeah, right. And Rusty doesn't watch porn on the internet because there's a parental control filter on the PC. Kids are smart, John. They find ways around it."

"Sane people don't crave semi-automatic weapons, Ruth. Only lazy hunters want them. Semi autos and pump actions are only good for vermin. What you're talking about is just one deeply disturbed individual who inherited a fortune that allowed him to buy weapons illegally and he used his money for evil. Or have you forgotten that he was always a trigger-happy piece of shit?"

In the shed thick with the scent of Hoppes No. 9, she can barely even breathe through her nose.

"I'll wait for you in the house," she says, suddenly dizzy.

As Ruth is walking away she stops, turns back and adds, "By the way, I didn't sneak up on you. You didn't see me."

In the backyard, tissue-paper thin white bedsheets flap on the slowly spinning Hills Hoist. As Ruth stares though the opaque cotton stratum she is peering through decades of time. When they were kids nobody had a minor's permit. On her brother's tenth birthday, at the same time that he started to help milk the cows, he got his first rifle. As long as he didn't target any livestock he was permitted to kill indiscriminately. By daylight he would shoot rabbits in the paddocks and ravens or parrots out of the sky but his favourite time to kill was when night fell. At night, the prey was possum. Their neighbours, the Whiteleys, would come over from the pig farm and while John and Robin stalked the bush with their rifles and spotlights, Ruth and Helen sat together at the cleared dinner table playing Old Maid, the edges of the deck soiled as brown as bread crusts from the caress of fingers. Occasional gunfire would not interrupt their games but if the shots intensified, a chaotic chorus of bullets, they would pause and look at one another over their fans of playing cards, knowing what it meant: if a possum became caught in the branches when it was shot then the boys would blast the crown of the tree until it exploded in a confetti of leaves. Like demigods, the boys would return from the thrill of the kill, basking in their glory. Sometimes they brought back orphaned joeys, which would hang by their tails from your finger. Helen once kept an orphan and raised it as a pet but as it grew bigger it nightly destroyed the kitchen in its search for food. So while Ruth was allowed to play with the orphaned joeys for the night, the baby possums would inevitably vanish from the Blundstone shoe box beneath her bed while she slept.

Before school the next morning, while the Kettles and the Whiteleys waited together at the church bus stop, John and Robin would delight in tormenting her about the fate of the joeys with their doublespeak, constant back and forth quips about *a dog's breakfast.*

At the kitchen sink, John washes his hands with detergent before taking a seat at the head of the table.

Pouring the tea, he glances at Ruth. "There's s'posed to be a south-westerly change coming. Could mean hail. You should find somewhere undercover to leave your car tonight."

"I didn't come here to talk about the weather, John."

John blows on his tea, takes a sip and then asks, "Why did you come back?"

Ruth knows exactly what he means but chooses to ignore it. There is the matter of her nephew and this minor's permit to put to rest before they move onto anything else. "Why didn't you tell me about the duck hunt? When we spoke on the phone, right before I came down, why didn't you tell me then?"

John looks sideways, into the dark hallway. "It didn't seem important."

"Jesus Christ, John." Ruth sighs.

John cracks his knuckles. "He's come on the hunt twice before," he says and then pauses to wait for her reaction.

Stunned, Ruth doesn't know how to respond.

"See, you didn't know that, did you? This birthday he finally got what he's been asking for, his own shotgun."

"Shotgun? What kind of shotgun?"

"It doesn't matter," says John. "Point is he's happy as Larry, like a child with a new toy."

"Well I'm outraged," she says. "Beyond outraged."

"You know what? To hell with your outrage! You've got some nerve, you know that? You come waltzing back with your holier-than-thou attitude trying to play the concerned aunt all of a sudden. Who do you think you're kidding?" John flicks his china teacup with the trimmed nail of his trigger finger. "Some nerve."

When his attention returns to her at the opposite

end of the table, his voice is flat, "It's the rabbit that's running away, not the man with the gun, that gets shot."

"Whatever that means," says Ruth, recovering her composure despite feeling sharp pains in her head and neck.

She presses her fingertips against her eyelids for a few seconds. When she opens her eyes she says, "Why tell me at all if you're just going to bury your head in the sand? What am I supposed to do with this information?" Ruth can feel her hands begin to tremble. "It's the wrong decision, John. It's very, very wrong. That's not what I think, it's what I know."

Ruth lifts her bag from the floor and is about to take flight when something prevents her, something visible in the whites of John's eyes and the trembling labellum-like lower lip.

The moment freezes.

"What happened, that had nothing to do with me at all." John draws in an exaggerated breath before continuing. "None of that was my fault, what happened at Port Arthur. I didn't do, do anything to s-s-set him off," John stammers.

"Didn't you?" she replies. "Then why do you sound so guilty? It's Carnarvon Bay, isn't it? I always had a hunch. All that time you spent there, it can't all have been chasing one girl. There must have been other reasons Carnarvon Bay was your haunt. You and Robin Whiteley, what did the pair of you get up to, John?"

Ruth's voice glows, red-hot like molten rock. It has the power to injure him—char his eyebrows, blister his skin, or melt the soles of his boots.

"I said, I didn't do—"

"Oh, don't worry, you don't have to tell me. I can

guess. If it was half as bad as what you did to me it's no wonder you're too ashamed to admit it." Staring at her brother, being burned and buried by his guilt, Ruth is tempted by pity, like a shiny red apple, but refuses to take a bite. "After all this time you've finally put it together," she says. "You made the connection, didn't you? Now you blame yourself. What is it, do you have nightmares? Panic attacks? Do you cry for no reason?" This flow, it won't cool instantaneously. It could take days, months, even years before he is undisturbed by her words. "Do you know what I remember about back then, John? I remember you being fucking horrible. You were a complete cunt for no reason. You were a bully, John, plain and simple."

It is John, not her, who rises from the table first, his voice barely audible. "Don't ever talk to me about this again, I'm warning you."

The lava moves slow enough towards him that he can escape. Eyes downcast, he backs carefully away from her, towards the front door.

John is warning her? Ruth would laugh if there weren't already tears in her eyes.

The bully is not a type endemic to the schoolyard or classroom; a weed, it invades all spheres of life. The last place Ruth encountered one was during a temporary contract within a City Council, of all places. For two months Ruth sat in an open plan workplace never noticing the vermin in the corner. Deceptively quiet and mousy, seemingly harmless, this bully was the type who pretended to work but spent the day gossiping via email. Occasionally she let slip a snide remark about a co-worker but only when they were out of earshot and always in the guise of a joke, one that was never funny—an aptitude for double-talk.

Still, Ruth paid little attention to her over the months, had only engaged in a handful of superficial but friendly conversations about pets. The woman was a stereotypical spinster, a cat lady who brought in her own disposable filter bags filled with loose tea from home. Despite this, she unofficially held the position of 2IC.

Ruth never saw it coming. In hindsight, it was an opportunistic attack. Afterwards, she came to believe that a bully's mentality is not dissimilar to that of a rapist. It is all about power and the abuse of such.

The incident took place at a business luncheon to celebrate a milestone in a project Ruth was barely involved in. On a Friday at noon, the team walked together from their building a few city blocks to a restaurant and lounge bar, the kind she usually avoided.

Around the large table wine was brought and glasses filled. Bit by bit, she relaxed on the stream of lubricated conversation.

Shortly after the meal, a few made excuses to leave, to collect children from school or meet friends.

It was the perpetrator who ordered the first spirits of the afternoon—rum and coke.

Those left at the table followed her lead. Ruth would have one drink and then leave, she decided. When the moment came to pay, she was informed, 'It's taken care of'. Despite her insistence, the waitress merely smiled and walked away. Apparently it was an open bar. When she finished her drink she ordered another.

Five o'clock came and went in a blur and Ruth found

herself at the table with the perpetrators. So eager was Ruth to fit into her new team and so impaired was her judgement from the alcohol, that when the attack began her immediate reaction was to explain herself, to try and correct what was clearly a misunderstanding.

Did she realise they all knew she had eyelash extensions? She wasn't fooling anyone.

For all Ruth went through having *cow lashes* growing up, the suggestion that she would go out and pay money for extensions was so utterly ridiculous it was a joke.

The alcohol removed Ruth's inhibitions. 'Here, you can touch them', she offered. 'Give them a pull.'

'They're your only good feature and they're fake.'

'Excuse me?' Ruth said in disbelief. 'You can't speak to someone at work like that.'

'This isn't work, it's the pub.'

Shocked, with her hands beginning to tremble, Ruth turned her attention to the Project Director. 'Can I please have a word with you? Outside?'.

'Don't bother', the perpetrator told her, 'he doesn't like you either.'

The Project Director wouldn't look her in the eye. 'Is that true?' Ruth asked him.

For a drawn-out moment he hesitated, tilting his glass on the table and then turning to her he said, 'You've been unfriendly'.

So this was all a case of her being the new girl in the classroom, on the playground? Were they serious?

'See?' The perpetrator said. 'No one likes you.'

Ruth listed off the colleagues she had never had anything but positive interactions with and for each of the names the perpetrator provided an account of backstabbing, each with just enough detail to make it seem plausible.

'You're harassing me'. Now Ruth truly felt violated. 'Seriously, stop. Or I'll make a complaint against you'.

'So what? You have no proof. I'll just make a complaint right back against you'.

Once again Ruth turned to the Project Director for help.

'Don't try and manipulate him!'

'Can you please just tell me ... am I not wanted on the project?' Ruth asked the Project Director.

He sighed and then his face hardened. 'If you want to stay on the project then stay on the project. If you want to leave then leave'.

The perpetrator smiled smugly.

For a few moments Ruth sat stunned. 'I can't go back to work now, can I?' she said finally, a realisation voiced aloud.

'Not unless you want to work somewhere that no one likes you and you know they're all talking about you behind your back', the perpetrator said.

It felt like a nightmare; it couldn't be happening. Ruth's brain was too slow to process the information. Due to the alcohol, her ordinary reactions were taking longer at a time when a quick response was necessary. Desperately, she looked around the restaurant and over to the bar where strangers sat draped on banquettes or sunk in Chesterfields sipping cocktails or imported beer. No one here could help her. With shaking hands, she picked up her bag and got to her feet. Before she left, she looked the perpetrator in the eye. At an utter loss, she made one final appeal to her humanity.

'You have to be careful how you treat people. Don't you know that? You can't go around harming innocent people. I'm from Tasmania, I knew victims of the Port Arthur massacre'.

The perpetrator sat back, was silent a few seconds, and then laughed in her face. 'Are you going to come into the office on Monday and shoot us all, Ruth?'

The entire weekend, Ruth ate nothing. Every time she tried, she would dry retch. As soon as she was sober on Saturday morning, she contemplated her options. Perhaps she could confide in another colleague, one who had left early, ask their advice?

Then she spent hours rehearsing what she would say to the perpetrator when she saw her on Monday. How she would defend herself against future attacks. To simply quit was not an option; she was dependent on the income.

By nightfall, she was experiencing violent flashbacks to school incidents. One in particular.

"Just leave her alone," says the soft voice of the class captain, untethered and too soon soaked up by the classroom walls.

"She asks for it," the perpetrator calls over his shoulder. "You go around telling everyone they have to be nice to her but I'm sick of it. She's a freak!"

Then directly to Ruth he says, "Sit still or I'm going to stab your eyeballs out."

The last thing she sees is the sharp arms of the scissors opening like the beak of a hungry chick. Then she feels the cold metal pressed against her eyelid and the pressure on her eye socket.

When she opens her eyes he is gone. Then she feels the itch on her cheek, close to her nose. She reaches up and wipes the skin with her fingers, expecting blood. When she looks at the fingertips there are short hairs stuck to them, like black miniature pine needles. As she realises what has happened, it seems very important to her, the most important thing in the world, that she keep her eyelashes. And so she stands up carefully, never taking her eyes from her upturned fingertips and that's when the teacher comes rushing back into the classroom, the class captain returning at her side.

"What on earth's the matter?" the teacher says, before she sees Ruth out of her seat. When she does, with a look on her face of disappointment or frustration, or perhaps both, she sighs and says, "Oh, Ruth."

On Monday morning, Ruth broke down and rang the recruitment agency in floods of tears as she told them she would not be going back to the City Council job, not even to collect her personal belongings.

Over the coming months, revenge fantasies became Ruth's constant companions. No guns, no shootings, no innocent victims.

Just the bully.

Poison: a hands-off, elegant means to an end. Not vainglorious, like a stabbing or an acid-attack. It didn't require muscle, like bludgeoning. Ruth required a weapon that would simply get the job done. Blackwood bark was very practical that way—practical and cold-blooded. Ruth was still in possession of a security pass for the building. The bully arrived early to work each morning, before the rest of the team. Ruth could slip in after her through those sliding glass doors with an inconspicuous syringe full of the concentrated solution. Then the moment of climax as she found the bully sitting helpless at her desk, as Ruth snuck into the kitchenette and injected all of her teabags with the toxin. Then, calm and satisfied, she would exit the building.

Consequences were of no consequence.

While Seamus records their details in the Walkers' Register at Fortescue Bay campground, Ruth stands motionless with her eyes closed, sunshine blasting through the lids, creating a hypnotic hot coal glow. The trance is only broken by Seamus's boisterous voice, "Ah Jesus, her da has given up all hopes of findin' her alive."

It takes a moment for Ruth to realise that he is talking about the Italian tourist, Pietra Toniolo, who went missing without a trace months ago.

A story from *The Mercury* sheathed in a zip lock plastic sandwich bag is pinned to the noticeboard beneath the modest shelter roof. Ruth reads the article for herself, still looking for a sliver of hope, but without any luck. The father has sent a heartfelt message of thanks to Tasmanians for a sense of *immense emotional support* the family felt during the search for his daughter. Although he may never know what happened to his daughter he said he had found comfort in knowing every effort was made to find her.

They say that the truth is stranger than fiction. All Ruth knows is that often the most haunting stories are the ones where the answer can never truly be known. Why else would cases like the death of Azaria Chamberlain–'My God, my God, the dingo's got my baby!'–occupy such a profound place in the collective unconscious?

Heading in the opposite direction from Cape Hauy, omnipotent now, that sound of waves in action. It resonates with Ruth. Not just the vibrations in her cochleae, like conch shells, and the way it sinks into her skin alongside the salt sprayed air and premeditated cold–it has penetrated her psyche. This time, as the pair walks the length of Fortescue Beach, Ruth has her eyes trained on the sea. So innocent, it appears, a pure daydream. Despite this, her jaw clenches and both hands grasp tighter the backpack shoulder straps at her chest. It might as well be a parachute she is wearing at this point. You took her, she accuses.

Pietra.

Inside Ruth's mouth, the syllables roll like a set of silent waves across her tongue: *Pi-et-ra*. Finally, lungs relent, and Ruth snatches a desperate breath.

Turning his capped head over his shoulder, Seamus asks, "Are you poorly? Sure, it looks like ye 'bout to boke."

In his Northern Irish accent, those consonants flick violent like flight feathers.

"No, I'm OK, not gonna be sick. Keep going."

While she may not be physically ill, it is true that she could easily turn around and go right back to the bothy and the sleeping bag. How can she make John listen to reason? It is not a question of moral superiority as he suggested but rather it is a question of common sense. Weapons and children are two things that you must never put together. Where was common sense the day the future Port Arthur gunman was given his first rifle, when he was the same age as Rusty? Ruth does not want to be asking that question about her nephew years from now. Neither does she want her brother to ask it about his own son.

Those who cannot remember the past are condemned to repeat it.

The continual tidal motion has worn into her substratum, as if the slow waves were on a loop, steadily eroding it away. A human being is not bedrock. Over years, decades and centuries, this fluid force even ate the heart out of sea caves, wore geo clefts into cliffs and left sea stacks towering off the coastal shore. Now she not only knows how it is accomplished, she begins to understand how it feels to be a casualty of this war of attrition, all without getting a toe wet.

"It's only ninety minutes," she says. "That's nothing in the grand scheme of things."

Looking at the sand, she imagines each unit of time as a single seashell, which will fit easily in the palm of her hand. All she has to do is carry it, light and empty, until she finds the next one.

Easy as a child collecting shells on the beach.

"Maybe not in this world," says Seamus. "But what 'bout the other world?"

Ruth is in no mood for one of Seamus's Celtic ramblings. "I don't believe in fairy nonsense."

The other world.

Is that where Pietra is hiding? In a land of eternal youth and beauty beneath the surface, where it is always summer and there is no hunger and no despair? A mirror image of the world above sea level?

Seamus just won't stop. "Spend three days there and it'll be three years where you came from. Spend three years, it'll be three centuries. When you go back home everybody you know will be dead."

"Well isn't that a pleasant thought," she says dryly.

"The principle of life is change, love. None of us wants to grow old, to die, but consider the alternative. There would be no growth, no new life."

"Blah, blah, blah."

Once on the walking track to Waterfall Bay, climbing to the cliff top, the view of Seamus's back just ahead of her is all too familiar. This is not the first time she has been left feeling, in his presence, as though she is merely tagging along for the ride. At least on the Three Capes Walk they'd have been able to walk side by side. That path was made wide enough, using a trinity of timber, stone and gravel. As they hike, the absence of conversation between them is not unusual. Seamus's mind is constantly churning. Right now he is no doubt engaged in an inner dialogue with himself. To witness firsthand the Peninsula's rock formations is something he has long been planning and anticipating, the artistry of geology combined with thousands of years of elemental weathering.

Of all the native tree species that surround them, it is the sheoak of the understorey that stands out to Ruth, assuring her that she is indeed on the coast. A hint of silveriness imbued in the dark green needle-like leaves is the promise of pristine sands below them.

Like a compass arm, Ruth points straight across a south-east sea to Hippolyte Rocks. "There!"

Seamus draws his camera and begins shooting. It is the water bottle Ruth reaches back to her hip for, taking it from the elasticised side pocket of her backpack. Undone in haste, the lid spins for a second on the tip of her index finger before it falls and her hand snaps shut like a trap to catch it. Chilled water spills down her throat as she snorts through her nostrils with exertion.

The size and shape of the rock has always reminded Ruth of the body of a blue whale with a docked tail, floating stationary on the surface, stranded without its rudder.

Before they set off again, Ruth steps up to take in the view back to their home base, Fortescue Beach. Straight down, the kelp is visible as deep as the eye can see, a subaqueous forest. Their destination, the Moai—one of the well-known, named sea stacks along with The Candlestick and The Totem Pole—is sacred, a shrine to the Rock Gods.

At Canoe Bay, Ruth falls back. Oblivious, Seamus hikes on ahead while she strolls by the empty camping area on the stony shore. The remnants of an illegal open fire are days cold and strewn by native scavengers. Facing this is a rusted sunken dredge, its Crocodilian head spying from the waterline. The flat arch of a cranial platform rises beyond a long rigid snout while the bulk of the body is hidden below the surface. Along this improvised breakwater, little cormorants are perched like sentries. At risk of losing sight of Seamus, finally Ruth summons him, "Coo-ee!"

Ruth's stentorian voice echoes back to her and for a second she is startled. This sonic boomerang has hit its target though, and Ruth rushes to meet Seamus returning along the track.

"Ye havin' a dander?" he asks.

"A what? A gander?"

"A dander," he says. "D for delta. Means a stroll, a slow walk, a dander."

"D for delta, got it."

"D for ..." Seamus breaks into a spontaneous jig. "In the deep, dark, dark cave lay a dragon being bold bossy and brave."

"What the hell?" she laughs. "Is that an Irish nursery rhyme or something?"

"Nothin'," he says. "Were a poem I had published in Primary Three at school."

"A poem you wrote? You remember it?"

"'Twas my first publication. Course I remember it. Sure, it's short and not very sweet." Only now, as they round the head of the bay, does Seamus notice the sunken dredge. "Prospectors? What were they hopin' for?"

"Probably sapphires. Sapphires, definitely." Ruth laughs. "No, I don't know. Never thought about it. It looks really old though."

As they approach the suspension bridge over Walkers Creek she whispers to Seamus, "Look, a pademelon."

Ruth knows he has never seen one before, only Bennetts wallabies and Eastern Grey kangaroos. Smaller than both, the pademelon turns its head to stare at them, seeming unafraid, used to the sight of walkers. Ruth never tires of encounters with wildlife. Crouching down to its eye level, she communes with the animal for a drawn-out moment.

Crossing the bridge, they enter the fern grotto. A frond furls like the fingers of a hand beckoning to them. A sudden peace descends. Immediate, an intravenous injection, it is the antidote to Ruth's troubled mind. At first her tongue slumbers in the bed of her jaw and then walking feels like floating forwards, effortless. Glancing back, she catches sight of Seamus's smile, teeth crown jewels atop his beard.

At Bivouac Bay, they stop for a toilet break.

The rest of the way, Ruth is busy reacquainting herself with the bush. Oyster Bay Pines rise above an understory of Bedfordia. The sight of stone cairns, when they first come into view, brings relief incommensurate with their role as landmarks. The stacked rocks recall the Cape Raoul track cairns, the ones that greet you as you emerge from the sheoak forest and continue between the shallow lake and the inlet.

"It's this way," announces Ruth, a gust of wind lending authority to her words as she overtakes Seamus.

Being a local, she would call this climbers' trail a wallaby path, although she spots no wallabies on the approach to the cliff top. Usually you hear the animal first, the sudden rustle of leaves in the understory or a stick cracking under hind leg as the animal bounds away.

Arriving at the Moai, the earth beneath Ruth's feet gives way to a 100-metre sheer drop and a vast expanse of sea. There is a painful blast of light in her eyes as sunshine reflects off the wave-pinched surface and the pale grey rock cliff surrounds. Squeezing her eyes shut tight, Ruth stands and waits a moment for the blindness to pass. Then, shielding her gaze with both hands at her brow, she opens her eyes, breathes in, and sees the Moai: a lone towering pillar of dolerite shooting up from the end of a rock platform, like a black altar, connected to the coastal shore north of Fortescue Bay.

"It's the fecking Paschal candle," says Seamus.

Alarmed, Ruth reassures him, "No, it's the Moai. This is it."

Wind whips hair around each of their faces as they stand in conversation on the cliff top.

"Did you say the Candlestick?" asks Ruth. "That's Cape Hauy, where we just came from. The Candlestick is beside the Lanterns."

Ruth gestures south, back along the coastline. Seamus crouches, camera resting on his kneecap. Peering over the cliff edge, Ruth finds a group of climbers at the base, having just completed their abseil.

"Damn," she says. "There are people down there. What do you want to do? Wait for them to leave? How long does an average rock climb take, anyway? An hour? Shit, shit, shit! I told you we should have gone to Cape

Raoul first. There are no rock climbers there."

"Aye, Cape Raoul. Sure, then we'd be followin' the tourists on *the Misnomer*."

Ruth can't help but smile each and every time Seamus calls the Three Capes Track 'the Misnomer'. It is a joke, really, calling the new dry-boot standard trail the Three Capes Track when it neglects Cape Raoul altogether. Growing up on Tasman Peninsula, it was not a compass rose you used to orientate yourself by. The position of the sun in the sky or the Southern Cross at night were of little consequence. The three capes were your cardinal directions and they formed a near perfect right triangle. The first leg ran from Cape Hauy straight down to Cape Pillar, the base leg from Cape Pillar across Maingon Bay to Cape Raoul and the hypotenuse was formed by joining Cape Raoul back up to Cape Hauy. Even the sports houses at Tasman District School were named after the capes: Hauy, red; Pillar, blue; and Raoul, green.

"They don't bother you?" she asks.

"Who, the pilgrims? Why'd they bother me? What right have I to be bothered by them? I know how selfish I am but arrogant?" Seamus shakes his head.

Pilgrims?

To Ruth they look like nothing more than ants crawling across an altar towards the sea stack. "What did you call it? Paschal?"

"Keep forgettin' you're a heathen," says Seamus. "Aye, Paschal," he repeats. "The fattest candles on the planet. After the first lighting of the candle you hear the story of the creation of the world in the first reading of the Easter Vigil. Sun and stars, sea and fish on it usually, symbolising life."

Amongst the climbers, the colour red is the star of the day. Blue is the understudy. Yellow is an afterthought. Bright are the t-shirts, cropped pants and caps they don, as are the helmets, harnesses, ropes and slings they unpack.

"Can I see?" asks Ruth, unable to resist the chance to share an eagle's eye through the camera's zoom lens. The sudden dissonance of distance turns her initial exhilaration to vertigo. As Ruth stumbles sideways, Seamus lunges to catch his camera, leaving her to fall. Landing on her hands she slides on the rock, grazing the heels of her palms. Once she has caught her breath she looks up at him in disbelief, a flash flood of emotion sweeping her to the brink of tears.

"Your skin will heal," says Seamus, unwilling to make eye contact. "The camera won't."

Pain burning deep in the dermis makes her turn up her palms. No blood has broken the skin's surface. It is an itch but not one that you want scratched. Ruth sees water splashing over her hands seconds before she feels the sting.

"Get off!" she shouts as she pulls away from Seamus's upturned water bottle. "Ow! That hurts, you fool!"

It is Seamus who laughs first, a spontaneous outburst. Quickly she joins him.

"Ye eejit," he retorts.

Giving up, Ruth lays down on her back, forearms cushioning her head.

It is at least an hour, but not two, when she hears the voices of strangers in conversation. Faces flushed with exertion, one by one the pilgrims begin to appear.

"I think we've got it," Seamus tells her.

Sitting up, Ruth combs her hair back into a ponytail

with her fingers, smiling with eyes half closed, as the two groups acknowledge one another's presence on the lookout with murmurs and nodding heads.

"Don't trust the piton!" a climber calls out, as he holds up an old rusty climbing spike.

"Congratulations." Seamus walks over to him. "You've not worn gloves then, for the big climb?"

"Just chalk, mate."

"Was it worth it?" asks Seamus.

"Everybody should climb the Moai. I want to do it again as soon as possible."

Seamus glances back at Ruth, eyebrows raised. Only then does she notice that each of the pilgrims has wounds on the backs of their hands, the skin rubbed raw, pierced and bloodied so that she can imagine the holes go right through. The sight hits her in the gut.

"They're all crazy," she whispers to Seamus upon his return.

"Love," he replies, "look at your own hands."

That night, a storm force southerly assaults Tasman National Park. The wind spits portent. Lightning is the sound of shotgun blasts, then thunder is tin sheets shuddering. Beneath that, are bullets of rain. Within the bothy, Ruth sits with Seamus at the plank table, candles burning bright in the necks of empty wine bottles to illuminate their game of Scrabble. Beside the board sits another wine bottle, two-thirds empty, and beside each of their tile racks a freshly filled mug.

The long-sleeved button up shirt Seamus wears appears to Ruth at odds with the sweat soaked band and miner's light on his forehead. An assortment of words, both real and imagined, crisscross the board: vadj, froq, netheme, blud, whak, drift, grow, bisexual and zap. They don't keep score. The beam of Seamus's headlamp darts like a firefly over their compositions, then rapidly from one end of the table to the other, before finally alighting on Ruth's shoulder.

"That wind sounds like a bloody banshee," Ruth complains.

"Careful now," says Seamus. "The banshee is twisted and cruel. She signals the coming of the carriage that will take you to the other realm."

For a few seconds, Ruth watches a single flame burn on the head of a candle, like a lady standing still in the wind, her long ginger hair blown back from the wick of her face. It makes Ruth think of *Redheads* matches and that the person who came up with this brand name surely witnessed a candle behave in the way she observes now.

"There's a million different stories about banshees in Ireland. Everyone's heard one. My gran herself had a story about seeing, or hearing, a banshee," says Seamus. "She was walking past a convent. It's surrounded by a wall that's about 12 feet high. I don't know if it's to keep people out or keep the nuns in but you can't see the convent from the town so it was always seen as a scary building. Kids would hurry past its gothic architecture and dark corners."

Ruth is dragged back, as by an undercurrent, to Port Arthur and the ruined church.

"As my gran was walking past one night, she saw something moving out of the corner of her eye and looked on top of the wall and saw what looked like the silhouette of a wee girl. It was silent as she passed but when she walked further down the street she heard a wail. Not a shriek, or scream, but just a long-drawn-out mournful cry. Like everyone in Ireland she knew the story of the banshee so she didn't look back."

For a few moments, with their eyes locked on one another, they listen together to the wind outside. Ruth feels a rush of fear, teetering on excitement; they are children telling ghost stories in the dark. Suddenly, all she wants to do is climb into bed and have Seamus's body wrapped around hers beneath the sleeping bags, her ears deafened by the pillow and his warm, bearded cheek.

She drains her glass and says, "Come to bed."

One of Seamus's eyes widens, the eyebrow lifting, and she sees that he has misunderstood. Sex is never far from his mind. At the sleeping platform Ruth steps out of her jeans. Seamus approaches holding one of the bottle candles in his hand. As he steps over her jeans on the floor, the flame tips and a rivulet of hot wax spills, the purlicue of his hand a tender net to catch it.

"Jesus fuck!"

Squatting, he lets go of the bottle. It rolls across the stone floor as he attempts to shake the wax off his hand but the wintry night air has already hardened it like a second skin.

When he takes off his shirt and lies down beside Ruth, she climbs over and sits on top of him, bearing down on his pelvis. With her elbows pressed into the air mattress above his shoulders she braces herself over him, but close to his face that she may kiss him. Although always wary at first of his beard and moustache, she finds his lips soft and welcoming. Ruth begins to rock. She is the waves of the sea that is drowning him. They rock together like this, her a siren slowly pulling him under. With his eyes closed Seamus sighs into Ruth's mouth, over and over, but it is not a sigh of passion; it is a death rattle escaping his body each time; it is plain enough, she is killing him. Sometimes Seamus is looking at Ruth and he is only looking, but there are moments when his eyes soften and look up and he is an infant gazing at his mother, he is Jesus Christ staring to heaven from the cross; he is a man in love, surrendering. Silent yet desperate, he is asking her something. Ruth can see the question in his face, in those deep brown eyes but she cannot answer him, even though she longs to.

When finally Seamus pushes Ruth off of him, letting out a heaving sigh, they are both wet through—he seeping up through his pants to stain her underwear and she wet inside them.

Despite this, Seamus says, "I'm tired of dry humping," and rolls over to face the wall.

Across his back freckles spread like stars—Ruth's Milky Way. Unable to think of a single thing to say to console him she invents constellations, traces them with her thumbnail, the bright red lines that appear on his pale skin arresting as stop signs, traffic lights. Quickly his skin turns cadaverous beneath her fingertips, the light strokes from the edge of her palm and the pressure of the luna mount. To warm him, she draws the sleeping bag up.

Chapter 5
John

With a candle burning on the bench, John rests his fingertips on the ledge of the transom window and peers out at the storm. The wind shakes the trees violently and John recognises this frenetic movement. The branches gyrate wildly like the lifeless limbs and floppy ears of a fresh rabbit in the jaws of a hound.

Throughout the house the wooden doors have swollen as a result of three days of heavy rain. They stick on the doorjambs. Condensation on the fronts of the windows tells of the cold beyond. The forecasters fear flooding. Swells are pushing seawater into rivers and creeks on the Peninsula, on top of predicted downpours. Troops of ants march in long lines across the floors, the barriers of insect spray now washed off the perimeter. It is the slugs in the dairy though that John takes notice of. Slithering in at nightfall they leave silvery trails on the concrete, which show up beneath the fluorescent lights in the morning.

When the power failed, John was in the kitchen at the refrigerator, eyeing off, on the bottom shelf, the cake he had baked and iced for cracker night. Of course he immediately closed the door to keep in the chill but in reality, in these temperatures, he might just as well have stacked the contents in an esky and left it on the porch.

The stove fire is the next thing John thinks about, that he must light it before it gets any darker. There are plenty of candles stored in drawers and there are a couple of lanterns in the kill shed.

Storms upset the cows, upset their milking routine. Back when they kept horses he had a mare struck by lightning in the front paddock. It survived but he had to put it out of its misery—the rifle way. Took a day or two before that stench of singed fur and burned flesh cleared out of his nasal passage and the taste out of his throat. Grim business.

The generator will power the refrigeration for the stores of milk in the dairy but the house is back to basics. John blows air behind his closed lips inflating the vestibule of his mouth and as he taps beside his nose with four stiff fingers the sound is similar to, but softer than, that of a basketball bouncing on a court. With a puff, he exhales the stored breath and checks in his pocket for the mobile phone. The battery is low and needs recharging. For the moment, he puts it in low power mode. So, no landline because the docking station has no power. The mobile he will save for an emergency. John strikes a match and holds it inside the stove, beneath the pile of kindling he built at lunchtime. Watching the tiny flame catch and grow he remembers the dual band radio. Since Christmas, they had tested it a number of times, he and Rusty, communicating between the two farms. Rusty was easily bored and John soon gave up trying to sustain conversations with his son. This will be their first real opportunity for a live run.

In the hallway, John trips on the runner and almost falls, in his haste to reach the bedside table drawer. As he enters the bedroom, out of habit he reaches for the light switch, then laughs at his own stupidity. John sits down on the bed, radio receiver in hand. While he plans what to say to Rusty, he tunes into the weather channel, sparing a thought for his sister right on the coast. The refugee couple can always come here to the house if Fortescue Bay Campground floods. When the power is restored he might have to drive over to Fortescue Bay to check on them and make an offer of temporary accommodation and board.

Rusty is not on the public channel. John calls Rusty's mobile but it goes straight to his voicemail. John sends a text message to him then tunes back into channel 67 for the weather. The warnings are only a guide. The wind speeds and wave heights can be up to twice the forecast averages. Anything over 25 knots and a warning is issued. At the moment, the gusts are only 20 knots, which still constitutes dangerous surf conditions with waves breaking close in shore.

After five minutes with no response from Rusty to his text message, John carries the radio back to the kitchen where he takes candles from the drawer to fill the candelabra on the dining table and put votives in clean jam jars on the benches.

John doesn't know what's gotten into his sister, usually she's as quiet as a church mouse. What was she playing at asking him what shotgun he bought Rusty for his birthday? Was she hoping he was going to say an Adler A110, so she could go on some delusional rant about the fact that it fires seven—now only five—rounds in as many seconds? Try and tell him it was no different to a pump-action shotgun? The way everybody goes on about the Adler you could be excused for thinking it is some kind of magic weapon, that it fires silver bullets that can kill a werewolf.

John recalls making Ruth cry on her birthday once, in this very room. Perhaps it was her tenth. Sitting at the dining table waiting for the cake to arrive from the kitchen, he had ribbed her until she burst into tears and ran to her bedroom. Now he can't even remember what he said but even back then he knew how to get to her. By that age he had years of experience on the school playground as well as on holidays spent with the shackies at Carnarvon Bay. It was his sister's pride that had ticked him off on that occasion, she was so proud that it was her birthday and had sat at the head of the table like a princess. It is not regret he is feeling, just an unpleasant vibration within the room. When they were kids he had never been violent towards his sister. It was only ever teasing. *Sticks and stones* was a lesson she never did manage to learn. It was only if he actually pushed Ruth to tears that he got reprimanded. John suspects she worked that out early on and used it against him—crocodile tears were her forte.

As the storm rages outside the house, John begins to be tormented by sharp pains that start in his back and side and move towards his groin and testicles. Unable to find a comfortable position in a chair, he paces the rooms, tugging at his eyelashes, ripping a couple out. When he can take it no longer, using a front kick John drives the heel of his bare foot into a stuck door, only just keeping his balance by driving the heel of his standing foot into the aged floorboards. When he looks back at the door he sees the wood has splintered near the handle. Turning his body side on, he launches himself at it shoulder first. It swings open. The sound that leaves his body is somewhere between a sigh and a groan, but the emotion is, through and through, relief. With the pain moving to his shoulder, he squeezes his elbows into his flanks gingerly and pulls the door closed once more. Then, he steps backwards, and he throws himself at it again.

Again.

And again.

It's raining clear pellets. John sits inside the vehicle with the farm expense ledger resting open on the steering wheel. On the car bonnet, wind moves the rainwater backwards towards the windscreen like a wave withdrawing across gleaming dark sand. The alarm on his watch sounds. At the same time, the mobile rings. It is Helen calling. John switches off the alarm and puts Helen on speaker.

"Hello?"

Hello, John. Are you with Rusty? He's not answering.

"No, I'm waiting outside the school. I think he had a detention for that last fight he was in."

What a nerve. If he's not out in five minutes drag him out by the shirt collar.

"Righto."

And can you get some ice from the servo please? I'm going to need a G and T, or half a dozen, tonight.

"Be there shortly."

John ends the call. Glancing up, he sees Rusty through the rain streaked driver's side window, the crimson red sweatshirt blurred as it approaches, a cap on his head beneath the raised hood.

"Have they made you switch your phone off?" asks John as Rusty gets in.

"That's it, Dad. Let's go." Rusty lowers the sunshade to look in the mirror as he lowers his hood.

"Thirteen minutes late," says John.

"Sorry. I couldn't help it. Let's just go."

"We have to get your mother some ice from the servo."

"And Coke?"

"It's a wonder you haven't lost all your teeth with that lolly water you guzzle. Dental work ain't cheap, Rusty."

"I never lost a tooth, only had a few fillings," he says.

John has steered the conversation towards the topic on his mind without even trying to and he realises suddenly that he may have hit on what is at the root of Rusty's problem. Rusty visits the dentist regularly and he's not a fan. There is a time and place for empathy but husbandry is not one of them. It isn't surgery for pity's sake. The only tool that's required is a pair of cutting pliers you can pick up at any hardware store, a bottle of surgical-grade disinfectant to keep the clippers sterile, and a couple of plastic rubbish bins, one to gather the piglets and the second one close by to deposit them in once they're processed. John has never clipped a piglet's teeth himself but he's seen it performed plenty of times.

You just hold the piglet like a football, cradling and tucking it between your forearm and body. Then inserting your index finger into the piglet's mouth close to the back you force the mouth open and use your other fingers to manipulate the lips to expose the teeth you need to get at. Helen didn't mention if Rusty had cut the lips or the tongue, or god forbid opened the pulp cavity or shattered below the gum line. At the very least he hadn't managed to yield a flat surface, leaving sharp areas, which meant she had to re-clip them herself.

Deciding to wait for the right moment to broach the subject, he starts the car.

Without warning, too late, John finds himself ghost driving, the vehicle heading the wrong way on the Nubeena Ring Road.

"Wait! Let's turn around," says Rusty, twisting his neck to look back at the dark, wet road through the rear window.

"What?" John accelerates. "No ..."

"Why not?"

"We can't stop here," says John. "This is bad country." And it is not geography of which he speaks, but genealogy.

A lot of violence has happened there. It must be the most violent place in Australia. It seemed the right place.

A chord struck.

Once again, John hears the bone chimes thud. Simply making their presence known. No sign does he see nor a specific message hear, only senses someone on the other side announcing themself at his door.

Leave your goddamned notch, he thinks, go on then. Do it, you bastard!

At the Port Arthur service station, a child in a raincoat rides their bicycle to shelter past the bowsers, forcing him to wait. John is about to broach the subject he has been sent to discuss with Rusty when his son opens the car door and jumps out.

"I'll go." Rusty bends his head in the rain to look back into the car. "Want anything?"

John passes him a ten-dollar note. "Don't forget the ice."

"Nah."

John watches Rusty walk towards the ice freezer thumbing keys on his phone. With only one hand free he drags a bag out carelessly instead of lifting it. John shakes his head and taps an anxious index finger on the steering wheel.

Holes, Rusty, holes.

From the wallet still held in his hand, John pulls out the polaroid photograph he has had stashed there for the last few years. John discovered it whilst searching for magnets for Rusty. Said he needed them for some new hobby he and his school mates had picked up from one of their teachers. As far as John could make out this 'magnet fishing' was just a new term for treasure hunting, which he was fine with as long as it was coins and tyre rims the kids were after and not safes or guns. Despite his initial suspicions that the PVN had put the idea out there in the community, that there was some environmentalism element to the whole thing, to have kids removing debris from bodies of water, John had given his permission.

The polaroid is more than thirty years old and of a bay mare named 'Delta'. The horse had come up to the fence one afternoon when he had ridden his bike to Carnarvon Bay in hopes of seeing her in a pair of denim shorts that all the teenage girls were wearing that summer. The camera he took without permission, risking an hour on the rice if he got caught by his father. To John's mind, it was worth the pain.

Although he hated to admit it, there was some truth to Ruth's allegations the other day. Is that why he can't let go of the memories of that time? He wants his first love to forgive him for what he did? Is it love or simply absolution he is seeking? John bites his lower lip gently and of its own accord it slips away from beneath his top teeth. Another vehicle speeds into the service station and pulls up beside him, a black sports car shining as if the exterior has just been waxed. The points of reflected light across the curves of its body like stars spread across a clear night sky.

Bang! Bang! Bang!

John's eardrums are pierced right before he turns to see Rusty exit through the door. Gunshots, is his immediate thought. Rusty has not lowered his hood to pay for the ice. John eyeballs him, searching for any sign of trauma. When he sees Rusty's hands deep in the front pocket of the sweatshirt, John's fingers fly up to his greying temples.

"Bloody Ruth," he mutters. "Damn her."

John exhales and waits for his son to get back. Without giving him the chance to close the car door behind him, he drives off. The mobile starts ringing.

"You want me to get it?" asks Rusty. "It's Mum."

"Leave it, son." John reaches to place an unsteady hand on Rusty's damp shoulder as he finally pushes off his hood. Overnight, it seems, or at least over the winter, with the cold weather clothes covering up his body, Rusty's neck has thickened like a climbing vine. The break in his nose from his last fight months ago has healed, leaving a slight bump on the bridge that is almost becoming on a young man. It is the kind of thing that makes for rugged good looks.

"Hell of a racket back there," says John. "What was it?"

"What was what?"

"What do you think? That noise, back at the servo, that's what."

"You mean the bottles smashing? Yeah, the guy who

came in after me knocked some bottles off a shelf. How'd you even hear that?"

"Bloody idiot sped in like he was on the autobahn," says John. "Lucky the kid on the bike had already passed through or he'd have knocked 'em over."

"Dad, can you watch the road please?" Beneath the bag on his lap Rusty squirms in his seat. "Shit this ice is cold."

Staring through the windscreen John blinks in time with the wipers, forcing from his mind the events of virtually a quarter of a century earlier, as if it is the moment in a film where in seconds the night turns to day and a subtitle appears on the screen to account for the viewer's time travel. New characters appear and one will say, 'A woman was killed here a long time ago'.

A close up shows the spot on the bare ground, now clean, where in the previous frame there had been spilled blood.

'I heard it was a shooting,' the other replies. 'I heard two people died.'

The first makes a gun with his hand and cocks it. 'Boom!'

"No, he took the man to Seascape and killed him later," says John, under his breath.

"Who?" asks Rusty. "Someone got killed?"

"What?" When John turns to look at Rusty the seatbelt locks up against his straining chest. "No, nothing." In his mouth the saliva tastes polluted, an unusual sweetness like blackcurrant. "Put your seatbelt on."

Once Rusty is strapped in, John begins. "You must have known your mother was going to tell me about your mishap with the piglets. Look, it doesn't take a genius to work out—"

"I'm sorry and embarrassed, alright," Rusty interrupts him. "But most of all I'm sorry for the worst week ever."

"For God's sake stop apologising!"

Rusty is always too ready to apologise, fit the word 'sorry' into the same sentence two, three times. It is like the boy is dependent on apology, uses it as a crutch. "There are things that go on at a farm that would make a city person's toes curl. If you don't have the stomach for husbandry you'd better start hitting the books. I'm not talking about the Cs, an occasional B you're used to bringing home, I'm talking straight As. That's the only way you'll get into a good course at university. It's about focus, Rusty. Focus and discipline."

Piglets undergo a battery of procedures during the first few days or weeks of life, not just tooth-clipping. There is tail docking, castration, and ear-notching or tagging or tattooing. All procedures involve a degree of tissue damage so of course the piglet is going to experience pain.

"A pig is not a pet," says John. "It's fifty kilos of meat that's high in protein and low in fat."

"They weren't pigs they were piglets," says Rusty. "Babies."

The boy was high on the dopamine release of cute little piglets and not totally prepared for the more hands-on task work.

"Right, well, if you want to apply that type of logic, do you think those paediatricians at the Royal Hobart Hospital don't sometimes have to hurt their patients, even babies, when they're helping them?"

Rusty shakes his head. "It's not the same thing though."

"Son, these chores are performed to protect the welfare of the pigs not just to improve production.

They're called *wolf teeth* for a reason. You can't have fanged piglets running around a farm. They're born with eight razor-sharp chompers. They fight with their siblings for teats and suffer facial lacerations, not to mention their sows getting udder lacerations and if a sow gets hurt it'll refuse to nurse the piglets and then what do you think happens to them?" John can hear the rising anger in his own voice. "Is it a girl? Has one of these girlfriends you're always talking about been filling your head with leftist, vegan propaganda? Is that it? You're trying to impress your girlfriend by being a young rebel?"

"My girlfriend isn't a vegan, Dad," says Rusty. "She eats fish."

"Since when is fish considered *meat*?" Only then does it dawn on John. What does all this mean for the duck hunt?

It is Cracker Night Eve and a reprieve from the rain sees John take Rusty across the front paddock of the west hill for the annual ritual of cutting down a sacrificial limb from their family's tree for the bonfire. This year, for the first time, it is Rusty who carries the hatchet, a sharpening puck in his hip pocket. The ground at the crest of the hill becomes rocky and the lush green of the grazing pasture fades out to native tussock grass with the occasional daisy. Lilies are commonplace, orchids rarer.

The lowest branches of the dead stringybark reach out far above John's standing height in Blundstones: six foot one. The stumps of previous limb amputations, most taken close to the trunk with a few leaving more branch remaining, speak of Cracker Nights past. Of course, Rusty sees the *Eucalyptus Obliqua* as a wooden jungle gym and has left the hatchet on top of a rock to start climbing it before John has even unwound the length of rope from his shoulder.

"Don't bloody swing on it!" he shouts. "Those branches are full of rot. They won't hold your weight. If you fall and break your neck I'll give your firecrackers to the neighbour's kids."

Rusty jumps down quick smart.

"Which one do you reckon?" asks John.

The thin crown above his head has died back substantially since last year. Walking backwards slowly, facing the tree, Rusty at last appears to be taking his task seriously. John fashions a lasso and flings it into the air, the loose end tethered firmly to the ground beneath his right foot. Over it goes, leaving a swinging noose within arm's reach.

"Right, too slow. I've got one." John is eyeballing a branch another six feet beyond his fingertips if he stood on tiptoe, right of the lightning strike crack that runs up the centre of the trunk where there is charred and missing bark.

"Pick up the axe," he instructs. "Get your stone out."

"There's no water up here," says Rusty.

"Use a bit of spit."

John plays tug-o-war with the chosen branch.

"Not too close to the collar," he tells Rusty. "Take your time, it's already dead. Couldn't be easier."

John keeps his focus on the boy though the sky up here always turns his thoughts to the swift parrot. "No need to take it back over your head like that." Where the pine forest now stands bordering Cripps Creek, swamp and blue gum once grew, the birds migrating each year. John was only a child then, younger than Rusty is now. It was those swift parrots that helped form John's enduring belief that a bird should never be kept in a cage. John can quote only one line of poetry, from the Blake poem, *Auguries of Innocence.*

A robin redbreast in a cage puts all of heaven in a rage.

It is the only bit of poetry John ever thought worthy of committing to memory and this fact had nothing to do with its namesake, his former friend and neighbour, Robin Whiteley.

Rusty has been splitting logs for firewood these past two years. It shows in the precision of his strike. John pulls on the rope putting downward pressure on the branch collar to aid him.

"Stand clear!" John raises one hand in the air to count down. "3, 2, 1..."

Rusty cheers as the severed branch hits the ground. John begins to feel a glimmer of excitement about the festivities ahead, just a spark of the spirit of Cracker Night ignited. In recent years the authorities have clamped down on the community tradition due to safety concerns. Now you need a permit. John doubts whether anyone even remembers it as part of Empire Day to mark Queen Victoria's birthday anymore.

For the rest of the bonfire fuel, father and son cross the hill to the fallen crowns of other families' trees. The hilltop stand of stringy bark stumps attests to the many generations who have gathered here around a bonfire at autumn's end to eat, drink and be merry together while children threw Tom Thumbs and Penny Bungers or watched the sparks fly from spinning Catherine wheels. Seizing the last chance to celebrate the turning of the seasons, the vibrant changing colours before the blackout of dead winter.

From the summit of the west hill John has an eagle's eye view of the farm. The land itself is something special. Convicts cleared this land. They did a good job of it too. It can't have been easy work back in those days, all done by hand and horse, no heavy machinery. This land is part of history. It is important for the culture. It has been, and remains, a privilege to work it. That's why it gets to him when outsiders, even his own sister, only see Port Arthur, and by extension Tasman Peninsula, for that one unfortunate day. The Peninsula has a legacy far beyond that simpleton.

Chapter 6

Ruth

Ruth is woken by a helicopter's rotor whirling through her dream. In the dream the sound became that of a heavily loaded washing machine on spin cycle. When she gets up off the sleeping platform the stone floor of the bothy is a mortuary slab beneath her feet, tender with sleep. Slipping on her anorak and gumboots she walks briskly down to the beach. Not yet have the campers surfaced from their tents or lit their breakfast fires.

Fortescue Bay laps like a wide wet tongue at the immaculate shore. There is nothing, just the light hovering above the waters. Ruth stands alone at the beginning of Earth.

The knowledge that the residency will end inflicts a pain tenfold more acute than the flaying cold of the Peninsula's winter dawn. That Seamus is a lover of the beautiful and the ephemeral is beyond her comprehension. Like a stubborn crab, Ruth will not let go.

As she is observing the still bay the surface is suddenly breached.

"Oh my god," she wheels around and says to no one. "It's a dolphin!"

Turning back, she sees there are in fact two dolphins, a cow and her calf. As if joined at their sides they arc together out of the water, a pair of short thick beaks followed by a pair of fins perfectly synchronised. Then the smaller tail, which is not completely trained in the fluid motion of its mother, smacks the surface at the last second.

Ruth considers running back to the bothy for Seamus and his camera but she does not know how long the dolphins will stay and she dare not miss them so she gives herself up to the moment, knowing that she will have no proof of the encounter, except in memory. Twenty metres from the shore the cow and calf play, at ease in the calm shallow waters, the mother teaching her young how to breach and breathe. Where the dolphins have surfaced a buckled disc appears like a vaccination scar upon the skin of the bay. Saltwater haloes float above the submerged cetaceans, so Ruth knows where to look for them. Further out, another dolphin, a bull's back, becomes visible. For a whole minute it stays stationary like a docked submarine and then he plunges down—then up—and the air blasts out of his blowhole so loud it scares birds out of the branches of a blue gum on the shore. He leaves behind a solid ring, which ripples out in concentric circles as if he is stating his status, his age determinable by counting these circles like tree rings from pith to bark.

At last, yet too soon, the dolphins head away, swim back out into open ocean, waving goodbye to her with their backs all the way. Ruth waits but eventually the surface of the water seals over and she knows that they are gone.

As she is stepping off the beach, Ruth sees a small

group of people standing together at the boat ramp. They hold onto one another as if their very lives are dependent on not being separated, not letting go. The arms of smaller ones wrapped beneath the arms of the taller, whose arms are wrapped around the others' necks, chin leant down and wedged between one's ear and another's cheek. They are root bound like a single vascular plant.

This is Pietra's family, Ruth assumes. They have found her.

Ruth is looking for a stretcher or a black body bag. Men in suits and ties wearing dark sunglasses are conspicuous as Roman collars in the wilderness setting. The lights of an ambulance flash silently. A woman stands alone, smoking. What at first appears to be a dressing gown is in fact a shell pink longline jacket.

"Morning," says Ruth to the warden. "What's going on?"

"A group of young fishermen put out a mayday on the emergency channel yesterday afternoon," he says. "Said their aluminium runabout was sinking. Weren't able to give an exact co-ordinate though."

When the warden speaks he does so mindfully as if speech is a resource to be conserved. Tim is his name, she remembers. Mid-thirties, ombré hair pulled back in a ponytail, short sleeves and a tan are his uniform. An earthiness emanates from him; here is a grounded human being. Ruth wonders how many days, how many weeks or even months on end he spends in the forest without leaving.

"Are they locals?" she asks. "Do you know their names?"

"I feel for the families," he says. "They've been here all night waiting for news."

Does the woman see her? It feels like she is staring right through Ruth.

"You think you might know them?" asks the warden.

"No."

When Ruth raises her hand and holds the palm still by her face like a light, shining it at the woman, she responds by taking her hand out of her jacket pocket and waving it from side to side as she exhales a breath of smoke, cigarette still burning in the other hand. Then she brings the cigarette to her face, her hand covering her nose and mouth like an oxygen mask as she inhales. As Ruth lowers her own hand, the warden beside her raises his to wave back at the lone smoking woman and Ruth realises, this is one of the missing fishermen's mothers.

"I thought maybe they'd found the missing woman, Pietra."

The warden turns up the brim of his cap at the mention of her name.

"Oh, you know about that, do you?"

"Only what I've read in the papers. Is there anything they're not saying?"

"I wish I did know more," he says. "I wasn't the last person to see her alive, I just saw her the day their group set off on the Three Capes Walk from the Historic Site. I happened to be over there to sign some paperwork and she was, well she, Pietra—"

Ruth nods.

"I noticed her because she was wearing like a neon pink windcheater and she was walking with her hair up in a high ponytail, just walking around the Site like normal, any other day. I didn't think anything of it until I heard one of the walkers was missing and they gave a description but I haven't seen that woman since then."

"Did you speak to her at all?" asks Ruth. "Did she say anything?"

"No, I only spoke to the cops. I reported the sighting and got questioned, the demountable got searched. It was a bit off-putting to begin with because I didn't know what was going on but they were cordial, just did the walk-through and were out in ten or fifteen minutes. After that though it really hit me. My girlfriend comes to visit sometimes and if I get busy she'll go for a walk on one of the trails, she always wears an armband with her music device or phone, and puts her hair up in one of those ponytails. It's gut-wrenching to know my girlfriend could have been out here and I go inside for a minute and she's gone," he says.

Back at the bothy, Ruth is met with a vision. The panels of the casement window coerce the early winter sunlight into a dozen distinct diagonal slats. Within the oblique light, Seamus stands at the bench warming his hands in the steam rising from a pan of baked beans, his fluorescent orange weatherproof pants ablaze. When he turns his head, above the pan his hands open as if releasing a dove. Though a moment ago Ruth was eager to tell him of her encounter with the dolphins, now she finds herself withholding it. It is true they have a shared experience of the residency and yet she has also found herself on her own separate journey, as surely as Seamus has been on his creative one.

"Been for a walk?" asks Seamus, scraping beans onto a plate.

Ruth sits down at the plank table. "I forgot how cold it gets right down at the water."

Only now do her teeth start to chatter. Once the cold gets into your bones the only remedy is a steaming hot bath or to sit before the fire as she does now, pulling up her chair. It is a juvenile, lit in the ashes of last night's conflagration, lacking the heat necessary to really thaw her out.

"You see the helicopters?" asks Seamus as he brings his beans to the table.

"I thought they'd found Pietra, the missing tourist," Ruth tells him. "But it turns out some fishermen's boat sank. They're searching for them."

Ruth rubs her hands together, close to the crackling flames. Finished his breakfast, Seamus puts another log into the stove fire. Sparks fly. Leaning back in her chair, having caught, finally, the heat of the flames in her cheeks, Ruth surveys the thin nylon ropes strung between the rafters as a makeshift clothesline. With her eyes she follows the green, interconnected web overhead.

Ruth has long since forgotten what island living is like. The first rule of ecology—everything affects everything else.

Do no harm.

If only it was that simple.

"I've a favour to ask you, love," says Seamus. "Only if you want to, of course. No pressure nor obligation. It just seemed to me like a good idea so thought I'd ask. I'd like you to prepare the canvases for me today. What do ye think?"

"Really?" Ruth smiles. "I'd be honoured."

Sitting cross-legged on the cold stone bothy floor, a blank canvas lain across her lap like a dulcimer, Ruth applies a layer of white paint. Each brushstroke is a meditation. While she waits for one coat of paint to dry she takes up the next canvas and repeats the ritual, taking each freshly painted canvas, in turn, outside into the sunlight to lay on an old bedsheet spread out in the clearing. When a canvas is sun-baked dry, she brings it back inside and takes up a sheet of sandpaper. Beginning at the centre of the canvas, she works outwards in long arcs, her hand rolling in a wave-like action, weathering the surface.

Visible in the beams of sunlight falling through the front windows, fine paint particles drift like grains of white sand. Drumming the canvas with her palms to loosen any lingering dust, the first layer is complete. Now she takes up the brush once more and begins to lay down the next layer. Back and forth with the brush, striking a rhythm. Her heart is a metronome, her wrist a well-oiled hinge. Canvas after canvas, layer upon layer. Layers of time, layers of tragedy, and layers of loss echoed in the horizontally layered dolerite and the flat-lying siltstone of the Peninsula coastline that surrounds her.

When Ruth has completed her task, she watches Seamus finishing a painting at the plank table. Whenever Seamus works his stance alters. Every movement becomes deliberate, measured. Even when he is simply crossing the room he moves like an artist. It is as if only part of him is physically present, the other part in a private world of thought—even more so than usual—and so she doesn't bother trying to speak to him until he is done.

When Seamus is signing his new work, 'SJLL', Ruth says, "I know Seamus was your grandfather but I've never asked you about the Joseph and the Luke."

Seamus glances sideways at her to gauge whether she is being serious or not. "That un's an embarrassing story."

This piques her interest. "Go on then, tell me."

"I never liked Seamus, too old fashioned, a spud-munchers name, but my ma did and I was too young to have much say in it. Joseph I can live with. Luke though," Seamus looks directly at her this time, "that was all my fault." Seamus stands back from the canvas. "You know us Taigs get confirmed when we're ten or eleven?"

"No, but OK."

While it seems it will take a lifetime to truly get to know Seamus, she has by now learned quite a few things about his *country of origin*. In Northern Ireland, *Taigs* or *Fenians* is derogatory slang for Catholics, *Huns* for Protestants.

"When you get confirmed you've to choose the name of a saint and I was a massive Star Wars fan as a kid. Han Solo was my favourite character, still is, but there was no Saint Han."

"Star Wars?" says Ruth, wrestling with her smile. "Are you telling me that you're named after Luke Skywalker?"

Seamus grins back at her, raising both eyebrows. Instantly she squeals with laughter. This man is the only person she has ever met who is able to make her laugh no matter her mood or the circumstances. Seamus's sense of humour appeals to her like no other.

"Sure, it's better than havin' no middle name at all. What was ya ma thinkin'?" he says. "Baptising babies is our tradition. In the old days newborns died all the time. You'd baptise a baby to save its soul from limbo. You'd baptise 'em just in case, so."

"When were you baptised then?"

"One month old, on Christmas day."

Seamus takes his paint brushes outside to wash, leaving Ruth alone with the painting. It is a lone sea stack, the Moai, painted down the bottom, towards the right-hand corner of the canvas. No sea; no sky. Just a vast empty blue space. 'Neutral space', he calls it. Although she doesn't fully comprehend it, she knows his artist's statement by heart. While it appears empty the space is in fact an arena in which to explore subjective relationships between physical geography and interconnected systems of identity. Ruth's initial reaction, looking at the painting, is to sense an unseen predator is on the prowl, as if this stack is a mouse trying to remain as still and quiet as possible in the presence of a fox. Ruth identifies the stack as the long-tailed mouse, the only rodent species endemic to Tasmania. What gives it away is its two-tone tail—light below and dark above and longer than its whole body and head. Seamus has taken the stack out of the sea, its home, and stuck it on its own, made it small and vulnerable on a big canvas.

Still, she keeps on looking.

When she has looked long enough, something happens. She begins to experience the space, not just the stack. No longer a flat surface, it billows like a storm cloud full of static. Within her mind is the sound of quickly changing television channels or radio stations, as she begins to contemplate the reasons, the outside forces, responsible for the feelings of fear and vulnerability that the painting evokes in her. It's us who decide where the wilderness starts and where it ends. Humans define the limits, the boundary between cultivated and wild. Nowhere is that boundary clearer than on the Peninsula. It is only natural that we fill the wilderness surrounding us with what we fear in ourselves and our society. It's the place that we banish all the elements we reject in ourselves, in our culture and in our society.

Seamus puts an arm around her shoulders and asks, "Where to from here?"

Then she has lost it, whatever it was, and she is back to seeing only wasted space on the canvas.

"What's it called?"

"Ach, titles," says Seamus. "Don't be botherin' me with the title, I only just finished paintin' it."

"Don't Trust the Piton?"

Seamus pulls his waistband up over his belly, beneath the swathe of wool jumper. Then he snaps his fingers. "Don't Trust the Paschal!"

"Abuse in the Catholic Church?" she asks.

"Now you're gettin' it," says Seamus. "See, that's your own meaning you've brought to the neutral space. Say, what do you call those sewing pins, the ones with the coloured heads on? They come on a plastic rose, rainbow coloured?"

"Berry pins, you mean?"

"Berries? They made of glass or plastic, those things? I'll be needing half a dozen red ones for this paintin'."

"Or pearl head pins, I think they're also called. What do you want them for?"

"Five grains of red incense to embed in the candle. Sometimes the Paschal is encased in wax nails, to represent the five wounds. Three in his hands and feet, the spear in his side and the crown of thorns. The cross is always the central symbol. I'll not be sticking these pins in the form of the cross, I'll be choosin' points along the rock climbers' routes to represent the pilgrims' own wounds, usin' the pins as pitons."

It is equal parts curiosity as a temporary resident of Fortescue Bay and genuine concern as a local that draws Ruth back down to the beach under the premise of collecting firewood. Ruth remembers clearly the breaking news stories of the drownings in 2006. The deaths occurred five days before the tenth anniversary of the Port Arthur massacre and the first public memorial service since the event, said at the time to be the last official commemoration. Ruth suspected the story was covered as widely, even by the world news, due to the coincidence, that news crews were already arriving on the Peninsula in preparation for the tenth anniversary and found themselves in the right place at the right time for another tragedy. The fact is that she has visited the beach more times in recent weeks than in her entire childhood living on the Peninsula. Other children learned to swim in the lagoon here but not her and her brother. As a Tasmanian, being able to swim was *as useless as tits on a bull*, according to their father.

Rescuers sit on their haunches with backs resting against the trunks of blue gums. A child holds a long stick, collecting ants on its end from a mound, twirling it to inspect the crawling passengers. When a sound from the bush startles the child he drops the stick and runs to the nearest adults. Ruth surveys the roadside leading out of Tasman National Park for any sign of an echidna.

A journalist is interviewing one of the SES volunteers.

"If they say find someone, I find him," says the volunteer. "It's my job."

"Nothing is stronger than the heart of a volunteer," says the journalist.

"Ah, good," he replies. "You're welcome.

"You heard about the miracle then," says the warden when he sees her.

"They found them alive?" asks Ruth. "All of them?"

The warden puts his hands into the front pockets of his pants. "Rescued by helicopter an hour ago. Boat had capsized but an air bubble in the bow stopped it sinking. They managed to get their lifejackets as well as put in the mayday before they got the hell off."

"Unbelievable," she says. "A happy ending."

"This time."

"I can't imagine it, spending the night in the freezing water," she says. "Scary."

"All those seals swimming around their boat? If it was me I'd go out and buy a lotto ticket today."

"Why's that?"

"Where there are seals there are sharks."

As she walks the duckboards, Ruth wonders if the experience will be life-changing for the fishermen involved. Young men in their early thirties. John was that age, thirty or thirty-one, when Rusty was born. After night fell and the conversation about survival tactics had run its course, their bodies aching, just their torsos and heads above water, did the individual fishermen take a good look at their own lives? If they survived, the things they would change, the things they would do that they'd never had the courage to? Seeing that helicopter must have been the best feeling, and the flight out of there the best experience, they'd ever had.

Ruth almost envies them.

Approaching the end of Stormlea Road, Ruth is again struck by how little things have changed in the years she has been away. The place looks just the same—the quiet, undulating paddocks bald spots on the wilderness, old scars inflicted by the earliest post-convict settlers, the power lines that stretch the distance from farmhouse to farmhouse the threads connecting the human presence in the landscape.

As they pass by it, Ruth nods towards the long windowless white shed perched on a rise to their right. "That's the Whiteleys' piggery."

Seamus turns his head over his shoulder to look. "A working farm still?"

"Yeah. John's ex, Helen, runs it now," says Ruth as she glances in the rear-view mirror.

The most significant effect upon her of her father's death when she was nineteen was that she quickly realised that to feel anger towards the dead was pointless, even ridiculous. Just two years after Port Arthur this realisation made her seriously consider whether someone like the gunman should be allowed to go on living. Was it possible his death would serve to alleviate the anger and pain of all those affected by his crimes?

At the end of Stormlea Road only a few walkers' cars are parked; it's the off-season. Seamus carries his camera while Ruth carries the backpack containing bottled water, sandwiches and extra jumpers. They must cross private property to reach the Cape Raoul Track. As they fill in the walker registration book at the stile a group of three young men, shirtless and carrying towels, return from a swim in the temporary rock pools at Shipstern Bluff—the payoff for the three-hour return hike. Locals, she decides, undeterred by the cold.

Ruth leads the way into a dense thicket of Bracken fern, neck height. Overhead a pair of musk lorikeets manoeuvre like fighter jets engaged in a firefight. When they emerge into a small clearing at the edge of the semi-open forest Seamus stops for a breather and a sip from the water bottle.

"You're not going to make it all the way to Cape Raoul," says Ruth. "Seriously, you can't do that walk if you're unfit. Shipstern Bluff, maybe. We can go as far as the lookout and see how you feel."

"I already got gypped when the bonnies were a wash out. I was lookin' forward to it, if I'm honest."

Blessing in disguise, Ruth thinks.

"If I miss out on Cape Raoul, sure I may as well've done *the Misnomer!*"

The track climbs through an understory of blanketleaf and wattle. Ruth soon resorts to locking her arms in front of her to part the tall thickets of cutting grass that cascade across their path.

"I've noticed the spectacularly bizarre weather patterns. It's like they say about Melbourne, that you get four seasons in one day. The southern isolation makes it more extreme here though," says Seamus.

"We get the Antarctic winds from the south," says Ruth. "As well as the warm high-pressure systems from the north."

When the forest opens up again, Fairywrens dart ephemeral from the Banksia shrubs. The uplifting scent of honeysuckle permeates the air.

Ruth does not warn Seamus when the track is about to burst onto the lookout and a sheer four-hundred metre drop but lets it come as a shock, the way it should do the first time you hike the Cape Raoul Track. For her, the sudden view across Storm Bay is like looking into the face of an old friend.

"Jesus fuck," says Seamus, as he hurtles towards the cliff edge.

Vertigo acts like a gust of wind at Ruth's back, threatening to push her over. With the peculiar fear that her body will betray her mind and jump, she drops her centre of gravity, collapsing on her backside on the wide flat rocks.

Seamus stands on the very edge.

"These cliffs don't bother you?" she asks, exhilarated by the height and her own fear. "They're the highest in the Southern Hemisphere."

"I'm grand," Seamus says. "I've no fear of heights. I could jump right off here no problem. It's the sharks and the creepy crawlies that have me worrying."

"Can you see Bruny Island in the distance?" she says, pointing. "That's where the first apple trees in Australia were planted, by Captain Bligh."

If you didn't know better you could mistake it for a long low-lying cloud.

"Where my nan lives in Bangor there's a coastal road from the harbour all the way to Belfast," says Seamus. "On a clear day you can see Scotland."

Ruth pulls herself to her feet. "Come with me, I want to show you something."

Most walkers reach the lookout and then continue on their way down to Cape Raoul but Ruth knows a secret. She leads Seamus to the right, on a little path between trees, and the vista expands to take in the huge cliffs towards Cape Raoul, down to Shipstern Bluff, and beyond it the great Southwest of Tasmania.

"It's like the bow of the bloody Titanic!" Seamus exclaims.

The whitewater breaking on the pointed wave platform of Shipstern Bluff creates the illusion of forward motion through the sea.

"I never thought of that," says Ruth. "I wonder why it's called Shipstern Bluff then? I guess because it sounds catchier than Shipbow Bluff."

The way Seamus stands, on his back foot with his knees locked, gives the impression that he is holding weight, an object much heavier than the camera in his hands. Ruth waits in silence while he is shooting.

Below them, a shy albatross soars across the bay with a wide white wingspan approaching that of an ultralight aircraft.

Chapter 7
Marina

On Friday afternoon, Moon and Marina travel up the East Coast of Tasmania with a volunteer from the Peninsula Vegan Network. Already Marina has forgotten her name.

In paddock after paddock, sheep carry avian passengers on their backs, others drink from dams and those that have been recently shorn stand huddled together in tight-knit groups, head to tail, sides pressed together for warmth.

To usurp the silence, Marina addresses the volunteer seated behind her, "How long have you been an animal lawyer?"

"Oh, I'm not an animal lawyer. I wish!" she replies. "It's a pretty new area of law in Australia. I just do the occasional pro bono work for the PVN and other groups. The rest of the time the daily grind is construction law."

"You realise we could all get arrested tomorrow?" Marina announces. "I thought lawyers weren't allowed to break the law. Don't you get disbarred or something?"

"That's more for crimes like fraud, unethical conduct, that sort of thing."

"Don't worry," says Marina. "I forgot, the lawyers don't go out on the water anyway."

The law Marina is intent on breaking is the one that says the hunters are allowed to start firing at daybreak but the rescuers are not permitted to enter the water before 10:00 am. The penalty for the infringement is a fine, which was always around $100 but in recent years has increased tenfold.

Marina's eyes, reflected in the rear-view mirror, continue to question her backseat passenger. Marina is well aware of their power to unnerve. She is experienced at asking questions and probing to gather information without saying much. The loose lips of others cause their own demise. 'Anything you say can and will be used against you', is a phrase any lawyer should be familiar with.

Marina's tactic works and her passenger responds to the pressure by continuing the conversation. "The Department of Primary Industries, Parks, Water and Environment are more interested in policing protestors—rescuers, sorry—than shooters. The Box Flat bird massacre mattered, and hasn't been forgotten."

Across the centre console, Marina and Moon lock eyes like they're staring down the barrel of a shotgun. As Marina makes a sudden move to turn on the car stereo, Moon glances over his shoulder, with an arched eyebrow and eyeroll, at the lesser woman riding in the back of the car.

The Tasman Highway presses its shoulder against the Prosser River, only a low stone wall separating it from the wide sheet of plate glass water. The road and the river court for kilometres. At some point, Moon opens a small notebook on his lap. At first glance the page appears to contain an unfinished self-portrait in ink. In sporadic peeks, Marina watches him draw. There is a likeness, she has to admit, the angular face that he shares with her and the eyes that dominate it, but this is an idealised self-image, tall in stature with an elegant silhouette, blinding blue bangs conveying a cool carelessness. It annoys Marina. This character is not only literally two-dimensional, it lacks the psychological complexity that would make it interesting. Flat characters no doubt have their place. Minor, supporting characters don't need to be complicated to be effective, if their role in the action is limited. As long as the main protagonist is a well-rounded, self-assured character with a lot of complexity. Self-satisfied, Marina commits her focus to the road ahead and leaves her brother to his doodling.

The promise of first light is what is holding the group of rescuers together in the cold camp ground at Swansea. They have been assigned their teams. After a brief, private conversation with the organisers of the action, during which she informed them that her brother is an emotionally sensitive boy who needs her, Marina has been placed in Team Two with Moon. The rescuers are being deployed to Moulting Lagoon.

From her room at the neighbouring motor inn last night, Marina spent an hour gazing towards Freycinet Peninsula across Great Oyster Bay, landlocked and sheltered from the wind in every direction. All the while she consciously avoided visualising what it was going to be like out on the water with the hunters. It occurred to her that in Greek mythology, where human beings are out doing something like hunting, conquering the wilderness, most of the time it ends badly. It's a way of saying *know your place, know that you're not a god.* Moon had echoed the sentiment when she'd killed the ants beneath the prayer flags of *Doo-No-Harm.*

We're only humans.

In fact, the Greeks regarded the wilderness as so terrifying that Pan, their god who inhabited it, is the root of the English word *panic.*

Now, it is time to prepare, each person in their own private way, however necessary. They disperse, some to their tents, others to stand in small circles, with hot tea or coffee clutched at their breasts, filling the space between them with visible breath and talk of their lives outside of this. In addition to army-issue ballistic goggles, all wear white shirts or tops and a white cap in order to make it harder for the officers to identify individual rescuers and prosecute them.

When Marina was crewing with Sea Shepherd, an hour before the action, she liked to have her own space, her own time. Listening to music was her way of getting into the zone. As the action got closer, her intensity increased. From a stretch, she'd go into an actual physical warm-up, the heart rate getting higher and higher. That's how she got pumped up.

This is different. Marina follows Moon to his one-man tent where he sits down in the entrance while she remains standing, facing him.

"You're wearing lipstick," he says. "Did you just put that on?"

"No, I applied it at the motel. Why? Has it smudged already?"

"You just look like you're back in Sydney about to go browsing designer stores on Oxford Street," he says.

Before she can respond, Moon gives a quick nod

of acknowledgement to someone behind her. When Marina spins around, she is met by the black eyes of the volunteer lawyer, pupils fattened by the darkness.

Marina smiles to reveal the fangs behind her lipstick as the hair at the nape of her neck bristles. Like a beta female, the lawyer slinks away.

"Esther thinks you don't like her," says Moon, feigning a light-hearted laugh.

"Is that her name? She told you that, that she doesn't like me?"

"No, Mari. What I said was that she thinks you don't like her."

"Esther," Marina laughs. "That has to be the ultimate dowdy, old lady's name. Ugh!"

"See?" Moon leans forward, the forearms resting on his bent knees unfolding and swinging down parallel to his shins. "Why do you always have to be so mean? You know, I remember when you used to be kind. When we were in primary school, you were one of the kindest girls."

Without realising it, Marina has been shining the torch beam directly into Moon's eyes while he spoke. It's as if the moment before she was sitting in a room lit brilliantly, with the blinds raised, by bright sunlight pouring through the windows so she was unable to see the dust surrounding her. Now, the blinds have been lowered, keeping open only a single slit, allowing a narrow ray of light to enter, and all the suspended dust particles are suddenly exposed. Disconcerted, she fumbles with the torch for the switch to kill the beam.

They are headed for the frontline. Marina expected the mood inside the car to be sombre. Instead, flippant conversation carries on the current of nervous energy and heated cabin air like a kite on the beach caught in a thermal updraft.

"You have such interesting names," gushes Esther. "I especially love yours, Moon because my name means *star* in Persian."

"You're not the first one to say that," says Marina. "Girls always love Moon's name."

"Our parents lived in the Huon Valley," says Moon. "Apparently my sister was conceived in the Kermandie Marina. That's what they named her after."

"Moon! Why'd you tell her?" says Marina. "Even I wish I didn't know that, Jesus."

Esther laughs. "They say a child conceived in love has a greater chance at happiness."

Glancing in the rear-view mirror, peering through and beyond the back window, Marina waits for the intervals when the fog lifts and the headlights of the convoy of rescuers become visible, stretching back along Coles Bay Road as far as the eye can see. A convoy of light threading through the darkness.

Vehicles slow down and begin to pull off the road just past the sanctuary, at Top Bank car park where a mobile veterinary clinic is being set up.

The hunters are based further down the road, in an unofficial camping ground that is not signed from the road nor marked on any map. The only facilities are fire pits. The fact that the wetlands become sanctioned killing fields for part of the year is a secret kept from the visitors to the Freycinet National Park, who, if they happen to catch a glimpse of the hunters' hides, which are permanent residents on the Lagoon, are likely to mistake them for bird watching huts.

Once out of the car the focus is on legs and feet. Marina pulls on wetsuit booties over her leggings while Moon leaves his Blackspot sneakers on beneath the unravelling hems of second-hand trousers.

Marina admires Esther's tall Wellingtons boots for a brief moment and then says, "Good thing you're not going out on the water. Wearing those things you'd get bogged in a flash."

When Moon passes Marina a pillowslip, another wave of reality hits: it's a body bag.

"Just remember," says Moon. "Be careful not to get the slip wet or you could suffocate an injured bird."

As Esther quietly chants in some foreign language—*Hineni Hineni*— Marina thinks of all the water birds out there somewhere in the darkness that know not what awaits them this morning—Armageddon.

When they are standing in their individual groups in the car park word spreads that the police are on their way, not far off now. The rescuers must get out on the water now. For them, the shoreline is the danger zone; both entering and exiting the water is when they are typically taken into custody.

Around the back of her head, Marina tightens and retightens the strap of her ballistics goggles. The greatest fear is blindness. Death is far less likely, for a fatal shot would have to be at close range. Although accidents are always a real possibility it would probably take a deliberate shot and while the rescuers are the targets of verbal abuse they are not the sport of the day.

Half a dozen other rescuers have joined Team Two and their team leader, Mike, makes eye contact with each of them as he gives last minute instructions.

"Stay ten metres from the shooters at all times. Don't

flush birds that are on the water or in reeds. When you see birds flying overhead use your whistles to scare them away from the guns, not towards them. We are about to enter the water before first light. If anyone is not OK with breaking the law, they should abandon the team now."

One last chance to back out. Mike waits, but no one deserts.

They leave the shelter of stands of silver wattle and swamp paperbark, marching in single file, torch beams on the heels of the rescuer in front of them. For Marina, that is Moon, moving as if into the wind, with his hood up, head bent and hands plunged in the pockets of the trousers falling off his narrow hips. They cross the salt marsh, passing through grass tussocks and sea rush and then emerge onto a belt of beaded glasswort.

The voice of an officer resounds across the silent lagoon, "Five metres! Stay five metres from the water!"

"Come on, team!" cries Mike. "Go, go, go!"

The mud flat gives way to water with little warning and there is no room for hesitation. Marina is on the Lagoon, leaving the safety of the foreshore, and the law, behind. As surging adrenalin numbs her body to the freezing temperature of the water in cahoots with the chill air, she focuses on controlling her breathing, staying relaxed, to make sure her reaction time is good.

They march in silence but for the sound of purposeful splashing until they are at, what Mike determines to be, a safe distance from the shore. As they pause in thigh-deep water, a few rescuers raise their torchlight and the vastness of Moulting Lagoon is revealed. Beneath a firmament burning feverishly bright, the Lagoon is a dreamscape.

"It's so beautiful," a female rescuer remarks through chattering teeth, bringing Marina back to reality.

Moon, beside her, says, "Keep moving or you'll start to feel the cold."

Marina starts wading slowly on the spot but it is too late. All warmth has already been leached from her body by the Lagoon.

"This is nothing," she says with bravado. "In Antarctica the air gets so cold you can't inhale more than a few breaths or your lungs haemorrhage. If you have to go out on deck to check something you have to wear a mask so the air warms up before you breathe it in."

During her time in Antarctica, Marina had it drummed into her that if she did end up overboard she must keep as much of her body out of the water as possible or, at least conserve body heat by staying as still as possible and reducing the body area exposed to it. It's advice that she's fortunately not yet had to put into practise.

In the east, behind the rocky outcrops strewn with Drooping Sheoak, Mimosa and Honeysuckle there is an ominous glow. A blood red sun is being raised like a poisoned apple. While Marina knows that first light means the killing begins, her body aches for the sun's warmth. The fires at the hunters' camp flicker on the shore, visible a kilometre away, to taunt the rescuers.

Wraith-like, the hunters begin to emerge silently from the dark shore through a veil of fog. Barely visible in their camouflage gear, they wade, some pulling small motorless boats, eyes fixed straight ahead, passing unseeing as if the rescuers in their white clothes and high visibility vests are not really there, are of some other world.

Marina stands stiffly as a hunter with a shotgun at his shoulder and an ammunition box in a small canoe pulled behind him passes them well within the requisite ten metres.

Moon greets him, "Good morning."

"Don't say good morning to me, mate," he spits back. "Piss off."

Marina watches him disappear into the fog and then she says, "I agree with him. This is a serious situation we're in. A deadly serious one. I don't understand why you would want to talk to him like this is normal. He's a hunter. He's one of them. They're the reason we have to be out here."

"Mum always did it. I think she saw it as good manners," says Moon. "Fair enough, they're on the opposing side but it doesn't mean we can't all be civil to one another. A lot of them will say good morning to you."

"Opposing side, like teams?" Marina shakes her head in disbelief. "Isn't the whole point of us being out here that we don't consider killing to be sport?"

Mike butts in, attempting to reclaim his position as team leader. "We all come from different backgrounds, with different political, religious and other beliefs but let's focus on the job at hand, please. We're here to stop the shooters killing and injuring birds. If we fail, we're here to rescue the wounded and get them to the mobile veterinary clinic."

Mike breaks them up into pairs, Marina insisting she and Moon stay together, and each set off to cover different hunters with the instruction to stay within eyesight of one another.

Marina soon finds herself standing with Moon in front of a hide concealing two hunters. To their right is another group with a boat. As Marina loses her footing, one wetsuit bootie sucked off her foot by the mud, behind her the hunters laugh.

"See that? Nearly went arse over tit," one says loudly.

"Ignore them," Moon tells her. "There's strength in silence."

"I couldn't give a damn what they say." Marina squeezes the mud from her bootie and raises her leg out of the water to slip it back on her foot.

As the sky lightens overhead, the fog begins to diffuse and swirls like smoke on the surface of the water, creating an illusion of the Lagoon on fire. Without warning, the skies erupt, a sound like Revelations.

Struck stock still, Marina's eardrums shudder.

"It's just guns," says Moon, taking her hand.

Marina is not concerned about the hunters out on the Lagoon; her sole concern is those hunters inside herself. These are dual wolves, one white and one black. The white wolf feeds on peace and compassion, the black wolf on anger and heartlessness. All she has to know is which one has the greater appetite.

While the birds that are shot dead fall straight down out of the sky, twirling and tumbling like skydivers tangled in failed parachutes, landing with high splashes, the injured birds sail down gracefully as if they are landing on a still pond. Once they hit the water the telltale thrashing begins, unable to lift off again they are easy prey.

Over the din of gunfire, Moon informs her, "He's going to kill it now. There's nothing we can do. Once they've shot a bird it becomes their property."

"Fuck what the law says. I will not watch a bird die right in front of me. I never saw a whale die while I was with Sea Shepherd. When we show up, whales don't die."

"You have to stay ten metres away from them," Moon

calls after her as she rushes the hunter.

Taking no notice of her, the hunter slings his rifle over his shoulder and then plucks the duck out of the water by its head and gives it an initial twist before raising it into the air like a bullroarer and whirling it around in fast circles, wringing its neck. The bird is no sacred instrument and this is not a ritual, no secret men's business. If the bird produces a sound, she does not hear it. Marina is going backwards; she is almost underwater; she is as good as dead. Opening her mouth so wide she feels pain in her jaw she howls. The hunter catches sight of her closing in, and turns sideways as she launches herself at him.

"Lunatic bitch!" he screams, as he attempts to shake his forearm free from her vice-grip.

Managing to stay on his feet, he raises his knee and lands it in her stomach. As the force of the impact knocks her over and into the Lagoon, the hunter flings the lifeless duck back into the water beside his hide, where it floats, tragically, like a defeat.

Seized by cramp in her legs, Marina remains calm. Forcing her heels downward into the mosses she draws her toes as far upward as she can. Momentarily it intensifies the pain but silently she absorbs it. Once the worst of it passes, she jerks her legs towards the surface, though not so high as to throw her off balance, backwards and underwater. A loud splash nearby turns heads. This is a larger bird, half a metre long.

"God, it's a swamp harrier," says Moon, before biting his lower lip, his head agitated atop his neck.

With shattered brown wings, it dips its head, trying to move forward through the water, like a bilateral amputee swimming breaststroke. As Marina attempts to stand up, the hunter fires again at the swamp harrier.

"Sir!" shouts Moon. "You cannot shoot birds on the water. Sir!"

The hunter snatches up the drowning bird and holds it, still flailing, upside down by its buff trousered, long yellow legs, offering it to Moon.

Guffawing, he asks, "You wanna shot?"

"Kill it!" Moon screams back.

"What are you on about? It's full of lead," he says as he tosses the bird of prey into his boat.

"It's still alive, kill it!" Moon pleads.

The hunter raises his gun until the barrel is perfectly vertical. As Marina looks up, searching the sky for birds, Moon's face suddenly appears in front of hers, kneeling in the water his hands cover her ears and he pulls her so close that their foreheads touch.

"Don't look up," he tells her, his breath scented by spiced tea. "He's shooting over our heads."

As the shot rains down impacting the water all about them the sound is like a severe hailstorm.

"They leave them alive to upset us," yells Moon over the gunfire, his face hardened. "Let's go. There's more shots coming from over that way."

Barely able to walk for the pain, Marina trails behind Moon. As they wade further into the Lagoon, the mud kicked up into the water appears before them in dark algae-like plumes.

Marina does not recognise the mental space that Moon inhabits. A space where he has accepted that birds will die and is only concerned that they die quickly and do not suffer. What just happened not only caused paralysis-like immobility in her body, it caused a sudden, involuntary onset of doubt in her mind. Muscles and energy cramped simultaneously. All she can do now is hope that the rescuers can scare birds off with their flags and their whistles. Persevere for the precious sight of that quick, angular manoeuvre a flock makes mid-flight to escape beyond the range of the guns.

Once they find more hunters, Marina waves her little orange flag with all the strength she has left in her arms, eventually adopting Moon's technique of using his whole body to create wide figure eights through the air, like he is bringing in a jumbo jet to land. For Marina, the flag becomes more than her weapon; it becomes a form of protest. So she stands strong and waves it not only to warn the ducks but for the hunters to see as well. The high visibility PVC triangle at the end of a solid piece of dowel is a torch in her hand, burning bright orange with her passion—a flame of defiance.

Unlike the flags, the whistles are almost a match for the guns and the hunters realise this. It's the reason whistles are officially outlawed.

"No whistles!" a hunter shouts at them. "Who is that? You're not allowed whistles!"

Marina keeps her back to the hunters, who have cameras, and to the shore where the officers have telescopic lenses.

When a flock of birds comes into view, or when the hunters see the birds first and fire, all caution is thrown to the wind. The rescuers blast their whistles with all the force of the air in their lungs. They offer their breath, give of their life force, in a desperate bid to keep birds in the sky.

When it is all over—five hours of wading through mud, waist deep in places, their shins continuously combing the submerged beds of Ruppia—Marina and Moon find themselves at Kitty's Mistake, a few kilometres south of Top Bank car park, separated from the rest of the team. Their pillowslips are empty. The pair lie on their backs, exhausted. The mud flat is a carpet of broad arrows, identical to those stamped on the historic uniforms of convicts: the footprints of water birds pointing in all directions. Right at the water's edge where the feathers of black swans amass, these pheon impressions become deeper and point only directly toward, or away from, the Lagoon.

Battle-weary, they stare at the sky where high above them a swamp harrier soars.

Eventually Moon sits up. "We should get back. We can get out through Middle Bank and walk back up the road."

Smoke from the hunters' fires rises through the treetops as they enter the bush. Common Brown Butterflies float and dart in circles around their ankles and knees. They are confronted with four-wheel drive vehicles and tents. The hunters sit on folding chairs drinking beer, a boy no older than fourteen amongst them. Marina notices the t-shirt he is wearing, some heavy metal band design. They are always Nazi colours, those things—black, red and white. When a woman's voice yells out they ignore her and keep on walking.

"What the hell do you think you're doing? You lot are a joke. Piss off on out of here," she says.

A man joins in. "I hope you enjoyed ruining our day. And getting paid a thousand bucks for doing it."

Marina stops. With his eyes, Moon pleads with her to

let it go but she can't. The words are full of such emotion she can barely force them out. "Excuse me? What did you just say?"

"Come off it," the woman says, "we know you get paid a thousand bucks each to protest."

Marina stands caped in wild fury. "We get *fined* one thousand dollars for entering the water before ten. We get *paid* nothing!"

Now the man seated beside the boy stands up, adjusting his black beanie. "What's your interest in duck rescue anyway? You're out here for a university assignment, are you?"

Moon presses his hands firmly together and holds them, fingertips always pointing upward, with thumbs resting lightly against his sternum. Bowing his head he says, "Compassion." And then turns to others nearby, "Compassion."

At first a taut silence stretches across the camp. Then laughter breaks out. Before she can stop herself Marina shouts, "I was at Port Arthur. I was there! So screw the lot of you. How can you justify still coming out, year after year after year, with your damn guns? This whole thing, it's nothing but showboating, machismo bullshit! You're the goddamn joke."

To this, a hunter replies, "Who do you think you are, sweetheart? The master castrator? Yeah, I know what *machismo* means. Bet that surprises you, doesn't it?"

Marina's eye is drawn around him, back to the man in the beanie and the boy, sitting beside their erected Raider tent with tan coloured walls folded down like resting moth wings.

"How old are you?" Marina directs her question to the boy himself, who looks immediately to his father for the answer.

"That's none of your friggin' business, lady. Who are you to pass judgement on him, on me as a parent?"

It is only then that Marina spots what appears to be some home-made portable feather plucker. The grotesque sight of feathers piled up beneath it the evidence of a ritual that is the inversion of the traditional moulting of waterbirds at the Lagoon, from which it gets its name.

Nearing the end of the second day out on the water, Marina is dead on her feet. It hurts to breathe. The thigh high water is bracingly cold and all that is keeping her upright. Torso swaying, she closes her eyes and raises her arms, bent at the elbows like a scarecrow, hands dangling at her sides. From the black stillness inside her head she hears Moon's raised voice, aimed at someone else entirely.

"I am not letting you shoot any more birds," shouts Moon.

Suddenly the sound of a rescuer's whistle is so piercing she snaps open her eyes.

A gunshot blasts close by.

The shot hits an object submerged in the water, which smashes like a china vase sending fragments flying up into the air.

A man's voice, vaguely familiar, calls out, "Where's my son?"

The only reply is the loud snap of a break shotgun reloading.

Then there are two sets of two sounds in swift succession, which remind Marina of the call of a southern boobook owl: *mo-poke mo-poke*. Only the call revolves at double speed: *m-pk m-pk*.

As Marina turns her head and finds her brother, she is like a smoker who looks at the cigarette held between their fingers transformed to a slender cartridge of ash beyond the butt.

A time lapse–Marina cannot account for the seconds, cannot recall what just happened. Before her eyes, there is not the smoke from a burned cigarette but a cloudburst suspended in the air. In slow motion, the water rains down into the Lagoon as silver particles.

Directly behind it, she can see Moon from the hips up, his white shirt stippled red at the centre of his chest. The image of the Nazi postage stamp flashes before Marina's eyes, red soldiers with bayonets, waves of fire at their backs. Focusing in on Moon, she watches him crumple, left arm flung behind his back while his right arm is pinned to his flank, the hand reaching out from a locked wrist with fingers curling into his palm.

"Ohh," he utters. "Ohhh."

As his body falls forwards and over, he is also dragged straight back through the water. Irrational, her immediate thought is that something beneath the surface has got him. A croc has him in its jaws and is about to perform a deathroll. Moon is dragged one arm's length, then two, away from her. Now his torso sinks. Only his head rises out of the water, the long fringe, dyed red, tousled by severe vibrations along his neck. Then his head too falls back and crashes into the Lagoon.

"No, no, no, no, no–" Marina projectile vomits into the water between them.

Just as quickly Marina recovers and her training kicks in. This is an emergency but there is nothing she can do for her brother out on the water so she must get him back to land immediately.

"OK, OK, OK," she mumbles as she attempts to reach him. "Moon, come on."

His left arm around her shoulders, the other pressing a hand to his chest wound, the rest of his body is limp as she drags it towards the shore.

Once, he falls back down into the water.

"Moon, Moon, you can't stop, you can't stop."

It is still so far away. Marina sees a hunter in their path, shotgun pointed at the sky. She does not recognise him and looks to Moon for confirmation. "Is he the one?" she asks.

Moon is unresponsive.

They back up, turn sharply, and try another direction. Marina can feel something sliding down her own brow right before she sees it dripping down over her eyebrow. Where Moon has clung feebly onto her head with his hand, he has left blood. Looking down to see it still running steadily from the wrist hanging over her shoulder, Marina begins to trot, bringing her knees up as high as she can raise them, her brother's body bouncing beside her. All the while her eyes dart back and forth across the Lagoon searching for other rescuers.

"Help!" she yells. "I need assistance! Please help us!"

Again Moon falls into the water, this time groaning in pain, and she hears shooting behind them.

"Let's go," she says. "We have to get out of here."

Then she sees it, a capsized kayak floating just ahead. Marina leaves her brother on his knees in the Lagoon, with his chin resting on his chest, and his hands floating supine in the murky water around him.

As Marina strains to flip the kayak over a pain strikes like an iron bar across her lower back. Simultaneously her ring finger bends back so far it feels like it's about to break off. Then she can no longer feel it; the finger is rendered useless as jelly. Panting through her mouth, she is about to cry with the stress and the pain but grits her teeth instead, closing her mouth and snorting through her nostrils. Underwater, she brings her ankles together. Standing tall over the righted kayak she sees Moon staggering towards her. Neither of them say a word as he slumps into the bucket seat, one hand reaching for the bungee straps on the back. Marina climbs into the front and grabs for the paddle.

"Moon, Moon! Hey, hey, hey, don't sleep, don't sleep," she begs, her voice tearing with emotion. "Moon? Moon? Don't sleep."

Marina does nothing but paddle. With each stroke the breath hisses through her clenched teeth as she bites down on her bottom lip, her face a grimace of determination. When she tastes her own blood on her tongue she does not stop.

The bow of the kayak hits the shore.

Boom!

New voices from afar call out:

"I see you!"

"We're coming!"

Marina turns back to check on her brother, and she catches sight of Moulting Lagoon, in all its splendour and devastation. A lamentation of black swans sail close to the shore, their bright red beaks and eyes an exact colour match for the shell casings floating all around them. Surely she is hallucinating. One trumpets. Its exquisite tail feathers curl like a pile of dark wood shavings.

It is a strange thing, that when something real happens to you, all else—even those things and those people you mistook to be the centre of your universe—falls away, disintegrates before your eyes while that which is real stands right before you like a giant, eclipsing even the sun.

From the bright shining path of reflected fluorescent light set out before Marina on the hospital's corridor floors, it is a direct connection to the headlights of the car on the night-time roads that lead from Hobart city all the way back to Tasman Peninsula.

In the blink of an eye.

On a mission, Marina opens the driver's side door before the car has come to a complete stop in the driveway of *Doo-No-Harm*. In seconds, her shoes clomp up the front steps, her already half unbuttoned shirt falling off her shoulders. The squeal of the screen door is her only welcome. Immediately she goes to the bathroom. Plugging the sink, she turns both taps all the way on and fills the basin with warm water. Without soap, she cleans her face quickly, scooping handfuls and then *rub, rub, rubbing* the mud mask from her skin before drying it with the hand towel. Marina's hair is tangled, darker and twice its natural volume due to the drying winds and sediment products of the Lagoon. What remains of her lipstick exaggerates the rawness of her mouth, spreading well beyond the lip line. The reflection staring back at her from the vanity is sinful and as unfamiliar to her as Catholic guilt.

In the bedroom, she pulls her shirt down. Past the small swell of her breasts, she lets go of it. Then steps out of the puddle of fabric, almost frozen stiff, on the floor. From the wardrobe she takes her staple outfit: a long sleeved black knit pencil dress. After slipping it off the plastic hanger, she dives headfirst into it with elbows locked.

Only when Marina enters Moon's room—dark, empty and silent— does she detect a whisper in her own head. It lays blame, telling her that it's all her fault.

You sacrificed Moon; your own brother means nothing to you; he was expendable; you saw him as useful only if he agreed with you; you totally manipulated him; he was forced to conform to your will.

Marina switches on the light.

On one wall is a raw edged cotton patch: HUMAN FREEDOM, ANIMAL RIGHTS. Above the patch, just beneath the ceiling, hangs a John Lennon *People for Peace* poster. In the corner, against his desk leans a beat-up acoustic guitar with a small rainbow petalled plectrum flower Blu-Tacked to the pickguard. On his bed, the doona is coverless, pilled and webbed with thread. Marina can never resist the urge to pick at it and nag him to buy something new. The cheap stuff is made in sweat shops and the expensive stuff is made with duck or goose down. This is the one he's had since he was a teenager. Somewhere along the line it lost its cover and no one replaced it.

Marina takes his suitcase down from on top of the wardrobe and drops it on the unmade bed. As she unzips the lid she becomes suddenly focused. Turning to the tallboy she reefs open drawer after drawer to take out t-shirts, underwear, socks and pyjamas, slamming each one shut as she goes.

In the kitchen, Marina wipes up the crumbs from lunch two days ago, before they departed for Swansea. With the orange dish cloth still in her hand, she strays to the refrigerator. Held to the outside by alphabet magnets is a child's drawing. The black outline of a whale is dissected vertically and filled in by a rainbow of coloured pencil. Smoothing down her mother's venerated keepsake with gentle fingertips, she begins to cry quietly, her cheek resting against the cold stainless-steel door.

Chapter 8
John

As John drives home to the Peninsula from the law firm in Sorell, a post-apocalyptic plume of smoke burdens the southeast sky. Umber, the smoke turns bronze as it gets closer to ground level, where it is backlit by the forest fire. The sight is a common one in autumn and no cause for alarm, just Forestry Tasmania conducting a fuel reduction burn. The animal people always throw up a stink about controlled burn-offs, totally ignoring the cold hard fact that it is beneficial to the forest to reduce the numbers of insect and mammal browsers. There is no alternative when the understorey of a Eucalypt forest becomes too dense and the litter on the forest floor piles up. Continuous regeneration relies upon major disturbance, like fire, to open up the tall canopy and increase the amount of sunlight reaching the ground. It initiates seedfall and triggers ground stored seeds. Not to mention that at times, these groups call on the shooting club to hunt down and put out of their misery the native animals, like wallabies, that get burned but survive these fires and are too difficult to rescue.

The solicitor seemed to be on John's wavelength, of the opinion that what happened at Moulting Lagoon was simply an accident and it was the fault of the rescuers who were running around illegally like lunatics.

Along the Arthur Highway from Sorell, the bus stop at Copping is still there and as he passes it, though John tries not to look, at the last minute he cannot help himself and sees him there, as he knew he would. Not on the roadside but reflected on the inside glass of the car window beside his cheek, like an apparition captured in a photograph. Standing with his head tilted to the left, blinding blonde hair blowing around his shoulders and into his eyes, as he hails the bus.

The memory is crisp and clear. Not a moving image but a slide-show of stills, only seconds between them. There is audible memory too. The sound of riding a bus, those gear changes.

It was a Saturday morning a few years before Port Arthur. John and Robin Whiteley were headed up to Hobart to see a new blockbuster called *Jurassic Park*. In the past few months John had heard news and rumours about the guy—that his father had drowned himself in a dam in a suicide, that the old Tattersalls Lottery heiress he was shacked up with died in a car accident that was his fault and he got away with it, that she was filthy rich and he inherited all of her money—but John had not seen him, or his sister, since their family sold the property at Carnarvon Bay in February so when he got on the bus wearing a ridiculous cravat, John's heart skipped a beat. All the seats towards the front of the bus were taken by seniors and so he moved further down the aisle.

When he sat down near two girls John was instantly relieved. Before long though there was a commotion and one of the girls ran to the front of the bus to speak to the driver. Whispers travelled back. *Rubber Lips* had tried to put his hand up one of the girls' dresses. For the rest of the journey he was made to sit, like a naughty school boy, behind the driver.

There was a single bus service between the Peninsula and Hobart each day and in the afternoon when they all returned to the bus to travel home *Rubber Lips* was not allowed back on. The driver stood at the door and barred his way, pointing and telling him to get lost. On board, applause broke out.

That trip home was the last time John ever saw *Rubber Lips*—before he saw him right before the Port Arthur massacre—and he was leaning out of the window of a taxi, which was following the bus, waving his fist in the air, shouting threats and obscenities at the driver.

John's thoughts shift to Robin Whiteley who pissed off years ago and came back with a wife, three kids and a Yank accent. Apparently he had made quite a name for himself in the States as a wood chopping champion. Now he lived in an affluent part of Hobart. It wasn't his money that John resented, or his family; John resented him for getting away, for going somewhere else. Last time Robin visited he'd towed his boat down and the two men went fishing at Fortescue Bay beneath the light of a full moon. Robin's intoxication was visible, spread scarlet across his nose and fat cheeks, and John took aim. 'Do you ever think about when we were kids?' For all his flash gear, Robin hadn't caught a thing. 'The beach parties with the shackies at Carnarvon Bay?'

'I don't remember much from back then', said Robin, turning his back.

You're lying, thought John.

'That one crazy night, we were all sitting around

the bonfire and *Rubber Lips* turned up and set himself alight. Do you ever think we should have let the bastard burn? We would have been doing the world a favour'.

Robin winced. 'Jesus, John'.

'You see what I'm getting at though?'

Robin sighed. 'We didn't know. I suppose I just felt sorry for him'.

'He should burn in hell for what he did ... doesn't deserve to be alive'.

That night when John is lying alone in bed, in the dark, Rusty asleep in the next room, he feels it is safe to return to his thoughts of her. John has been dreaming about her more than usual. Dreaming about the times down at Carnarvon Bay, except in the dreams they are grown-ups and she is always facing away from him, will never let him look upon her face. It was a more innocent time.

Falling asleep, John begins to drift between memory and dream.

John was thirteen, Robin was fourteen and Helen was twelve. While the boys were veteran Carnarvon Bay goers, it was Helen's first summer holidays with the shackies. There was lightning and thunder over the state forest between Mount Arthur and Black Mountain. Overhead, clouds raced across the sky like dogs to their master's whistle. Beneath the clouds, a great dark shadow was dragged across the bush.

Robin asked him, "What happened with the firewood?"

Helen chimed in, "Where were you?"

"Where's the firewood arsehole?"

"I'm sorry, mate," said John. "I forgot it, sorry."

"And here we were waiting like idiots," said Robin.

"God you took too long," said Helen. "Look, it's going to rain."

Robin pulled a beer from the esky and passed another to John. "Cheers ... to this sunny weather. The problem with the fire is that there's no firewood."

"Cheers before it starts raining!" toasted John.

"Don't you mean before it rains even more?" said Helen.

The two boys banged their cans together.

"Dude, you gave me an empty," said John, realising his friend was playing another trick on him.

"Truth is he's in love," said Robin. "This dude fell in love with Rubber Lips's sister. Wait, what's his real name again?"

It was true; when John was thirteen, he found his first love. Robin called her brother 'Rubber Lips' because of the pursed lips he always made along with squinted eyes, as if he was trying to figure something out that was just too difficult for him. At first John thought this nickname came about because of the fires the eighteen-year-old had been lighting in the bush around Carnarvon Bay. The way he stomped them out before they could take full flight meant that the rubber of his gumboots had melted and reset so many times that they no longer fit his feet and he had to get around everywhere barefoot. Something about shoes having tongues and Rubber Lips's melted gumboots, that's what led John astray. Eventually he caught on though.

"Speaking of piss," said Robin. "Rubber Lips pissed the bed until he was your age, Helen. Twelve years old, man."

"No way!"

"Yeah, how disgusting."

"You shouldn't blab about it after so many years," said Helen. "Take it easy."

"Why, do you still piss yourself, Helen?"

"Don't be a pig!" she said.

"We're just talking about his pee. What do you mean don't say it? Why are you defending him? By the way, at what age did you stop pissing the bed?"

John was startled by a loud noise. "Did you hear that?"

Robin laughed.

"Listen, I'm serious, there's something over there."

"Where?" Helen's eyes were wide and her mouth hung halfway open so you could see her top teeth, which were a perfect match to the albumen in her eyes.

"It's probably him," said Robin. "It's Rubber Lips!"

"Listen!" urged John.

"Let's check it out."

"There!" John pointed. "Look, right there!"

"Calm down," said Helen. "It's probably just a wallaby."

"No, let's go and see."

"Yeah, it's a wallaby alright," said John dryly. "A six-foot-tall wallaby with a rifle."

"Where arsehole?"

"Right there mate."

"Let's go back to the beach," she said. "This is boring."

"Aren't you worried about who was spying on us?" asked John.

"Probably it was just an animal," she said. "Or a camper. I'll just wait for you back at the beach."

"Come on, Helen," said Robin. "Don't be such a party pooper!"

"This is stupid," she said.

"Grab your torch."

The sky was still blue through the branches of the forest canopy, the dark blue of deep saltwater. The yellow torch beams that crossed their path were tepid light at best.

"Be careful," John told Helen. "It's slippery. Careful where you tread."

"Are you sure you saw something?" she said.

"Shine the light to the left," said John.

"Why don't we go back to the beach?" she said.

"No, let's check this out."

"Are you sure?" she asked.

"Holy shit! Did you see that?"

"What?"

"It went over there!"

"He's right," said John. "To the left like I said."

"No the other way."

"I saw it," she said.

"Yeah, trust me," said John.

"Fine, we'll follow you."

"I can't see anything now," she said.

"I told you it went to the left," said John.

"I think I heard something," she agreed.

"Watch out for spiders."

"Stop it!" she said. "I have something in my shoe."

"Hey, did you hear Rubber Lips caught an echidna and pulled out all its spines while it was still alive? Gave 'em to the Old Possum to use as knitting needles. She's always on that spinning wheel or knitting on the porch watching us. Have you seen her with the binoculars?"

"He tried to tear apart a cat with his bare hands too," said John. "That mate of his from the city had to stop him pulling it apart like a barbecued chook."

"Whose cat?" asked Helen. "Robin, stop touching my arm!"

"I dunno," replied John. "Just said he didn't like cats."

"This sucks."

"How can you see?" she said.

"Now what?"

"I dunno. I've got no clue."

Snap!

The full weight of a man's body standing on a wet stick. They spun around to face him as lightning struck.

"Nice one, psycho."

"I knew it was you," said John.

With a silly grin on his face, Rubber Lips followed them out of the bush, giving a detailed account of their every movement for the last hour.

John derails this train of thought, connected carriages of conscious and subconscious, throws back the duvet and swings his legs out of bed. Switches on the bedside lamp.

From the kitchen he fetches a pack of batteries and lifts a chair from the dining table. Rusty is standing in his doorway with a look of concern on his face.

"It would have kept me awake, knowing the batteries needed changing," John explains. "Go back to bed, mate."

With fresh batteries fitted in the smoke alarm, John pushes the chair against the hallway wall and returns to bed, satisfied.

Robin thinks he is better than everyone else, has always thought he was superior, but if there is blame, the larger share must be apportioned to him.

Once again John throws back the duvet and stumbles out of the room in the dark.

"What now?" Rusty calls out from his room.

"Well it's no good only changing the batteries in one smoke alarm, is it?" John calls back.

"Dad, you keep waking me up!"

"Better than us dying in our sleep," he says as he picks the chair back up.

Chapter 9

Ruth

While the sun sets behind the Banksia Camp Ground, Ruth collects firewood. As a resident artist, Seamus is neither required to pay for this nor to line up with the other campers and wait for the warden to dole out logs. At a nearby tent an overweight man on a folding chair who is anxious to cook the day's catch casts dirty looks at her over his shoulder, cursing and complaining to his female companion.

Blocking him out, Ruth focuses instead on the scent of the wood, which she knows is freshly chopped; pieces of firewood go stale as sure as loaves of bread.

On Rare Bird Farm it was hers and John's nightly chore to carry the firewood in from a store piled in the shelter of a bisected water tank in the backyard. John would stand and stack logs into her waiting arms until she could barely see over the top.

With relative ease, Ruth pushes the wheelbarrow along the duckboards through the forest. In the distance, at Agnes Creek, the birds sound like screeching primates.

On the bothy stoop, Ruth leaves the load for Seamus to deal with.

At the sink washing her hands, she says to him, "That really is an ugly clock."

"What?" Seamus looks up from stacking the firewood beside the stove. "The pilchard?"

"We should take it down and put it away."

"Leave the poor old clock alone! It's kitsch, kitsch for the kitchen. There, I've said it. I'm a fan of the Lucky Pilchard."

While Seamus takes the empty wheelbarrow back to the camp ground Ruth finds a bottle of Mercury Cider and places it out on the ledge to chill before shutting the window. Leaving the candles unlit, she pulls up a chair from the plank table and sits to watch the twilight unfurl. Beyond the glass the atmosphere turns blue, the intense colour the backdrop for the black silhouettes of tree branches. Ruth is aware that she only notices this distinct colour, appreciates it, because of Seamus, her artist in residence. In gratitude she christens the phenomenon—the ever deepening, darkening hue—St Patrick's Blue.

The sounds of human voices echoing through the forest eventually startle Ruth out of her reverie. For a second she thinks she sees rain in the clearing but it is a swarm of insects whorling through the air like handfuls of rice thrown on newlyweds. With preternatural speed, the voices grow loud and clear.

Seamus has returned, inexplicably, with her brother John at his side.

From her dark corner Ruth stares silently as Seamus, not having yet noticed her, takes a box of matches and lights the candle in the empty whisky bottle on the mantel. John finds her. The candlelight illuminates his face and casts his shadow, like a sinister twin, on the wall behind him. For a moment his eyes trap her.

John has brought fresh cream, butter and eggs from the farm. Seamus wastes no time peeling potatoes and chopping shallots for his signature dish, champ, which he will top with the poached eggs. Whistling as he works, he leaves the siblings alone together at the plank table in some semblance of privacy.

"Listen, there's no easy way to say this ... there's been an accident. The duck hunt turned serious for Rusty at the weekend," says John.

Ruth blinks, then replies, "Didn't I tell you, huh? Didn't I warn you about putting guns into the hands of children?"

"Well it was obvious pretty early on that he wasn't a welcome addition to the hunt. The protestors resented him, I'm sure. They certainly told us at various times that they weren't happy with him being there. All sorts of things ... I think at one stage they ... the Old Quacker's kid, I know there was a fairly major issue with him."

"Is Rusty OK?" Ruth demands to know. "Just tell me that he's OK!"

"That's the first thing Rusty said too, 'Is everything OK, is he going to be alright?' and the other protestor said, 'No, you've shot him'. Just a terrible, terrible moment, the sort of thing that you never want to have happen in the field. Rusty was too shocked to speak after that."

No, no— wait— wait, wait, wait. Ruth's mind scrambles to block John's words, so she can escape from the facts. It can't: this. Finally, she laments, "Oh this can't be happening."

Ruth finds herself tucked into a wave of pain. It is an absolute monster.

"Are you even listening to me?" asks John. "I told you, Rusty suffered a bit of shock, like anyone would. Now he's fine and with his mother."

"Oh thank god," says Ruth. "Thank god."

"When I gave my interview to the cops, I stressed to them that I'm a licensed gun owner, an experienced hunter." John cracks open a fresh beer. "I've always taught Rusty to be careful with firearms, to treat them with respect. The way they were carrying on you'd think it was some old, rusted, falling apart shotgun, some antique held together with radiator clamps. It's bloody brand new."

It is only then that Ruth registers the fact that her teetotal brother is drinking like a fish.

After supper, with John's account of what happened at Moulting Lagoon finally clarified and beginning to sink in, the three of them sit ensconced in candlelight. Tapers burn upon the mantel, on the hearth and along the tabletop. Holding court, Seamus has opened a third bottle of cider, John keeping pace with him, while the glass in her own hand has grown warm and flat.

"I'm weirdly proud of my fucked up little country now," says Seamus. "It's had quite an impact on the world for somewhere so small. I remember thinking growing up that the rest of the world was peaceful and how unlucky I was to grow up in Northern Ireland. It was just life for us. I still find it strange when other people in the world haven't grown up with armed soldiers on the streets or didn't check under their cars for bombs or haven't seen the damage of a blast or walls riddled with bullet holes. That was just a normal childhood for me."

Now it is Seamus who is being insensitive, bringing up *The Troubles*, events from decades ago, while her family was presently in crisis. No doubt this is due in part to being intoxicated but that is no excuse. Are these men all the same? Ruth is about to dethrone Seamus when he unexpectedly changes the subject.

Quaffing his cider then resting the glass on his knee Seamus says, "I also wished I were a Protestant."

"Why?" asks Ruth.

"'Cause Catholics were the minority, plus Protestants rarely went to church," says Seamus. "They didn't get the statue of the virgin once a month, a stupid idol sent from family to family. Every time it turned up we'd to get on our knees and say fifty Hail Marys and five Our Fathers after dinner for a week. Most of all, they weren't forced to be altar boys and therefore escaped being buggered by a priest."

John laughs at this.

"Basically I thought they'd the easier life," says Seamus. "I'd rather have been out climbing trees, playing footy or nick-nack."

"Nick-nack Paddy-whack, give the dog a bone?" says John. "Didn't realise Paddy in that meant the Irish kind."

Ruth looks away from the smirk on John's face to Seamus but her brother's barb appears to have missed its target.

"It's where you get some newspaper, a lump of dog shit and light the paper at someone's doorstep before knockin' their door and runnin' like hell," Seamus explains to both of them. "They come out and try to stamp the fire out and cover their shoe in shit. That game amused us for years."

"Oh that!" says Ruth. "I didn't know there was a name for it. That's funny."

“Not if you’re the one walking dog shit through your house,” says Seamus. “It gets called different names in different areas, but the premise is generally the same. Dog shit is optional but the more amusing.” Seamus empties the last of the bottle of cider into his glass. “Did you pair not terrorise the neighbours growing up?”

Ruth only smiles, intending to remain silent on the subject and is surprised when John speaks up. “Ruth would have told you about the shootings we had down here?”

Seamus leans back in his chair and with bloodshot, bleary eyes looks from one sibling to the other. “Aye, horrible, horrible event.”

Ruth’s eyes sweep the floor in front of her.

“Did she tell you that we knew him, the one responsible? And his sister. Ruth went to pony club with her.”

Too boisterous for the subdued candlelight, Seamus says, “What’s this?”

“I didn’t know her,” protests Ruth. “Don’t exaggerate.”

Slowly, John taps one foot on the stone floor and Ruth can see he plans to continue.

“You’re drunk, John,” she says.

“Sure, we’ll walk you back to your car,” says Seamus. “I fancy the fresh air if I’m honest.”

“If he’s drinking he shouldn’t be driving,” says Ruth. “Look at the state of him.”

“Ruth’s right,” says Seamus. “Time to call it a night.”

John snorts and watches Seamus rise out of his chair. Just as she recalls, her brother is not only a bully but a coward. Disgust eclipses her anger as John obeys Seamus’s command, getting up from his own chair and following Seamus outside like a chastised dog.

Once on the duckboards, Seamus begins to sing. Not at the top of his voice but loud enough to wake sleeping campers.

"Seamus, hush!"

"Don't shush me, wee girl. I've a fine voice. I'm a grand singer, my gran always told me so."

"Did she have dementia?" says John.

"Aye, I'd always sing for her when I was a ween. I'd be stood there on her sofa like it was a stage, and I'd sing for her. I'd sing ... *She Loves You* by the Beatles, and *Green Door* ... whoever that's by." Seamus stops on the path in front of her and she almost runs into his back. "Johnny boy? Who sings *Green Door*, Johnny?"

John's reply comes close by Ruth's ear, skimming her shoulder. "Don't know it, mate."

Seamus carries on. "At the weekend we'd take family drives in the country and my gran would always lead the singing. *Two Little Boys* or *Old Shep*'. Great times now I think of it."

Ruth wishes, not for the first time, that she'd known Seamus as a child.

When they reach the day use car park John heads straight for the toilet. Seamus spins in slow circles with his head thrown back. Then he stops and turns his drunken face toward her, pointing at the sky. Seamus's wide eyes beside her shine in the dark. "They're upside down. See that, can ye? They're upside down, every last one of 'em."

The freckles that float across his nose, suspended in the moonlight, are her private stars. Upon his Irish skin a testament to his boldness, his sense of adventure. In his eyes there is childlike wonder. Never in her life has she wanted to kiss a man like she wants to kiss him right now, even if his lips were poison. Appearing out of nowhere, John clears his throat loudly and Seamus takes a discreet step away from her.

"I've been a lot of places and tasted and smelt it all, John," says Seamus. "It's a big place and it's beautiful but every time I got home and I looked out and seen God's little acre sprawled out, green as far as the eye could see, my wee heart soared."

John opens the door of the ute and stands with his arm resting atop it.

"You know, I did find true love," he says. "That girl was the reason I never married."

"Eh? Just wasn't meant to be?" asks Seamus.

"I hesitated," says John. "Anyway, I s'pose she took it as a sign I wasn't interested. We never got the chance to share our feelings. What can I do? Nothing I can do but suffer in silence."

A man forlorn, John eases himself into the car.

"You're away?" says Seamus. "Safe home, John. Safe home."

Returning together to the bothy, a spontaneous burst of courage wheezes out of Ruth and she tells Seamus, "The one thing that hurts more than anything is that I wasn't here for Port Arthur. It happened the year I left home."

"This young buck who did the shootings, Johnny said you knew him?"

"My big brother always had a crush on his little sister. John was almost a stalker."

"But he said he suffered in silence."

"What a joke!," says Ruth. "John used to hang around outside their house, all day sometimes. I remember thinking it was funny every time he called from a phone box and couldn't get through to speak to her. John deserved it, losing his money like that. How humiliating. I got the feeling that he blamed the fact he couldn't get her attention on her brother, like that's what came between them, the way her brother constantly ran him off. In John's mind her brother ruined his one chance at true love or something."

"Fecking hell."

Ruth raises her right hand to her mouth, bares her teeth and bites down on her middle fingernail.

"You know where I was? Do you want to know the truth?" she says. "I was at a college Soiree all afternoon, drunk and having the time of my life. When I finally did hear the news it felt like I was the last person in the world to know."

A week passes and sitting opposite Seamus with the unwrapped fish and chips between them on the bench, Ruth thinks of the children's game pass the parcel. Sheet after sheet of butcher's paper just like this. It was the anticipation, not what lay inside. The gift itself was invariably a disappointment.

Ruth burns her fingertips on the hot chips, slick with tomato sauce.

"Happy days!" he declares between blowing breaths.

"Down there used to be the dog line," Ruth tells him after a time. "To stop convicts escaping Port Arthur and getting off the Peninsula. The soldiers would starve and beat their animals until they were really wild and then chain them up on rocks out in the sea."

Seamus is momentarily distracted by the scourge of full-blown crescents on the skyline, the sails of kite surfers cruising Pirates Bay, a neon nylon eyesore.

Ruth dusts the salt from her chips before she eats them. "There's a famous story about a convict who disguised himself in kangaroo skins and tried to hop past but his disguise was too good and the guards were hungry. I can't remember if they shot him by mistake or if he surrendered."

"Port Arthur is famous, ye know, at home I mean."

Ruth looks up, half a broken fillet in each hand.

"The Marcus Clarke book?" she asks. "I keep telling you, that was Macquarie Harbour."

Ruth sets the fish back down on the paper.

"What's wrong?" he says. "No good? Want to swap? The flake is grand."

Ruth shakes her head, casting her gaze at the ground. Tears are the last thing either of them need. Ruth just can't bring herself to talk to Seamus about her decision to stay on the Peninsula at the end of the residency. Repeatedly she's having difficulty finding the right word to even begin. Also she's afraid of substituting the wrong word, either knowingly or without even realising, like she wants to say 'pass the tomato sauce' but will say 'pass the apple sauce' by mistake. After wiping the grease from his fingers Seamus wraps the leftovers up, and Ruth grabs a piece of her fish at the last moment. If her mouth was full she could not be expected to talk, be drawn into any lugubrious conversation.

The tessellated pavement is an intertidal seaward platform of Permian siltstone. Having walked halfway across it, Ruth halts, suspended in a thought. The pavement is emblematic of human life, chequered with good and evil. Which squares are light and which are dark determined by whether they are wet with seawater. The element of chaos injected into the game. No rules of play. With each tide the board changes and also with the weather, sunshine to evaporate the darkness or only diffused light. At times, the game washed out by rain.

Ruth looks at Seamus with his camera. In their time together he has taught her a little about photography. In a negative image the lightest areas of the photographed subject appear darkest while the darkest areas appear lightest. That means then, that the white parts of the negative image are actually unexposed particles and the black parts are fully exposed. Cameras relied on the same elementary principles and performed in similar fashion to the human eye. The epitome of evil, fear and malice, Ruth remembers the Port Arthur gunman's hair and eyebrows were so white they looked bleached. Almost white, also, was his uncommonly pale skin. It would not be correct to call him *albino* even if that was one of the many names her brother did call him. Such a clear image he presented, almost angelic. Did he only appear white because of the parts of him that were unexposed? Ruth remembers the newspaper coverage immediately after the massacre, the criticism directed toward Australian media for using photographs of the gunman with eyes digitally manipulated to make him appear deranged, even demonic.

"This tessellated pavement is the closest thing to the Antrim Coast that I've seen in Tasmania. It's hard to believe that it's natural, the rocks are so evenly spaced, like a giant's chessboard," says Seamus. "What's the story behind it?"

"Ah, wave erosion," she replies, on autopilot. "The entire Peninsula, it's all wave erosion."

"Aye, I mean what's the myth, the dreamtime legend about how it formed?"

"I dunno," she says, feeling that she ought to know.

As Seamus walks the Pavement she imagines he listens for what it has to tell him, for his series, about the invisible links between human beings and physical geology, past and present. Clearly Ruth recalls words lettered in chalk on the blackboard in a classroom. Simply, 'Geology gives lessons in the past, throws light on the present and foretells the future'.

"Aye, 'Masonry', I think that's got to be the title ... title with a double meaning. The mosaic pavement belongs to the Freemasons. You often see the chequered floor along with the blazin' star and the other symbol. The dual quality of everything connected with terrestrial life and the physical groundwork of human nature."

Crouching, Seamus is about to pick up a shell to inspect it when she seizes his shoulder with both hands and says, "No, it's a limpet. Don't try and lift it off the rock, you'll kill it. At the very least wound it."

The shell reminds her of a woman's nipple, although not her own. As they cross the Pavement together to return to the stairs and the car, Seamus says, "What this reminds me of is a place called the Giant's Causeway. It's something you see, not a place you visit."

"It does look like a giant's chessboard," she agrees.

"It's a World Heritage site so it attracts the tourists." Seamus begins to pant with the physical exertion and this punctuates his speech. "The story goes that the giant Finn challenges a Scottish giant to a fight and they build the causeway across the North Channel so that they could reach one another without wettin' their feet. Finn sees the Scottish giant first as he's much bigger. Finn loses it and runs home to his wife, a small woman. He begs for her help and she wraps him in a blanket and when the other giant turns up he sees this giant baby. Now there are different versions of what happens but my favourite is when the Scottish giant looks at 'baby' Finn and says 'if that's his baby I don't want to see his dad' and in terror he runs back to Scotland tearing the causeway up as he goes, only leaving the Irish side."

Just in front of him, on the top step, Ruth's back stiffens, her hand gripping the railing. Seamus waits, expectantly. If there was something she wanted to say, she thinks better of it, and silently moves on.

In the passenger seat she is his navigator.

"What's this place?" Seamus says as a sign welcomes them to Doo Town. "A local joke?"

"It's just a quaint shack town famous for its whacky signs."

As she says the words *shack town*, Ruth experiences a jolt so strong it's as if a seat warmer had suddenly been turned on beneath her. It's Carnarvon Bay, that's what she's thinking of, the *shackies*. She hasn't been drawn into the orbit of actual memory but just feels something; she becomes aware of her connection to the events at Port Arthur. There is more to tell Seamus but this is his residency and he has made it clear he doesn't want any distractions. It is something best kept to herself. Perhaps later, when this is all over, there will be a right time to share it with him.

"*Rum-Doo,*" Seamus reads aloud from white weatherboard. "Don't mind if I do!"

At the Blowhole car park, Ruth asks if he wants anything from the kiosk.

"I'm no tourist wanting a cappuccino with my wilderness experience," he says. Then, checking the blackboard, adds, "I fancy some of that rabbit pie on the way back!"

As Ruth orders herself a takeaway coffee Seamus carries his camera down to the lowest viewing platform at the landward end of the tunnel. An invisible revolving door, you are supposed to take your turn to see the Blowhole in action and then move on so the next in line can enjoy the view without feeling crowded. These sights are not the kind to share with strangers; they speak of solitude, and isolation. To conserve space, Ruth stands above him on the higher platform, warming her hands on her coffee cup, while others slip easily around her.

Now, the sea comes.

Through the dark tunnel the swell rushes, expecting more than this shallow pool of seawater at the other end. Too late it finds itself trapped by rock walls, dotted with tourists and their flashing cameras. Slamming into the rocks with an explosive thud it erupts like a white fireball into the air.

The swell is sucked backwards through the tunnel. Seamus turns and calls up to her, "I think we've got it!"

There are fewer people at the Tasman Arch than were at the Blowhole and for this Seamus appears grateful. A cliff-top path provides the vantage point. The Arch rises out of the water as tall as a cathedral ceiling while below the surface lies a deep underworld of submerged cliffs and caves. This wound foreshadows a disaster yet to come. The Archway will lead inexorably to the collapse of the roof.

"When the roof collapses this will be another Devil's Kitchen," says Ruth.

"Another *devil's* kitchen or another *of the* devil's kitchens?" asks Seamus.

It is difficult enough sometimes to understand what he is saying, she isn't about to start playing *Norn Iron* grammar games with him. Besides, Ruth doesn't believe in God or the Devil, only mother nature. As Seamus shoots, Ruth is captivated by the sounds of the churning sea far below—womb water. If the Blowhole embodies a procreative masculine energy, the Arch embodies the unconscious aspect of the feminine. Shadowy and seductive, a narrow passageway into the unknown, it invites a deep dive into the dark realms of the soul. The opening is guarded by towering dolerite sentries. At their feet lurk the flesh-loving waves ready to fall upon and devour those who risk passing through in uncertainty, in fear or out of mere curiosity.

Ruth leads him along the cliff-top path to the Devil's Kitchen. Triassic, Jurassic, Permian-age—this is what millions of years looks like, hundreds of millions of years, and it is simply crushing. With each step Ruth seems to be walking deeper into her own sadness. As if the weather is influenced by her emotion, the sky overhead is squid ink. When they stop Seamus gathers up the hair at her neck and whispers into her ear. "What's the devil cooking in his kitchen?"

Ruth doesn't hesitate. "Souls."

"That rain is kickin' off like rioters' boots," Seamus has the last word.

Chapter 10
Marina

For days after the duck rescue, Marina woke just before first light, unable to fall back to sleep. The sounds of nocturnal forest insects were the whistles of rescuers on the wetland. Though she washed her hair repeatedly, the scent of gunpowder still clung to her and that it might be a phantom smell made it no less disturbing. In fact, it kept reminding her of an overheard conversation between her parents a long time ago—less than a year after the murders—when her mother was fired from her job at the Antiques store in the Huon Valley. Looking back, it is as if the murders marked for her mother the beginning of a trajectory of personal change that was directly related to Port Arthur. Ultimately, her mother being fired led to them selling their boat in Kermandie Marina. The comment of her mother's, which has stayed with Marina all this time, is that her being told she was 'fired' was what upset her most of all, the way her mother's boss put the dismissal into words. 'Of course,' replied her father. 'Being told you're fired is a military reference, it associates the experience, metaphorically at least, with shell shock. That's all this is, you're in shock'. This, combined with the fact that Marina had turned fifteen and begun boarding at the Friends School in Hobart, must have created for her mother both a psychological and physical distance from the trauma of Port Arthur and the prior life they all shared. Marina now realises it was this very distance that was traumatic. It must have felt like the phantom limb sensed by an amputee: it is clearly absent and yet the sense that it is *there* keeps returning time and again.

With Moon due to return home from the hospital any day now, Marina can take it no longer. Pulling back the covers, she swings her legs out of bed and gently places her bare feet on the polished timber floor. Still, four days after the duck rescue, the tender arches feel like they have been beaten with short rods.

Leaving the rooms unlit as she hobbles through the house, eventually she emerges into the breaking dawn. Stiff blades of frozen grass cut the delicate skin between her toes as she crosses the lawn. Arriving at the garden shed, standing face to face with the aluminium door, Marina hesitates. She tugs on her left earlobe. Might there be spiders inside? Neither she nor her brother had volunteered to tackle the job of clearing out the shed so until now she has not felt any urgency to locate her old journal. Marina lets go of her ear, covers her breasts beneath the nightdress with her forearm and slides the bolt back. As the door is opened the shed yawns, the subtle scent of mould on its breath. When she turns on the lights, Marina's lips part and her mouth half opens, the sudden brightness reminding her that she is not yet fully awake. She stands in the entrance facing the light with arms hanging from her shoulders, only her neck moving so that she can look sedately around the cluttered space. All the while she can feel the cold semi-dark at her back. Against the far wall of silver aluminium a dozen wooden chairs rise in two stacks pressed together. These, she knows, are for Quaker meetings. Here on the Peninsula where there is no official Quaker House they gathered for silent worship at a Friend's home, a different one each Sunday morning. Never again at *Doo-No-Harm*. Marina reaches out to the left of her to touch a tall ladder splattered with white paint. Her fingertips come away filmed with dark dust. There it is, to the right, the antique writing bureau. Marina remembers the first time she ever saw it in the store where her mother worked, two stories of rooms filled with olden-day treasures. Drawing in an audible breath when sees the keyhole in the single drawer is empty, she enters the shed proper. One, two, three, four, five steps to the desk. Opposite it she sits down on a steamer travel trunk pushed against the wall. One foot taps the concrete floor. The key, where could her mother have put it? Or, was it lost? For a second she thinks of calling Moon to ask him about the whereabouts of the missing key, then she remembers that he is still at the hospital. Even if he wasn't, it is for the best that he not get involved, it is her private business and if she asks after the key he is bound to have questions of his own. No, she will handle this herself. A screwdriver is what she needs, to bust open the lock. Marina stands up to begin the search for her father's old toolbox, it must be on one of these shelves, bowing under the weight of plastic tubs full of old photo albums. Beneath the raw electric light globe at the centre of the shed a small white feather floats down through the air. In the same instant, it seems like, Marina realises two things. Firstly, that the feather must be from one of the hens, probably stuck to the light bulb, released by the heat of the electricity running through the filaments. Secondly, that the writing bureau drawer may in fact be unlocked.

It is when she is finally in the shower that Marina begins to feel it, unmistakable, something she has not felt since childhood: dread.

Standing naked beneath the streaming hot water Marina is absolutely dreading going back to the hospital. They took the Port Arthur victims there that night. Later, the burned gunman. It was rumoured that individual hospital staff refused to treat him. While the hospital filled with the wounded, a nearby church filled with families and strangers, mourners keeping a vigil as television reporters stood on the church steps, collective candlelight glowing through stained glass windows. When he took his bag of guns to Port Arthur that Sunday morning this is not the fate he anticipated, to be locked in a cage. What he expected was to go out in a blaze of glory—literally. When he lit fire to the Seascape Guesthouse during his last stand he had expected to perish in the flames. Even after being locked up he tried other ways to die, the obvious methods like hanging himself with his bed sheets and slashing his wrists with razor blades but also more inventive ones like swallowing a rolled-up tube of toothpaste. Dr Philip Nitschke, the leading Australian 'right to die' advocate, had come out saying that his ongoing incarceration amounts to torture and given that he will never be released he should have the right to take his own life, if this is what he wants. Society says he has no such right. Despite Marina's reverence for life, which underpins her veganism, if she could forfeit his for just one of those that he took that day, she would.

Live and let die.

Marina braces herself with both hands against the tiled wall and waits, wasting litres of water. Eventually the emotion passes and she turns off the taps. Only then does she realise that she has been sobbing, that tears still spill from her eyes, run down her cheeks into the corners of her downturned mouth. Stepping out of the shower she takes a folded towel and presses her face into it, muffling some curses. Wrapping the towel around herself, she walks about the house switching on lights. It is almost June and staying darker for longer and longer each morning. Marina has not dried off thoroughly and she leaves wet footprints on the polished wooden floorboards as she returns to her room.

A round red sticker.

Of course, how could she have forgotten that? Marina glances again at the date in the top righthand corner of the journal page: 1st May 1996. Almost two and a half decades ago. For some, that was a lifetime. More than a lifetime for others. It makes sense that she might lose a small detail in that gulf. The owners made every visitor to the Site wear a round red sticker to show that they had paid the price of admission. Targets, as it turned out; Marina had obediently stuck a target on her left breast directly over her heart.

It's a beautiful day, a smile wouldn't kill you.

Did her mother really say that to her? Unbelievable! Marina doesn't remember that at all but she must have said it because Marina wrote it down.

Prematurely, she stops reading and reaches for her

cup on the bedside table. The saucer rattles as she takes the handle. The steam that washes her face as she sips is as much a comfort as the sweet tea. A fragment resurfaces, not a memory exactly, more like a dream returning. A bain-marie in a café, waiting to be served and wearing a round red patch on her clothing. Just as she is about to snatch it out of the ether the fragment slips away from her.

Marina was never in the Broad Arrow Café at Port Arthur. Not for a moment.

As she sets down her cup, Marina glimpses out of the corner of her eye a fresh impression of *Vivid Cerise* upon its white lip.

When she blinks it has vanished.

Startled, Marina scrambles across the bed, away from the teacup, wiping at her bottom lip with her thumb. Instinctively she rubs thumb and forefinger together before her eyes but there is nothing on the fingertips. Marina is not wearing lipstick. With her heart racing she spreads back out and tries to ground herself.

Their family separated that Sunday, her father taking Moon with him to the golf links near Port Arthur to be his caddy. The course looked over heath and rolling farmland to the dolerite cliffs of Cape Raoul where soldiers had long ago shot at the sea columns for practise leaving the tips of a geological wonder ragged and uneven. Marina and her mother were dropped at the Historic Site in time for the walking tour. Marina's best guess was that there were more than five hundred but less than one thousand visitors.

It was busy, even for Port Arthur, she has written.

Marina kept checking her digital watch, she remembers that. It was 1:30 pm each time she looked.

Then I saw a rabbit.

A rabbit? What rabbit?

There was an explosion.

Then it comes back to her. A rabbit running. Marina's eyes were chasing a rabbit in the grass, through the sound of laughter and the legs of people standing around her, when the first gunshot exploded in the Broad Arrow Café. The rabbit heard it first. Marina watched it bolt. By the time the sound wave hit the group of visitors the rabbit had vanished.

Everyone was saying it was a re-enactment.

Just a play put on for the tourists. Even her mother told her this as gunshots continued to ring out. Marina heard *more than a dozen* shots in as many seconds.

Along with some of the other parents present, Marina's mother took her hand and began to lead her away from the group towards the re-enactment.

I told her we should wait.

Was it the rabbit, she wonders, did the sight of the animal fleeing spook her? Or was it just a Godly child's respect for authority that told her they should wait for the tour guide? Marina cannot remember. Whatever it was, she had dragged her heels that day.

She has written down:

A policeman or person in a uniform ran past us.

Marina sighs. Flattens her hand on the open page. Outside raindrops gently graze the window pane. A sun shower spurts, tapping louder on the glass. She tries to think back. It must have been someone already onsite because no police arrived at the scene until much, much later. Probably around 3:00 pm. Before that it was only the volunteer paramedic trucks and of course the helicopters droning overhead, a continual relay of patients from Port Arthur to the hospital in Hobart. Marina can still see in her mind's eye the image of a helicopter loaded and heading away with one door swinging open in mid-air. Leaving her tea to grow cold she reads on, still unbelievably grateful to this day that she narrowly avoided all seven circles of hell waiting inside the Broad Arrow Café.

They looked like they'd seen a ghost.

That's a blank but this next bit she remembers only too well.

Get out! Leave! Run! Get out! Get out! There's a gunman in here!

As Marina reads the words they are as familiar to her as a nursery rhyme from childhood—Ring-a-ring o' roses, A pocket full of posies, A-tishoo! A-tishoo! We all fall down—and like so many Nursery Rhymes the true meaning of the words were not apparent to her at the time she first heard them. In fact, none of them could comprehend it. They all stood stock still staring with mouths open as metal flew from the café door like tossed kitchen scraps.

Fire! Get out, fire!

The 'don't cry rape cry fire' technique, Marina recognises now. Then she saw a tincture of blue smoke drifting on the air and was pulled back by her mother, off her feet almost it had felt like.

There was a car park between us and the Information Centre where we just came from.

Marina scratches the back of her neck, crossing the hairline. So many cars right in front of them, cars in which you could get in and drive away, escape. None of them hers. The sensation of helplessness she felt at that moment returns to her now and she is overcome.

A sadness rises up before her as great as any she has ever felt—a dragon.

Suddenly I could smell dusty carpet. I had a flash of the emerald coloured carpet in the house where we were before we came to Port Arthur. During worship I felt the presence of God in the circle. It was like an invisible but real light in the middle of the room, falling down like a waterfall. You were supposed to be still of body as well as spirit and mind. I was sitting so still that my whole body was starting to ache. I kept getting distracted by the Friend sitting beside me. He scribbled away with a short pencil in a spiral notepad. At the end of the meeting when he offered me his hand and smiled at me I only let him shake my fingertips. When we were praying in the Parsonage I suddenly wished that I had looked over at the notebook, just to see what was so important he had to write it down during worship but it was too late.

Anyway, Marina's stomach is empty and her bare arms cold. With unspilled tears in her eyes she looks away from the page. During her momentary retreat from the past she puts on her unwashed black cardigan and makes breakfast, a crumpet with honey she finds in the pantry. If Moon was here she would have to justify herself, explain to him that the fact he eats sugar makes him a hypocrite. More insects are killed harvesting sugar cane than in apiculture. Strictly speaking, honey is an animal product but Marina makes her own rules, and occasionally breaks them. The point is she eats in peace. The moment her brother is released from hospital and returns to *Doo-No-Harm*, under her care and supervision, cannot come soon enough. The shrapnel wounds he sustained to the left temporal region, to the chest and wrist are healing to the doctors' satisfaction. Order will be restored. Rinsing her plate in the sink so as not to attract the ants, she opens the curtains and lets the daylight in.

Driving home from the chemist at Nubeena with Moon's prescriptions, three boys walk shoulder to shoulder down the side of the road coming at her, hands in their front coat pockets, straps of their school bags slung diagonally across their chests. Any one of them could be the young hunter from Moulting Lagoon. Full of rainwater, a cluster of potholes in the road under the tyres cause her gaze to bump up to the rear-view mirror, her forehead and eyes reflected like a passenger in the car with her.

When between the shacks at Doo Town Marina sees Pirates Bay flicker she winds down her window a fraction. The sea peeled back forcefully from the beach sounds like something delicate being torn. A distinct sound like slicing that makes Marina wince to hear it, that slow laceration tearing delicate skin and soft tissues. It is a perineal tear. Over this, the crashing whitewater screams at the top of its voice as the sea gives birth to inshore waves.

When she was a small girl Marina stood here with her back to the open mouth of Pirates Bay and asked her mother a question, 'What would you do if one day I disappeared into the sea?' At this her mother laughed, 'You're silly! You're Marina! How can Marina vanish into the sea? She's *of the sea*.' 'What if a shark got me?' 'Then you control it with your superpowers. That's it. And he'll go his own way'. 'What if my powers don't work on the shark?' 'Then I'd get your father's diving gear and jump into the water to rescue you. Even though I can't swim and I'm afraid of the sea, I'd rescue you. I would'. Then their mother had turned to Moon. 'Does Marina's little brother fear the sea? Does he?' 'I only go in if it's shallow'. 'Moon, look!' Their mother held her arms out as if she was holding up the sky above them. The moon was visible. Pale. Moon had inched backwards as a wave crept towards his toes on the sand. 'Do you want me to find you a beach without any water?' Marina asked him. 'It's called perigee', their mother said. 'When the moon is the closest it comes to Earth. A full moon at perigee makes the highest tides of all. So you see, the moon controls the tides. The moon can cause the whole beach, up and down the coast, to flood. It can make the sea bulge or shrink. That's Moon's superpower'.

Arriving home, she finds the internal doors of the house all closed: from the entrance hall to the living room; and, from the living room to the kitchen. They are unlocked so she passes through without concern, closing each one after her.

In her bedroom she takes a scarf from the shoulder of the dresser mirror and stretches it around her forehead, brings the ends around and ties a firm but comfortable bow at the nape of her neck. Before she goes to see Moon she checks her reflection to make sure the look is *chic* rather than *pirate*. The autumn tones through the scarf pattern make her pale blue eyes pop. The red lips have lasted.

Marina does not knock on her brother's door, her footfall on the wooden boards is obvious enough.

"What were you doing out of bed?" she asks. "You've only just this morning been released from hospital."

"Thank god you're back," he says. "I'm itchy all over.

Look!," Moon props himself up on his pillows.

Marina unbuttons his shirt and rolls back the singlet.

"It's red, isn't it?" he says.

"Yes, it is." Marina reaches behind her for the talcum powder on the desk, cornflour the main ingredient. "Just lie back down." Leaning over him to inspect the skin more closely, she sprinkles talc onto his chest and then taps it in gently with her fingertips. Next she unzips the cosmetics case and takes out the thermometer to check his temperature, a measure she herself has instituted rather than the doctors. With the thermometer in his mouth she rolls him over and straightens the fitted sheet ensuring it is secure on the corner of the mattress. When she taps his shoulder he rolls back over and she takes the thermometer from between his teeth and reads it.

"Your temperature is low," she announces. "Is that why you closed all the doors? Were you cold?"

"I couldn't get warm."

"Well, I didn't mean to give you a hard time." Marina sits down in the chair she has brought in from the kitchen. "I've got to go feed Yoko and Ono. I didn't have time to let them out this morning. Do you need anything first?"

Moon turns his face on the pillow so he is looking directly at her. "I got a text message from Mike."

"Mike?"

"Activist Mike," he says. "From the PVN."

"Oh him," she says, lifting herself off the chair to pull the covers up under his chin. "What did he want?"

"They're doing a protest at Clark Cliffs Cemetery. The funeral director is going to be doing a five-hour spotlight shoot of native animals. They have a permit from the DPI, Mike says."

"At Clark Cliffs Cemetery?" says Marina. "Why are they shooting in a cemetery?"

"They reckon the wallabies and pademelons eat the flowers on graves."

"Can't they build a fence?"

"Bullets are cheaper."

Marina gets up out of her chair so she is standing over her brother. "You're not thinking of doing it, are you?"

"Don't worry, it's after I have my outpatient appointment with the physio. I checked," says Moon. "I am going though and I understand if you don't want to, after what happened to me at Moulting Lagoon. Nobody will think any less of you. They know about ... well, they just understand."

"Understand what? You've been talking about me behind my back?"

"Mari, sit back down."

"No, I want to know what you've been saying. These people aren't your friends, Moon. You can't trust them. Just because they're vegans and activists they're still strangers. You have no right to be sharing my personal business with them. People gather precious information about you to try and blackmail you, to destroy you. Anything you say can and will be used against you. I know what I'm talking about, Moon and you're a very innocent person."

"Innocent? What does innocence have to do with this? Look, I'm proud of you. You are an inspiration. It's amazing that you went out on the water in the first place. After the experience in your past you have more reason than any of us to fear guns. Since finding out what happened to you, Mike has a new-found admiration for your involvement at Moulting Lagoon. You're not that teenage girl anymore, helpless. The trauma you experienced, the violence you witnessed, you've transformed it. It's like some kind of alchemy. You've transformed it into direct action for the most vulnerable, for the voiceless."

Moon's expressiveness disarms Marina. Defenceless against him, she withdraws from his bedside and leaves the room.

In the yard, the wind is cold and blows directly in Marina's face. Putting her head down she pulls the cardigan tightly around her body. The smell strikes her first, before the sight of the empty cage. It is the smell of violence, recent violence. There is no sign of either bird as she circles the henhouse. Sighing, she bends down to unclasp the coup.

"Come out, come out, wherever you are."

On the ground are smashed eggs and chicken shit. A tunnel has been dug in the earth beneath one wall and there are feathers there, a bloody mass of feathers. Marina's stomach cramps up.

"Goddammit!"

The wire is supposed to have been planted deep enough to prevent this from happening. What was it? A fox? A dog?

Then it hits her: an odour most foul. The kind of odour released by a stressed devil. They can bite through metal traps, and use their strong jaws for escaping captivity so why not breaking into food storage?

Walking back around the coup, Marina clutches the wall of chicken wire and scans inside. Across the dirt floor brown feathers are strewn like fallen autumn leaves stirred up by a dust devil. Even here, caught in the wire close to her face. The hens were trapped, she realises. No escape. Marina lets go of the wire and steps back. Wiping her hands first on her dress, she tucks her hair behind her ears and keeping her distance she paces back and forth searching for remains. There appears to be nothing. Only the mess of feathers. A single egg has been cracked open so that what is left of the shell resembles an off-white baby's shoe, a tapered toe opposite a round heel with a wide opening in-between. Whatever it was, it has stolen them, taken both birds out whole through its tunnel beneath the fence. Did it kill them one at a time, taking the first one out and to a safer place before returning for the other? Or did it kill them together in a frenzy? Probably they weren't killed quickly or outright. It only needed to disable the birds, stop them flying frantic up the walls. A scent lingers on the air that wafts from the scene, a distinct scent that attests to terror. Sweat, urine, blood, saliva, dirt, torn feathers. It told a story, one without a happy ending. How will she break the news to Moon? This is the last thing he needs, the last thing either of them needs. Yet some part of Marina feels like this is just the thing that ought to happen, that would happen, at a time such as this. It is those ripples, one action like a stone thrown sidearm skipping on calm water. Nobody, not even the sidewinder, knows how many times it will bounce before it sinks, each impact sending out its own capillary waves. If not for the tragedy of their mother's death the siblings would not have been at Moulting Lagoon on the weekend with the hunters. If Moon had not been injured by shrapnel out on the water Marina would not have forgotten to free the hens and they would not have been easy pickings for the mystery predator. And so it goes on, trauma after subsequent trauma, all traceable to a single flat stone.

For her own mother, it began with prayers and led to a diagnosis of obsessive-compulsive disorder and comorbid post-traumatic stress disorder. Based on Marina's own observation and experience, the two disorders are on the same continuum with overlapping symptoms. Not only did Marina witness the interplay between obsessive–compulsive disorder and traumatic experiences, she made a personal study of it, collecting empirical evidence in her memory.

The murders at Port Arthur hit her mother like a giant wave, the kind the surfers had to be dragged out by jet skis and dropped into at Shipstern Bluff. The aptly named Devil's Point—'Shippies'—was somewhere in the Tasman National Park between Cape Raoul and Tunnel Bay and by all accounts one of the wildest and most dangerous big wave surfing locations in the world. After Port Arthur it was like her mother became stuck inside the pipeline, the hollow formed by the breaking of this very big wave. For the better part of a year, the house in the Huon Valley was transformed into a hoarding epicentre. At work, she would wander through the two stories of rooms filled with pre-owned treasures and see only a visual manifestation of human transience, ephemerality, loss and demise. The antiques would have her obsessively pondering the lives of the person or persons who once owned them. Even an antique photo frame, she saw as a discarded vessel of someone's failed effort to preserve and display his or her own personal memories. It was as if the photo frame was a device that represented just how imperfect and vulnerable were our own bodies and minds.

Marina went to one extreme, denying the preciousness of *that of God in everyone* while her mother went in the opposite direction, extending that preciousness to objects. Not only did she hold on to her belief that there was *that of God in everyone,* she began to believe that each person's possessions were of unique worth, valuing them all equally, and opposing anything that may harm or threaten them.

Rolling up her shirtsleeves, Marina heads for the shed to fetch a rake to gather up the feathers. She tries to think if she heard anything last night. You would expect that the girls put up a fight, at least set off the alarm. Surely she could not have slept through it, not unless she was in the throes of a night terror at the time, which was possible.

Inside the house, as she is scrubbing her hands with soap at the bathroom sink, from nowhere comes a craving for a sweet biscuit and a cup of hot sugary tea. In her mind's eye she is seeing a shortbread finger, a finger broken from its mate. They used to eat them as children. It has been many years since she has enjoyed one. It is probably the shock of finding the hens attacked, this sudden sugar craving.

Mum told me to make sure it was 'hot and sweet'.

The importance of tea in the immediate aftermath. In hindsight, that she was volunteering at Port Arthur at all was questionable. Both her and her mother could just as easily have been on the receiving end of the aid. At the time, Marina didn't question it, was on autopilot.

They were Friends. Shortly before they arrived at the Site that day they had been gathered for an hour in a circle with other Friends in silent worship, waiting to hear the voice of God. Perhaps some message her mother received that morning influenced her decision to stay and help others when they could have left. Marina will never know and sighs, resigned to the facts.

Marina has never felt anger towards her mother for making her stay at the Site, has only ever directed peace and compassion towards her. Marina witnessed her slow disintegration after the murders. It was not just her family either. The aftershocks from 1996 continued, year after year, often in the life of the individual more devastating than the Port Arthur massacre itself. Yet always the subsequent tragedies could be traced back to that unspeakable Sunday.

Since their arrival, Marina has been collecting the hens' eggs every few days and, unsure of what else to do with them, placing the eggs temporarily in the storage grid on the inside of the refrigerator door. After what has happened it seems not only a waste but disrespectful to toss them out with the trash. Marina makes an executive decision: boiled eggs with soldiers. How long has it been since she has boiled an egg? It must be twenty years. There isn't much to remember. Crouching to open the bottom cupboard she takes out a small saucepan. The lid falls off and she leaves it to rattle on the shelf. If she remembers correctly it is cold water, slowly heated to a gentle boil, lest you shock the shells and they crack open. Filling the pot from the sink tap she recalls what the dietician at the hospital said about high quality protein for optimised muscle building and vitamin D for mood elevation. With a tea towel she wipes the bottom of the pot before setting it down on the hotplate. The light comes on when she opens the refrigerator making it easy to inspect the individual specimens. Brown splotches on the shells, what does that mean? Marina scrapes one with her thumbnail but it does not come off. Just to be safe she takes out the three spotless eggs. Easing them into the cold water she is a little surprised to see how buoyant they are, had almost forgotten that eggs float. No doubt it is a sign they are fresh, good to eat. Marina turns the temperature dial to the midpoint and checks the time on her phone as she picks it up from the kitchen bench.

Still shaken by thoughts of the devil in the henhouse, Marina returns to her journal. With Moon home, she wants to get it done with without delay, this peeling of the old onion.

Helpless also to stop the other people moving in the wrong direction, heading *towards* the café.

I didn't know what to say.

How about 'No, not here' or 'Make a run for it' or even, 'Lay dead still.'? The question she kept hearing on the day was 'Oh what's that?'. Others said 'Must be a show going on. They've got the muskets out'.

There were maybe fifty or one hundred people in the car park who ran for their lives. A few ducked behind cars but the rest went up the hill towards the toll booth. When we went past the Information Centre the people in front of us ran into the bush there, behind it.

What Marina really remembers is that she squeezed her eyes shut as bullets whizzed past her into trees and she felt urine trickle into her underpants but couldn't stop it. Later she would turn her skirt around so that the tell-tale wet patch was on her hip instead of her crotch.

When her mother tried to pull her towards the trees where the others were dodging from trunk to trunk she resisted.

I shouted NO. I don't know why. I just didn't want to go near the trees.

When Marina had pulled her hand free she felt so much better, relief as if it was a hot coal she had been holding rather than her mother's hand. It wasn't just the bullets hitting the trees. It was that but it was also something else. There was a woman running with a tan leather handbag held on top of her head and a couple running holding one another close with heads huddled together. It looked so much like they were hurrying to get out of the rain that Marina had bent her elbows like the wings of a fledgling chick and held her supine hands out at her sides for an instant to test if they got wet. All the while the thunder of gunfire echoed around the natural amphitheatre of the Site. In an electrical storm you must never stand under a tree, she had been taught. Lightning targets trees so it was the worst place to stand if there was a strike. Marina was confused and in a state of shock. This is why she desperately sought to avoid, at all costs, those dreaded elms.

I saw a dead man lying on his back on the ground like an angel with blood around his head.

The words—*a dead man ... like an angel*—pulse on the page. That face—the grey skin, the lips blue, eyes open when they should not be—jumps into her head. Marina can actually see him. It was all wrong, except for the halo, which looked two inches thick and shined a holy red. At least that is how she sees it now. Later, she would pass the man again, this time a tea towel covering his face and the halo congealed and grown dark.

Already, Marina needs another break.

Closing her eyes she draws with the tip of her nose a figure eight sideways in the air, a yoga warm up exercise to gently stretch the neck muscles. Half a dozen times she repeats it, until the tension she has been holding there is released. Halfway down the bed she crosses her ankles.

What came next?

We ran with our heads down through Government Gardens.

Marina ran with a weight on her back that felt like a burden basket with its strap pulled taut across her forehead and temples.

Here a page is torn out. Marina knows it was her who did it but she does not know why. She checks the stub at the spine. A single page. The journal recommences at the following page with the words *laughing gas*. What stands out in her memory about their time sheltering in the Parsonage is a young woman trying desperately to keep a baby silent. Mostly failing. Also, the fact that her mother eventually confiscated her wristwatch because she kept checking it so often. Of course, they prayed continually, for what seemed like many hours but in reality was less than two.

When she did at long last emerge from the Parsonage, Marina was quite shocked that there was still daylight outside. Inside, it had felt like the dead of night.

The question of what she knew at the time, how much she realised, vexes her and she flips forward through the final written pages with no relief, no real answer. At the time the event was something that was happening to her, the most unexpected and terrifying turn in an otherwise normal day that you could imagine, but still a day in her and her family's life. Marina knew about the tragedy at the school in Dunblane a month earlier, she knew more than other people her age because she was a Friend. Both at school and at home, what happened to the children in Scotland was talked about, their names and short lives honoured through the creation of a patchwork quilt, which all who were moved by the tragedy were invited to contribute a patch to. The Friends had only just posted it to the United Kingdom the past fortnight. So Marina understood, on some level, what was happening at the Historic Site. Still, this knowledge of Dunblane didn't prepare her. Nothing could have prepared her for what she saw, what she felt and what she ultimately lost at Port Arthur that Sunday.

It began with simple, seemingly superficial things. At that age, amongst the girls at her school, Marina had set the trends. Like wearing the long sleeves of their shirts rolled up well above the wrist, the hem tucked into their waistband before being eased back out almost to the point of untucking so it would billow over the front of their skirt or shorts. Within six months of Port Arthur the cheekbones had cut through her once round face, her spine and shoulder blades were merely a hanger for the t-shirts she wore beneath slip dresses. The curls that had reached down to her lower back had strayed from light golden brown with honey yellow highlights into a uniform dark, rich chocolate brown. Then she cut them off, so that the ends only just skimmed her collar.

There were counsellors meant to help with what was happening below the surface. Marina had suffered significant structural damage like a house after an out of control car crashes into the front of it, the driver walking away unharmed. Marina was seething with anger. It was her personhood that had been violated.

Despite all the pastoral care, what she didn't tell anybody, what she couldn't begin to bring herself to say, was that overnight she had lost her faith. 1996 was the year her faith was fossilised, like an insect caught in the blood flow of a giant swamp gum, dead and trapped forever in amber. Not her belief in God. No, it was much worse than that. She lost her faith in the Godhead. That of God in everyone? Not if you were there. And she knew, only too well, that she was one of the lucky ones, the survivors, not even wounded. Not in any visible way at least.

Marina has been so close to death but it has always been at a few metres distance. The people behind her, trapped in the Broad Arrow Café she was running away from, were the ones who were killed, those ahead of her on Jetty Road were the ones wounded, her brother beside her was the one hit by shrapnel. Marina cannot put it down to providence. How much easier that would be. As she cannot, that particular period is like a chapter in a book. She started the chapter, finished it and then turned the page. Marina continued, more or less, with the story of her life.

Marina closes the journal, unable to face what is to come. Simply walks away—a luxury nobody at the Port Arthur Historic Site had that day.

When she returns to the kitchen stove there is a lid on the pot and it is jumping. Jets of steam shoot out around its edge towards the ceiling. Rushing over, Marina grabs a tea towel to grasp the wet handle as she transfers the pot to the sink. At her back she can feel the radiant heat as spilt water sizzles on the hotplate. When she turns back to switch it off she sees that the temperature dial has been turned all the way up to high. Pulling the lid off the pot she finds exploded shells, the eggs inside turned the blueish purple colour of lividity, a water-related death.

"What the hell?!" she shouts and it echoes in the empty kitchen.

Then the realisation hits her. Moon did this. It feels like him delivering a symbolic kick in her face. Momentarily stunned, she retreats to her bedroom and closes the door, conscious not to make any noise. Being superstitious, she cannot help but think that her bringing the old journal into the house and reading it was bad luck. Would the devil have ended up in the henhouse if she did not? The deaths of the chickens are not her fault, she knows that, but with Moon home from hospital her focus must be on taking care of him not revisiting the events of the past. Standing over the bed and seeing the grey cloth hardcover, the word 'Notes' embossed in gold, Marina is tempted to simply dispose of the journal; however, she knows if she does this she will be left with the nagging shame of a job half-done, like cleaning out the kitchen cupboards but not getting to the backs, which were the part most in need of attention. The past is a tricky thing, our own memory, as well as the memories of others, constantly working to protect our present. Remembering is self-preservation in action. Marina has witnessed this phenomenon time and again with her and her brother. Discussing the same occasion from years ago at which they were both party, each of them will retell their own version of the past and swear it is the truth, that it is what actually happened. No doubt the past is slippery, not an animal easily caught with your bare hands, it is an elusive eel.

Drawn back to the journal, which now exerts some kind of power over her, as if it could foretell the future, more than simply her own words, recollected only days after the events transpired. Marina lifts a pillow from the bed and places it on the hard wood floor at her feet. Kneeling, she reaches for the journal once more.

Volunteers is where she left off. Yes, there was the Red Cross, Tasman Peninsula SES, Fire and Ambulance.

The care of a nurse with the love of a mother.

Surely this is an expression she heard afterwards and has merely repeated here, so powerful prefaced by the words: *their devotions*. It seems like something a Friend would say. Probably her own mother, in fact. Or is it an instruction? There is no way now to know for certain.

Further down the page: *I saw the police when the first helicopter landed.*

The ambulance must have been there for some time before this because people had been triaged. Patients lay on camp stretchers.

They were using towels and blankets from the Motor Inn.

The bodies of the dead were covered but she could still see pieces of their clothing poking out from beneath the tarpaulins.

'There's been a massacre'.

Someone shouted this repeatedly at them when they appeared on the scene. Marina feels a sudden chill wash over her. Touching her fingertips to her lips the cold is not too bad but when she bends her knuckles and presses the backs of her stretched fingers into her cheeks she finds them frigid. Rubbing her hands together it is just the fingers that are affected as if she'd slid them underneath the lid of a freezer and held them there a good minute. Checking the time on her phone she is surprised to see that she has been at it for almost an hour. Holding the edge of the bed she rises to her feet and feels the sudden claustrophobic urge to be out of the room, indeed out of the house. The words will still be here when she returns, she tells herself. This time she doesn't close the journal, only turns it over, pushing its face into the duvet.

From her cane chair at the top of the sloping backyard Marina considers the Hippolyte Rocks. Something is bothering her. There is still the house to clear out, a burden that falls to her alone now, with Moon recovering from his injuries. This is something else. The sun is shining but with no discernible warmth. Insects fly around her head. Not mosquitos, too small to be moths, what are they? Their tiny opaque wings are lit up, like her eyelids if she chose to shut them, so that Marina can easily observe their movement through the air. That is until they fly across the bright white borders of faraway clouds in the background and become camouflaged. In a nearby tree a spider's web is strung between two twigs like nimble fingers giving the peace sign, so closely woven it resembles fine silver mesh. For a moment Marina watches, waiting to see if one of the insects will fly into it. Then she looks away, conscious that Moon is in the house, imagining the conundrum he would face if he was to witness such a happening.

Should he rescue the caught insect? What about the spider who needed food to survive?

Marina knows suddenly what has been bothering her. What she has been carrying like a parasite gnawing away at her gut. With her free hand she clutches her stomach. It's right there below the cutaneous fat, as if she could sink her fingers in and grab it by its rotten neck. It's the everyman. An important man in her life, influential and trusted: that of God in everyone.

Marina was mortally wounded by this man. Although not her own father, grandfather, brother, a boyfriend or male friend, he was not a stranger. After the murders there were whispers at the Friends' School about the gunman, who was a former pupil. Marina was still a cub then but through play she was learning to hunt. And she soon learned what it meant when the teachers were huddled together away from the students. Marina learned to disguise her stalking as playful behaviour. As a student he didn't even last a year, they said, before the headmistress suggested a more suitable school to his parents and told his mother to take him to a child psychologist. Even the Society of Friends rejected him. If what they said was true, he was a bully-victim who was both victim to, and perpetrator of, bullying at different points. After the trial nobody was surprised to learn that at the time of the murders he still had the mental capacity of an 11-year-old child. Whatever the reality of his own past, at Port Arthur he crashed through the boundaries of her world like a bolt of lightning. A fiery, unpredictable demon striking at will, he ripped apart her innocence and she was powerless to stop him.

Is it any wonder she was left angry, and eventually turned vicious? The only way to survive was to cauterize the wound once and for all by turning the tables—that's exactly what she did.

More than once she has risked her life for a whale willingly, unquestioningly, and yet she won't do the same for a fellow human being. Why? The reason she is quick to empathic anger for animals is because they are not only voiceless but also innocent. The everyman, like the victim at Remarkable Cave, why did he deserve the same compassion? Even if he wasn't a stranger, if he was someone with whom she had an established relationship, why would she put herself in harm's way to help him? Why should she?

Sitting alone in the garden, only her shadow beneath her, a thought comes down like a bee to sting Marina. One hand in its sleeve flies up as a stopper to her open mouth.

You were afraid of being superseded by a superior helper.

It was time to go back inside.

Marina flips over the journal to face it for the final time.

One helicopter flew in and one flew out.

23 wounded.

It was a relay, like the cups of hot, sweet tea. That slowing of the blades as the helicopter set down on the grass, the *whomp whomp whomp* is still fresh in her mind, as if she could hear it through the windowpane right now. And the pain, the pain in a stranger's body, visible, audible. It was a truly terrible thing to witness another person's pain and be helpless to stop it. Even the memory of it was enough to keep you up nights.

Someone brought lollies.

That's right, lollies from the Broad Arrow Café. Imagine that. Going inside to fetch confectionary. That was a soldier's mission, make no mistake.

There is a little more that she has written down. After seeing so many dead people you were thinking who is next?

'Get us a gun down here'.

The last words she heard as the lights went out, everyone secured in absolute silence to listen to the gunshots outside.

Bang. Bang. Bang. Bang. Bang ... Bang.

Bang. Bang.

Bang ... Bang. Bang.

Bang. Bang.

Chapter 11
Ruth

Ruth stands stoic as a martyr at the centre of the bothy as Seamus sweeps the stone floor around her. The palms of her hands and the front of her dress are stained with the ash from their farewell fire, complementing the grey regrowth like a tiara balanced on her forehead. It had made her sneeze to clean out the stove, and when Seamus told her *bless you* she knew that he meant it. There has been analgesic talk about coming back together, maybe two years from now, but Ruth knows he won't return. When she scratches beneath one eye it leaves a bruise of soot. Seamus rests the broom against the plank table and, wetting his thumb on his tongue, comes to her to wipe clean her face.

"You really are disgusting," she complains but does not avoid him.

Ruth helps Seamus carry his paintings, *The Antipodean Series*, wrapped in reusable shopping bags and Sellotape, along the duckboards to the car park. Following her, as he often has this past month and a half, Seamus fills his lungs with the air of Fortescue Bay and bursts into spontaneous song. "Waltzing Matilda, Waltzing Matilda, who'll come a Waltzing Matilda with me? And he sang as he—"

"Oi! I wouldn't give up the painting if I were you," calls Ruth over her shoulder.

At the car boot, as Ruth passes her load of paintings to him he turns from her and smiles and she wonders if it wasn't to save time that he had her prepare these canvases but to have her hand present, underlying his work. Seamus closes the car boot and takes Ruth by ashen hand to walk down to the beach for one last time, and she wonders now whether her dolphin sighting was a mere vision. Suddenly Ruth wants to tell him about it but it is too late.

"Do you want to go in for a quick dip before you go?" she asks.

"I can't swim?"

"That's why I said *dip*," she says. "Don't be a scaredy cat."

"It's no handicap!" he says.

"I just thought you were afraid of sharks."

"Aye, that as well."

"Take off your shoes," she orders, slipping off her own without letting go of him.

"I need hands if I'm to unlace my boots."

"Use your other hand."

Seamus sighs but cannot refuse her and bows to pick at the knotted bows with his long nails.

"Come on!"

"Give my head peace, wee girl!"

Barely does he have his socks off and she is dragging him across the sand, cool mercury between his hairy toes. Only now does Ruth let go of his hand and he rolls up his trouser legs. Facing east, arms held out Moses-like at his sides as if to perform a miracle, he withstands the small waves. At the opposite end of the beach, beyond the river mouth the forest is dark beneath an incubus mist.

Back at the bothy, shins stinging with saltwater, Seamus locates his pocketknife and kneeling beside the sleeping platform he carves his initials and the dates of his residency into the white paint.

"Ruth?" he calls over his shoulder. "You've to leave your mark here too."

"That's OK," she says. "I was never officially here."

Seamus holds out the handle of the knife to her. "You're such a heartache, you are."

After carving only her initials she looks around the bothy for the last time. On the windowsill above the sink is a dead moth, beside it a cork coaster. LEAVE NO RUBBISH it instructs on the splashboard. Seamus places a folded newspaper on top of the woodpile. They'll leave candle wax and dream residue, the friction of real conversation and the scent of paint behind.

"I wonder who is coming next," says Ruth.

On the bench they have left the next resident an unopened bag of white rice and a roll of paper towel. Sighting the wooden draughts box Ruth thinks of Seamus's painting of the Tessellated Pavement.

"Should we pinch it?" asks Ruth, nodding towards the game.

"No," he says, lifting a garbage bag. "It belongs here."

It had seemed a good idea when Ruth made the booking. A night in the Comfort Inn as a symbolic return to civilisation before returning to the mainland. As well, being the only accommodation on the Port Arthur Historic Site, the idea of spending the whole night here can be a kind of penance. It will be a vigil of sorts to make amends for the fact she did not come all those years ago for the uttering of prayers and the releasing of white doves.

While Seamus checks in at reception, she waits in the car. The scent of house paint wafts through the cabin, a scent she will forever associate with her partner. Ruth inhales a deep breath and holds it. Saves it for later, much later. It's a good thing they sailed down on The Spirit of Tasmania because there's no way he'd have been getting on an airplane with all these flammable solvents. When he returns he hands her a plastic token.

"What's this?"

"It's how we get access to the Site for our ghost tour."

"Oh no, Seamus."

"It's booked and paid for, sprout. We've just enough time to stop in at the pub. I fancy a wee drink, don't you?"

Ruth bites her tongue. If a ghost tour is what Seamus wants then it is the least she can do for him, considering.

Theirs is an Officer Row room. Ruth slides open the glass door and steps out onto the shared verandah where there is a view of lawns, ruins and the water of Mason Cove in the distance. Standing here, Ruth recalls the sounds of gunshots echoing up from the café, which were caught by a visitor, who thought they were witnessing an historical re-enactment, on shaky video footage and broadcast around the world in the days that followed the massacre. Listening to those gunshots, Ruth was acutely aware that many of them were taking lives. She could not help but wonder if one of those shots captured in the video, one of the lives taken, was her friend's. Ruth couldn't listen to the sound of the gunshots more than a few times for she knew if she did that it would become her own infernal symphony.

The pub patrons are a mix of locals and motor inn guests. Ruth can barely look at Seamus across the table so she pretends to be watching the small television set perched high in the corner behind the bar while she sips on her whiskey. As she sits silently, listening to him speak about his ideas for his new project—to reprint damaged negatives and put them in second-hand picture frames—to her ear his accent is like a rough-hewn piece of wood.

Seamus quaffs the last of his Guinness. "Right, we're away."

As they leave the pub one of the local men sitting outside calls out, "Goin' on a ghost tour, are ya?"

The other men around him laugh.

In the dusk, they deposit their token to open the gate. Their destination is the Visitor Centre behind the Memorial Garden. They find their way in the dark by the sensation of the street beneath their feet, flanked by lawns and the houses of former officials: medical officer, Catholic chaplain, accountant, magistrate. Seamus takes her hand as spectres fly across their path—startled wallabies.

"It's different at night," he remarks.

How blessed Seamus is to not know Port Arthur as she knows it. In the darkness he can still appreciate the beauty of the stars overhead, the ruins lit with floodlight. As she walks with him it is as being aboard a doomed ship and staring out at a murderous sea, she a fortuitous survivor. Although she was absent from the Site that Sunday she can see clearly in her mind's eye what occurred, the view from this exact spot, thanks to that infamous footage taken by the misguided tourist with a video camera, heard to remark that it is 'all action down here at Port Arthur today!'.

Directly ahead, in the distance, are the Penitentiary ruins, partially lit by a moon rising in the east over the Isle of the Dead and by ground lights. In the cold air Ruth sniffs, wishes she had thought to bring a tissue. Sniffs some more.

"Are you poorly?" asks Seamus.

"No, I'm OK," she replies, wiping her nose with her jacket sleeve. "Are we late?"

"I couldn't tell you," he says. "Can't see my watch face."

"Nobody wears watches anymore."

"They do if they care what time it is."

"You can just check your phone."

"If you carry a phone," he says. "I've decided I don't believe in carrying a mobile phone."

A chilling scream resounds across the Site. The long, drawn-out cry of a woman or a girl. Across the lawns wallabies scatter. Ruth's immediate thought is of the banshee. Seamus stops her with an arm across her chest as they hear another caterwaul.

"Christ almighty," says Seamus under his breath.

Ruth tugs at his shirt sleeve, "Come on."

This is not what Ruth wants. She does not need this right now. The panic is immediate. Bats let loose in her brain. Another person's pain, such a godawful sound. It is difficult to breathe.

"Over there," says Seamus, turning her body by the shoulders. "It's coming from the old church."

Stepping from the street and crossing a lawn they have a view of the convict-built church illuminated by floodlight. Together they stand and try to interpret the scene. An ambulance is parked outside the church walls, its headlights on high beam. A pair of paramedics attend to a grounded figure, while another, tall, a man, looms. The paramedics lift somebody onto a stretcher.

The screams come at brief, regular intervals like advanced contractions. Seamus tries to move towards the sound but Ruth holds him back, refusing to budge.

"What?" he says.

"There is an ambulance there already," says Ruth. "Don't get involved."

With that she lets go of his hand and turns her back on the scene and the incessant screams. Blindly she hurries back across the lawn, the stars shuddering overhead.

"Ruth?" Seamus calls after her. "Love, stop."

Reaching the street she waits for him, thinking what a stupid idea this was, for her to even attempt this. A stupid, stupid idea.

In the Visitor Centre the assembled men, women and children are oblivious to the commotion outside. Wearing beanies, gloves and scarves they stand in pairs or small groups, bristling with nervous excitement. Ruth notes various foreign accents amongst the waiting crowd as she and Seamus walk up to reception to announce their arrival. The woman behind the counter is talking on a mobile phone. It is obvious from what she says and her strained expression that she is dealing with the emergency. Finally she puts down the phone and attempts to smile.

"We just walked over from the Comfort Inn and saw the ambulance," says Ruth. "What happened?"

The woman answers in a hushed tone. "We've had an

injury on our last tour. So we've called the ambulance out. It's rare but it does happen occasionally. I've just directed them where to find her."

"They've found her," Ruth tells the woman.

"If you didn't mention what you saw to the other visitors, that would be best."

"We won't talk about it," Ruth assures her.

Their ghost tour guide arrives conspicuously, wearing a flowing black cape and carrying old fashioned lanterns on her arm. A shock of blue through her raven hair.

"Oh, I wanted him," a woman nearby laments, as a tall male tour guide in a Driza-Bone and an Akubra hat disappears down the stairs with his group.

They are like school children as they follow their caped guide out into the night, tittering, nudging with their elbows and already trying to spook one another.

The ghost tour guide introduces herself as Lilith. Surely not her real name, Ruth thinks, as she asks for volunteers to perform the role of lantern bearer. Seamus is the first to step forward to collect one.

They walk in single file with one lantern bearer leading the group, one in the middle and brave Seamus at the rear.

The tour takes them all the way up to the Commandant's House, across the water from Point Puer. In the skies overhead they witness one shooting star after another as Lilith recounts tales of the ghosts which visitors frequently mistake for staff dressed in period clothing, the grave digger who went mad living alone on the Isle of the Dead, the surgical procedures undertaken without anaesthetic using sharpened whale bones as knives and the daring but doomed escape attempts of convicts.

All the while, Ruth cannot keep her gaze from drifting down the hill and across the water to the Memorial Garden and the Broad Arrow. While the rest of the ruins across the Site are lit, these lie in darkness. The ghost tour guide has made no mention of the most recent of the Site's violent history and it is only when the group is walking back to the Visitor Centre and comes within metres of the Broad Arrow that anyone else takes notice. As two young men part from the group, Ruth overhears part of their conversation and trails behind them to listen.

"Port Arthur is Australia's lame arse version of 9/11. A lefty firing from his right hip and hitting all those people? No way. The best marksmen in the world would be struggling to be as spot on as he's accused of being."

"Who said he shot from the hip the whole time?"

"Well, if you're standing in a café, in a trained assassin stance for close quarter combat with a longarm, you would need to stand in the one spot and swivel, heel lock into the hip and spin. That's not something that gets taught at Special School for half retards, that's Mossad, seal, special forces shit."

"Don't be a stupid cunt."

Despite Ruth's initial recoil at the vulgar language being used in such close proximity to this sacred place in the landscape, the sentiment expressed by the second man, the one listening to the conspiracy theory, has pretty well summed up her own response to it.

Back in their room at the Comfort Inn Seamus gets straight into a hot shower and surfaces from the bathroom wearing boxer shorts and a plaid shirt. As he rolls the sleeves up Ruth notices the slenderness of the forearms as well as his calves. Seamus's limbs have become bow-like. Ruth focuses on his pale, luminous hands, strong yet slightly feminine, beautiful hands. One takes a bag of crisps from the minibar, the other the TV remote control.

"Happy days!" he exclaims, settling back into the pillows beside her on the bed and choosing a television documentary about the cosmonaut Alexey Leonov and the first spacewalk.

"What's the difference between a cosmonaut and an astronaut?" she asks him.

"No difference, just the Russian name for it."

Ruth shuffles back to the bedhead. "You disappointed you didn't see a ghost?"

"I don't believe in ghosts, pet."

"Really?" Ruth recalls their game of scrabble in the bothy and Seamus's tales of banshees. "Why did you want to go on the ghost tour then?"

"Just because I don't believe in something doesn't mean—"

"Seamus, something's wrong," Ruth interrupts and takes his hand. "I can't go back with you tomorrow."

"Ruth, what the hell is it?"

"It's serious."

Seamus's fingers curl and she senses him withdraw like a wave sucked back from the shore. Although she can feel the warmth of the blood in his hand, she knows it is not carried from his heart. "I guess that answers that question. This is about the past."

"We may be through with it, but it's not through with us," she whispers.

"Aye, have ye talked to your John?"

Ruth summons a lie. "Yeah, I was on the phone to him when you were in the shower."

"What did he say?"

"I don't know, he had bad reception and then we got disconnected. I wasn't able to reach him again."

"What's the last thing he said?"

"He said ... 'Help me'," she replies. "Seamus, he sounded scared."

"Then this is all preliminary." There is hope in Seamus's voice, but it is unwarranted. "Ruth, please tell me, what's this all about? This is about the shootings? Why'd you not tell me about your family's connection to it before? Least when you knew we were comin' down here ourselves?"

"What about you?" she counters. "Why haven't you ever told me about what happened to your father? All I know is that he was shot during The Troubles. How am I supposed to know what *assassinated* means? What happened to him? You never talk about it either."

"You know enough," says Seamus as he yanks on his pants. "I'm down here with ye and I know next to nothin'."

"This isn't helpful," she says.

"Dead on, love. Let's look at what we know," says Seamus. "There was this mishap involving your nephew a few weeks ago. Your Rusty is unscathed and the other lad, he's goin' to recover. Accidents happen. There's nothing more for you to do here. This moment is not about waiting to see what happens. The only thing we can control is what we decide to do in the present."

"So what, what are you saying? What are we going to do?"

"I'm going to get on the road in the morning," he says. "And I only have one question for you. Are ye coming with me?"

"That just sounds so wrong."

Seamus's eyes fix on her. "They'll always be your family, Ruth."

Thrown from across the room, his words hit her like a medicine ball. Seamus snatches his wallet from the bedside table.

"Don't just leave," she says, becoming frantic. "Where are you going? Why won't you talk to me?"

"Ruth," he says, "sharpen your pencil, 'cause I'm goin' to tell you what happened. Gary Lavery was killed in a case of mistaken identity on the thirteenth of November in 1986. He was 46 years old. Loyalist Ulster Freedom Fighters shot him nine times, in the head and neck. The office in Belfast was riddled with bullets, leavin' no chance of survival." Seamus tosses back his wet hair. "Now do ye feel informed, righteously so?"

Some hours later Seamus stumbles back into the motel room reeking of whiskey. Ruth pretends to be asleep.

"I've worked it all out in my head," he says, falling into bed fully clothed. "I've it all worked out."

Giving up the rouse, Ruth rolls over onto her back. "You do realise you're going to be hungover now for the ferry trip home?"

"I'll be grand," he says. "I'll be grand."

"You should get some sleep, Seamus."

"Look at that face, you're gorgeous, aren't ye?" He

leans over her. The lamplight illuminates his forehead and the bridge of his nose, the wet glistening lower lip. His eyes are wide and winged as a mask across his face, the pupils, which should be swollen with consumed spirits are pinpoints. "I remembered something, I've not thought of it for years. This thing I read when I was a lad. I was perhaps thirteen. It was in the newspaper, a story about a man, a true story. I cut it out and I put it, I put it in my pocket, the pocket of my school shirt. It was an Israeli man, I think, who'd gone and shot himself in the head and left behind a suicide note. The newspaper printed it. It was to me, to me it was the most poignant thing I'd ever read. It said, 'I apologise to those I've left behind but I die not in misery or for ill reason. I've realised today that with my loving wife, fantastic kids and beautiful life, that nothing can get any sweeter and so I've chosen this moment because life can't get any better. Goodbye'. I thought the sentiment was beautiful, anyway." Seamus lies back down on the bed and stares at the ceiling. "When my ma did the laundry she thought I was mental and her and my da questioned me for ages thinkin' I was suicidal. I didn't have the words then to describe why I found it so beautiful. Sharing this residency, with you, Ruth, I know how that man felt."

Ruth reaches over and switches off the lamp, knowing this is their last chance. They kiss passionately—tongues and teeth and breath. For Ruth it is a moment of abandon, abandoning everything and everyone to find Seamus in the dark. They make love and it is a reaching deep inside of one another as if they could find God there, or at least escape death by climbing inside the other's soul.

When Ruth sleeps she dreams of a child in a pond

being dragged underwater caught up in a line. A parent in a boat nearby begs her to help the child. Ruth plunges down into the water. The only way to save the child is for her to switch places with them and let them rise up, or else she has to give up and rise to the surface herself. Suddenly she perceives that there is someone else at the other end of the line who is pulling it down. Ruth thinks that she could ask this person to come to the surface too, thinks she will help them. They appear. To her surprise it is just another child, ten or perhaps eleven years old. The three of them reach a place where they can all breathe, an air pocket, but have not yet surfaced. Ruth feels a deep sympathy for the child who had been pulling the line down. As the dream ends a sing-song voice says, 'Why can't you be yourself? Is it just too hard to cry?'

Ruth wakes into a sunlit room alone in bed.

"Seamus?"

As a strange man steps out of their bathroom, Ruth screams into the pillow.

"'Bout ye." A familiar voice.

"Jesus Christ." Ruth stares at Seamus, clean-shaven with short hair for the first time since she's known him.

"Not anymore."

Beyond the new haircut, it's his face—Seamus has dimples in his cheeks and a cleft chin.

"You look so different, I can't believe it," she says, sitting up. "C'mere, show me what you've done to yourself."

As he walks about the room packing up the last of their belongings she cannot take her eyes off him. "Why the change, Seamus?"

"Everything's changing," he says and she can sense

his coolness. Right now he is out of her orbit. No use asking him to elaborate.

"Come back to bed," she whines.

"It's time to go."

Ruth checks the clock radio beside her. "We've got half an hour before we have to check out."

"Aye, but I want to see some of Hobart before I drive up to catch the ferry back."

"Well I'll come with you."

"And then drive you all the way back?" Seamus raises an eyebrow at her.

"I can catch a bus back," she says, suddenly breathless. "Or we can take two cars. I'll borrow John's."

"Come on, get dressed. I'll drop you at the farm."

Silence is the dam wall holding back Ruth's tears as she and Seamus make their final journey together to Rare Bird Farm. She doesn't dare contemplate how much she will miss him. That he is also silent, she knows, means only that he is engaged in an internal dialogue. Those still waters run deep.

For her own selfish reasons, over the years Ruth has bestowed on Bass Strait, the great separator, a power even more potent than the mythology surrounding its mysterious losses and disappearances of people, planes and ships. Now the distancing power of the Devil's Strait is to be hers and Seamus's painful reality.

At Highcroft, what appears at first to be the common sight of a forest raven pecking at carrion by the roadside turns out to be, as the car draws nearer, a much rarer sight: a brown falcon taking flight with a rabbit carcass gripped in its talons and alighting on a power pole.

The natural beauty of Stormlea presses in on Ruth, almost unbearable. The dapple created by the shade and shadow of the gums and blackwoods in league with the morning sunlight, which has only just thawed the paddocks.

At the farm gate, Ruth risks a long look at Seamus. It makes her think that God must be a tailor. Those dimples look just like an artful stitch pulled through one cheek and out the other. More than anything she desires to put her tongue into his mouth and strum the thread, cause the dimples to appear, disappear and then reappear. Instead, when she takes his face in her hands and forces a kiss upon his lips she thrusts in her thumbs.

Ruth watches Seamus drive away. Stands and listens to the sound of the engine, as if it was his heartbeat, as it grows fainter and fainter, until it is simply gone.

While she enters an empty house—her brother out in the dairy—she is not alone. Ghosts inhabit these rooms.

In her old bedroom, Ruth puts down her rucksack and sits on the edge of the antique double bed that at one time, a time before her childhood, her parents shared. The coverlet is cool beneath her palms, the ceiling low overhead and boasting its own galaxy of mildew. A dark milky way. Ruth lies down on her back on the bed, closes her eyes and is comforted by the silence.

Late that afternoon, Ruth is still waiting for a call from Seamus, a call to tell her that he has arrived home safely. Ruth tries his mobile again but it goes straight to voicemail.

"It's me. Ring me back when you get this. I want to

know you got home OK." She pauses. "I love you."

Then she realises, Seamus didn't take his mobile on the residency so perhaps he has not even found it or has not yet recharged the battery. Ruth calls their home phone and is answered by her own voice telling her that they will be away until the fifteenth of June. She leaves the same message, adding, "You should change the message on this thing."

The house is draughty.

"John?" she calls out, thinking she has heard a voice.

Silence.

The ute is parked in the drive.

Beside the cold stove is a single gaunt piece of firewood. Putting on her gumboots, she ventures into the yard to fetch more. Outside she takes great lungfuls of air. Over the course of the residency she has become addicted to it, the scent of the bush with an accent of the sea. It awakens her senses.

Close by, a cow bellows. Ruth looks up. Overhead the first stars are out. By rights, all of the cows should be stowed away in the back paddock. Again it bellows. Ruth leaves the firewood and walks to the dairy. Growing up it was out of bounds to her. Only John ever had the dubious privilege of working with their father.

As soon as Ruth spots the animal she recognises it as a *down cow*. She stands motionless with her feet in a film of water on the concrete floor.

As he sees her enter, John, gathering up a hose, says, "That's 163."

"What's wrong with it?" asks Ruth.

"Calving paralysis," he says.

Despite its frozen hind legs, the cow seems bright and alert. Ruth approaches cautiously and crouches down to pat its neck.

"Can you help it?" she asks.

When there is no response, Ruth takes a handful of hay and feeds it to the cow while peering into its eyes.

As Ruth is walking back to the house she hears the telephone ringing. Just as she steps inside and is rushing to pick it up, the ringing stops. A sudden dryness in her throat causes her to swallow reflexively. Over and over again. Putting the receiver back down she enters the kitchen and fills a glass from the tap. Drinks. The water helps to clear her vision and she sits down and dials their home telephone number with no thought as to what she will say to Seamus, hoping with each ring that he will answer, that it will not go to their voicemail. In her head she counts the rings, as if waiting after lightning for a thunderclap. Finally Seamus answers.

"Thank God," she says. "I've been worried about you. Did you just call?"

Seamus blindsides her with a comment about making a short trip home to Northern Ireland and then, without letting her gather her thoughts, begins a spiel about some new project.

It occurred to me on the ferry home that you can print degraded film as per usual. I've just to get hold of all my family's old negatives, see what turns up on the perished film. What I'm thinkin' is a forbidding presence in an otherwise mundane, ordinary moment, foreshadowing inevitable loss and demise, human mortality and transience.

This is not even a conversation, Ruth realises; it's a

rationale, an artist rationale.

Without saying a word, she hangs up the phone.

By the following day, Ruth recognises that she can no longer simply avoid conflict. Settling her nerves with a beer, she feels ready to start a rational conversation with Seamus. Having had the chance to prepare mentally and emotionally, she is confident her feelings won't burst out in an uncontrolled way.

When Ruth phones home and Seamus's voice answers, she knows immediately that it is only a ghost of him, a recording. And so he has already left and changed the message to reflect their continued absence.

At the tone, Ruth bursts out laughing. Then realising she is being recorded she quickly muffles the mouthpiece at her breast and hangs up. This initial, ridiculous reaction is quickly followed by disbelief. With a trembling hand she puts the receiver to her ear for a second time. Dials their number. This time her heart races as it rings and she is desperate for him to answer. Wills him to pick up the telephone in their house on the mainland. The message arrives as dreadful confirmation: Seamus has returned to Northern Ireland. Suddenly the earth becomes flat and she is tipping over the brink of some eternal waterfall like a tall ship to its doom.

Ruth goes back to bed. Lying in the dark she recalls Seamus's dream. The yellow papers. The light. Just as it affected her when he retold it at the plank table in the bothy, her arms tingle with goosebumps and her heart thuds hard in her chest. Sitting up in bed she takes her phone from the bedside table and begins to search online for the mysterious yellow papers.

Quickly, her suspicions are confirmed. The answer is the Western Union telegram. During World War II, the sight of one of their couriers was feared and dreaded because the War Department used the company to notify families of the death of their loved ones serving in the military.

On eBay, Ruth finds a Western Union telegram sent by the navy to the wife of a soldier during the Second World War.

> *FROM THE VICE ADMIRAL, CHIEF OF PERSONNEL. I DEEPLY REGRET TO INFORM YOU THAT YOUR HUSBAND PRIVATE FIRST CLASS NORMAN F CALLAGHAN, IS MISSING IN ACTION IN THE SERVICE OF HIS COUNTRY. YOUR GREAT ANXIETY IS APPRECIATED AND YOU WILL BE FURNISHED DETAILS WHEN RECEIVED. TO PREVENT POSSIBLE AID TO OUR ENEMIES AND TO SAFEGUARD THE LIVES OF OTHER PERSONNEL PLEASE DO NOT DIVULGE THE NAME OF THE SHIP OR STATION OR DISCUSS PUBLICLY THE FACT THAT HE IS MISSING.*

Loose lips sink ships.

To tell Seamus about her discovery is not enough; Ruth must place the little yellow paper in his hands.

With trembling fingers, she clicks:

Buy It Now.

It occurs to Ruth as she is driving on the Nubeena Ring Road that it holds special significance. From the cemetery at the top of the ring, the road links to Nubeena and then down to Port Arthur. These three points are spaced almost equal distances apart: the place where her friend died; the place where she lived and where her parents still do; and, the place where she is buried. A tragic ring in many ways. Yet it also speaks of cycles, of life cycles, of the generations. At its centre is the Clark Cliffs circuit bushwalk. The road itself has a reputation for being the worst in the state. Not long ago an elderly woman was killed here, John mentioned. The countryside Ruth drives through belies the danger. Large swirls of hay bales in flat empty paddocks of pale green grass beneath heavy, unbroken rain cloud. The township was once a convict outstation. Ruth had passed the historic cemetery many times growing up but never had reason to stop. Today it is a sense of duty that brings her here. To walk amongst the graves of locals who died at Port Arthur, to visit her friend's grave for the first time, and also to be able to say she knows the cemetery more intimately than a feature on the drive to Nubeena or White Beach.

The simple chapel where the funeral services were held is no larger than the abandoned yellow church on the border of Highcroft and Stormlea, with those same lancet arched windows and a two-tier gable roof like a double rainbow. Without a coat, Ruth at first wrestles with the winter air but soon submits, the cold strangely comforting, evidence that she has been touched, that she is connected to the natural world. In a graveyard, any sensation symbolises life and should not be taken for granted.

Ruth pauses at the shared grave of husband and wife who died over a century ago.

Dear parents, tho we miss you much, we know you rest with god.

By far the most common epitaph she reads is, 'Peace, perfect peace'.

Amongst the graves, too, are victims of the massacre. One:

Who was tragically taken from us at Port Arthur on the 28th of April 1996. Leaving to wonder why her husband, parents, sister and their families.

Although now it seems almost unthinkable, she has never asked why, has always known the answer to the question of why, why they died. At least she thought she knew. The gunman said it himself, albeit too simply: he'd 'had a gutful'. No longer is this knowledge enough. This question of why is much larger, far more complex than that and perhaps in the end unanswerable. Is it even the right question?

When Ruth finally locates the grave it comes as a shock. Of course she knew it would be here and she was expecting to find it but the reality of the cold marble is like a punch to her gut and her eyes begin to water. It is a child's headstone and the text reads as she would expect it to. The flowers she knows were left by the mother, a clear plastic sleeve protecting the delicate petals of pink roses from the elements.

Ruth didn't return to Tasman Peninsula after Port Arthur, to attend the funerals, for a number of reasons. When she first got to the mainland and started studying full-time, she was just too poor. When Helen found out that Ruth would not be attending the funerals, using this excuse, Helen offered to pay for her airfare. Ruth told her that she'd think about it and then avoided her phone calls until after the services.

Ruth's biggest reason for not returning was that she had no idea what she would say. Ruth had no words to describe her own friend or what she meant to her. This young woman had been possessed of *something*. In Ruth's imagination this unnameable quality takes the form of the spirit level used by carpenters and stonemasons. A glass vial incompletely filled with liquid, leaving a bubble in the tube. A slight upward curve ensuring the bubble naturally rests in the centre–the highest point. At slight inclinations the bubble travels away from the marked centre position. Sensitivity is the key to a spirit level; its accuracy depends on its sensitivity.

Crouching at the foot of the grave, Ruth catches sight of her own reflection in the dark, gleaming marble and, feeling a chill on the back of her neck like an icy hand, she snaps her head over her shoulder. Not another living soul in the cemetery.

As Ruth sighs the sound is more than just the expelled air leaving her body; the sound is practise, a practise at dying. She falls to her knees.

No doubt when the parents' lives end they will be buried here also, perhaps in a shared grave, alongside their daughter and join the other families, generations of Peninsula residents beneath the earth.

Not her family though. They were cremated and their ashes scattered from Cape Raoul.

Ruth smells the sea as she rises to her feet and turning, sees storm clouds above Cascades Bay as it flows out into Norfolk Bay. The clouds inspire in her a sudden sense of urgency. Ruth kisses two fingertips and presses them to the engraved name, thinking rather of her rosy cheek, and leaves the dead to rest in peace.

Only now, this very moment, does Ruth find the word she has been searching for so long: compassion.

She was unusually compassionate, even as a child.

She was the first person in Ruth's life to show her that emotions are valid–not just her own emotions, but those of others too. When Ruth was bullied in school, she didn't join in with the popular crowd. Instead, she said by her actions 'You will not be treated this way'. Instead of saying, 'Poor, unfortunate girl,' as others, including teachers, so often did, she said through her actions, 'We won't stand for this', and stepped up to offer assistance. When Ruth finally left school, and the Peninsula, the last thing she ever said to her was, 'Go get 'em, Ruth. You're tougher than hell, aren't you?'

Ruth believes in the memory of water. That when a substance is diluted in water, the water can carry the memory of that substance even after it has been so diluted that none of the molecules of the original substance remain. Ruth believes this because it is the same with her, and the people who enter her life. They remain part of her long after their last molecule is gone. When connections become diluted by so much time that others forget, she remembers.

Chapter 12
John

John is not sure what to make of it at first.

"Stayed?" he repeats down the phone line. "I've never heard of it. What does it actually mean? It's what, like probation? A suspended sentence?"

Once again he listens to the solicitor at the other end and tries to take the information in.

"So after this twelve-month period we're in the clear? For all practical purposes it's like it never happened? There will be no permanent record?"

"Right, well that isn't gonna happen so the case is closed," says John. "Listen, this news is terrific, has anybody told Rusty yet?"

"I see. Well I'm also his legal guardian, his mother and I share custody equally."

"No, no, I understand. You're just doing your job."

"Oh, before you go, tell me, any news on the protestors?"

"No, I mean can they be prosecuted beyond the good old fine for being out in the field before 10?"

"Yeah well don't look a gift horse in the mouth, eh? Anyway, thanks for the call. I appreciate it. Cheers."

John hangs up.

Stepping from the dark hallway into the no man's land where kitchen crosses over into dining room, John's gaze is arrested by the day outside. Walking towards the windows at the front of the house, his white shirt becomes engulfed in sunlight. John is reminded of the immediate aftermath of the event itself, when he stood on the bank of Moulting Lagoon with other hunters, soaking wet from the chest down and shivering with cold, within metres of protestors, a lone photographer capturing the moment. Already he could see the sensational headline 'Ceasefire' or perhaps 'War is over'. John knew better though. The reason the hunters and rescuers stood in such close proximity was not some truce resulting from the shooting accident; it was merely the price of admission to a rhombus of shared sunshine.

As the family leaves the pig farm, John driving with Rusty on the seat in between himself and Ruth, he sees his sister is watching the quad bike riding out to patrol the fences on the Whiteley property. Even at a distance, the rider's long golden hair flying behind her is unmistakable.

For a time after she left home, Ruth exchanged letters and phone calls with Helen. Whether Ruth wanted the correspondence or not, John does not know. Helen was the instigator, relaying news from the Peninsula, perhaps in an effort to make Ruth feel part of the community despite her self-imposed exile to the mainland. Glancing in the rear-view mirror Ruth asks him, "Do you remember our horses wouldn't ever go anywhere near the piggery? It was strange. They'd rear up and carry on, throw us off even. Mum always said it was because given the chance pigs would eat a horse and the horses knew that."

"Rubbish," says John. "They could smell the slaughterhouse. Animals can be funny that way."

Ruth might not have much common sense but she did go to university, even if it was only an Arts degree she graduated with in the end. If Rusty spends a little time getting to know her, he'll see that if his aunt could do it, then he definitely can. Ruth is no role model but she has set an example for Rusty, at least in this one regard.

John leads them on the familiar walking track, beyond the lookout and over the shoulder of Mount Raoul.

"Why do we have to do this again?" says Rusty.

"You know, even the disabled don't sit in their rooms all day, they go out and do things like everybody else."

"You're supposed to say *people with disability*, not *the disabled*," Rusty tells him.

"What about the old adage 'sticks and stones may break my bones, but words will never hurt me'? Or don't they teach that anymore?"

"You mean verbal abuse?" says Ruth.

John casts a glance her way, and then responds with stony silence as they descend the southern slopes.

The forest becomes damp. Moss is bright underfoot and lichen is sprayed over rocks and the trunks of the trees that stand suddenly taller and closer together. It was here, amongst the dogwood, that as a child his little sister would search musk burls for the faces of native animals like spirits trapped in the wood.

"Cool sneakers," says Ruth.

"Online," replies Rusty.

The forest dries up and opens out and when the track emerges once again onto the cliff top they catch their first glimpse of Cape Pillar and Tasman Island in the east.

"Online," repeats Ruth. "What does that even mean, *online*?"

"It means that's where I got them," says Rusty.

"Yeah I know that, but I mean what kind of answer is that? Like how about what kind of sneakers they are and which online store did you get them from?"

"They're Vans and I got them from SurfStitch online."

"But that's not what you said though. You just said 'online'. A single word."

"Waste not want not."

"You realise, that's the least you could have said to me and it still be considered a conversation? Actually, that's not true, there is something shorter, one syllable from that one word. On ... *On*."

"What do you know about cool shoes anyway? You don't have any kids."

"And you sound just like your dad."

"Do not."

"Cool sneakers, Rusty. *On. On.*"

Predictably, Rusty shakes his head and rolls his eyes.

On.

The way Ruth is saying the word sounds like there is an ice cube stuck on her tongue, some strange onomatopoeia, "*On on on, on on on.*"

Then, it thaws in the warmth of her mouth, which releases other imaginary words.

"*Vadj, froq, blud, whak,*" she utters.

Finally it becomes visual, the onomatopoeia of steam: *netheme.*

John sees the breath leave her lips and condense as an intimate cloud in the cold of the air. He recalls winters so brutal that the Antarctic gales, howling from the south like wolves, literally took his breath away and blurred his vision.

"Hey do you still have any of those muesli bars?" says Rusty.

"Oh you want one now?" Ruth slips one shoulder out from beneath a strap and reaches around to unzip her backpack. "Typical."

Ruth passes Rusty a bar she has already opened and he takes a bite.

"You don't have to unwrap his food," says John. "He's fourteen not four."

"What do you think?" says Ruth. "It's tasty right?"

First Rusty coughs and then begins a dramatic choking fit.

"Nice try," says Ruth.

"That's really good," says John. "That's really funny. You can make jokes all you want but you're the one who's wasting his life sitting in your room playing video games."

"Yeah, and what are you doing?" says Rusty. "It's been two years since you and Mum split up. Shouldn't you be on Tinder or something?" Rusty turns his attention to his aunt. "You know, these actually aren't that bad."

Ruth laughs. "Screw you."

As they continue their descent along the cliff edge, the only sound is the water below, their footfall muffled by a thick carpet of needles. Abundant sheoak shelter them from the wind.

"Rusty, did you know that Glossy Black Cockatoos only eat sheoak cones and seeds?" says Ruth. "They're an endangered species now, on the mainland."

“What’s a Glossy Black Cockatoo?” asks Rusty. “You mean like a Black Cockatoo?”

“Well, you don’t get Glossies in Tasmania but they’re the smallest of the species,” says Ruth.

John is becoming increasingly agitated in his sister’s presence. The fate of the bloody Black Cockatoo is not Rusty’s problem. In John’s eyes, hours playing video games is no different to being a gambling addict. It is all just chasing the same hit of *feel good* chemicals in the brain. If something isn’t done about it, Rusty is going to stunt his emotional growth and lose his ability to tell right from wrong. John has resolved to not let that happen.

Emerging from the forest, they come upon the first stone cairn. Although John knows it to be a simple landmark, in the moment it appears sepulchral. Cairn after cairn, like tomb after tomb, takes them between the shallow lake and the dramatic falling away of the south-facing inlet until they are skirting the fluted, dolerite cliffs of Cape Raoul.

“The feeder pipe for the dolerite was located due north of here,” says Ruth. “They know that by the shape and orientation of the sea columns.”

“It was in the Jurassic period,” adds John. “Like the movie, *Jurassic Park*.”

“John, he wasn’t even born when *Jurassic Park* came out.” Ruth laughs.

“I’ve seen *Jurassic World*,” says Rusty. “And *Fallen Kingdom*.”

“Well, have you learned at school yet about the epic volcanic explosion that covered up to a third of Tasmania? Or, did your dad tell you already?”

“What was so epic about it?”

"It's why these cliffs exist today. After the volcano, the Tasman Sea and Southern Ocean formed and then rocks came up to the surface and constant wave erosion shaped all the sea stacks and cool geology we get here."

Having delivered them to the family's sacred place, John stands tall at the tip of the Cape, like a Captain at the helm of some monumental ship with ragged prow, surveying the Great Southern Ocean. Below, the fierce barking of the seal colony could be the bawling of convicts or crew. This ship will never heave, sway or surge; it has been docked here for millions of years.

John's gaze is steady as a compass. Looking east, Mount Brown sequesters Crescent Bay and its cache of gold dunes, which as children they flew down on waxed real estate sign toboggans. Beyond Mount Brown rises the dolerite cliffs of Cape Pillar, 100 metres taller than Cape Raoul's and the kingdom of rock climbers. On the spine of Cape Pillar, Cathedral Rock at the very end is the atlas vertebra. Just off the Cape, Tasman Island rises out of the water like an iceberg, once covered in Casuarinas and Banksias, now from felling and fires just a towering bare flat, a century-old lighthouse its lone inhabitant. To the west, Bruny Island in the distance is viewable from a new angle.

In this panorama, Port Arthur is conspicuously absent.

The decision to buy the gelding is not made precipitously nor is it a reward for *getting away with it*, as Ruth so spitefully put it when John told her. No, the purchase of the horse will kill two birds with one stone. First off it will give Rusty an extracurricular activity other than computer games. The simulated violence in these 'shoot 'em ups' is something John has never approved of. Running around killing and maiming virtual people on a screen without a tincture of reality was not just unhealthy for a boy Rusty's age, it was irresponsible of Helen to condone it, indeed enable it, by buying the bloody things for him. You better believe he told her so. In the end she agreed to pay for half the upfront cost of the gelding plus new saddlery and ongoing vet bills. What Rusty needs is to spend less time in the virtual world of violence and more time involved in positive social experiences like horse riding and recreational hunting.

Second of all, owning his own horse was going to address this problem Rusty was having with anthropomorphism.

Rusty's first question when he lays eyes on the animal is, "Do I get to name him?"

"The horse already has a name," replies John. "You want to give it a human name, is that it?"

"What is it then?"

"The name?" says John. "Cobber."

"Cobber?" Rusty leans back on the yard rails. "That sucks."

"It's an Aussie word for 'mate', Rusty. It's a sound name."

"Can I call him 'Cob' though?"

John shakes his head but it is not a 'no', the accompanying eye-roll tells Rusty it is a resignation.

"That's cool," he says. "It's like Children of Bodom."

"Children of what? Did you say children of boredom?"

"*Bodom*, Dad. It's a band. You wouldn't know them. It's metal."

"Heavy metal? What, like Black Sabbath, Ozzy Osbourne? He once bit the head off a live bat, did you know that? A real sicko. This band, they're not devil worshippers? It's not Satanic music, is it?"

"They're not Satanists," says Rusty. "They're Finnish."

Rusty sits up on the top rail watching as John sets about hobbling the gelding in the round yard. John is distracted momentarily by the earth inside the yard, the hoof prints like gibbous moons, the small rocks like meteors. Cob is in a halter with a rope wrapped three times around the saddle and tied off around the fetlock so that the horse is forced to stand on three legs. It tries to pull the leg free from the rope and when it cannot it turns its head and looks at Rusty, its ears pointing forward stiff as horns, before it lifts its head as if to whinny but doesn't make a sound. When Rusty does nothing to aid it, the gelding turns its head away. Yanking at the rope harder, pulling up its knee, the animal builds some momentum and turns on the spot. Now John cracks the whip and to reassure his son, says full-throated, and with commanding bass, "It's not cruel. It's for troubled horses that have too much pride in themselves. You need to gain their respect. When they're done, they fall."

Slowly at first, Cob stumbles forward.

Another crack of the whip. "A very prideful horse."

It is something between a trot and a canter and no doubt disturbing for Rusty to witness but that is the point. Around and around the yard on three legs. It does not take long before Cob begins to pant heavily and the head thrashes around in time with the gait.

"This is what we want," says John. "Cob is starting to surrender."

When he begins whipping at the rump it sounds

deceptively like cutting.

"It's alright," says John. "It sounds worse than it is."

After two more times around the yard the horse stops at the fence and turns its head to Rusty again with glazed eyes.

John sighs. "It's holding itself up."

From the yard, John tries to gauge Rusty's reaction. John is half-expecting to see hatred towards him coming from the boy, at least unease. Instead, he finds him standing up on the fence leaning into the yard to get a closer look.

"Cob's starting to want to lay down now," John tells him, emboldened. "Cob's almost surrendering to us."

The horse raises its tail high in the air and turns and takes off in the opposite direction, kicking up clouds of dirt, the mane flying and the coat shining brightly with sweat.

"They usually just lay down but if they don't you have to do something else."

"You have to pull him down?" asks Rusty.

"Go and get another rope."

To show that he is serious, John sends Rusty ahead of him on foot to the dam while he waits and follows ten minutes later in the ute. It gives John a kick to think about what his son might have told his schoolmates today, having been given only one cryptic clue about what he was to receive: *it flies*. A dreamer, Rusty had begun spouting off guesses immediately: 'A GPS enabled drone with camera? A Radio Control Helicopter? A 3D Mode Quadcopter? An FPV Vapor ultra micro aircraft with aviation headset?'. No doubt these toys are all extortionately priced items, most of the specifications of which John has no idea about. The look on Rusty's face when he realises, that is going to be priceless. Really, this is a gift from Rusty to him, and to a lesser extent, his mother. They might not be within their rights to kneel the boy on raw rice but John feels certain he has devised a way to leave a lasting impression on today's youth.

When John gets out of the vehicle to unlatch the gate he spots Rusty with a long stick in his hand sparring with a Bedfordia bush. John presses his hand on the car horn, holds it down for five seconds until the boy solemnly lays down his weapon. John drives across the empty paddock to the body of water.

A circular bowl, the dam is more or less one hundred metres in diameter, depending on the current season and rainfall. Despite the overcast afternoon its surface reflects, across the east crescent in high resolution, the crowns of a pair of Eucalypts that stand halfway back to the house, as well as the washed-out grass that frays like a distressed denim hem around its bank. As John brings the vehicle to a stop at the water's edge Rusty jogtrots over, making a bee-line for the tray back, standing there drumming the impatient fingers of both hands on the canvas canopy.

"Bet you've been waiting for this all day, haven't you?" says John as he lifts a corner tantalisingly. "Told all your mates you were getting a present today?"

"Yep."

"Good," says John. "Now go stand right by the water and close your eyes."

From the tray back John takes out a box the size of a real family TV set, before the plasma flat screens hijacked the market.

"You alright over there?" John creates a double coil by looping the electrical cords in his left hand, the weight of the console born by his supine right hand. Slowly, deliberately he curls his thumb over the back end and gets into position, spreading his feet shoulder width apart standing straight on the mound of the bank with the toes of his Blundstones dangling off the edge.

"Dad? Dad, is that mine?" Rusty is straining his neck to see. "Dad did you take that PS4 from my room? I swear to god ..."

John cannot keep the smile off his lips and so keeps his chin down.

"Let me see it!"

"It's your present, son."

"Dad!"

"Don't you want to see it fly?"

"Give it to me, I'm serious. I'm not joking, Dad. How would you like it if I came to your house and took all your shit? Oh you don't have anything, Mum took it all."

That is his cue. "Rusty, that's enough."

John shifts his weight to his left foot and at the same time lifts his right leg until his thigh is parallel with the ground below. John reaches back with the PS4 in his hand until he feels it hit the sweet spot then he pushes off with full power, extending his throwing arm as far as he can as he lets go of the console, cords and all.

Throughout, he keeps his balance.

John watches the water rather than the air and sees the dark shadow land on the still surface first. A second later the console nose dives into the dam, tipped by the air resistance on its descent. It is almost impossible to distinguish which comes first, the sound or the sight of the ever-widening blast radius as it ripples out. The splash follows both, spray rising in the air like a breath, the spray of a humpback whale shot straight up out of its blowhole.

As the water rains back down, the console sinks.

"Are you drunk?" shouts Rusty. "I'm telling Mum."

John laughs at him. "This present is from the both of us."

Rusty looks up from the water for the first time, sniffs. John feels his eyes on him as he goes back to the ute to take out his father's old pump action shotgun from the cabin. It is wrapped tightly in a grey, moth-eaten wool blanket, another item destined for the bonfire.

"What's that?" asks Rusty.

"Curtain rods," replies John.

"Yeah right." Rusty gets up off the ground where he has been kneeling. "Dad, I'm sorry. I didn't mean it, what I said. What did I do wrong? Just tell me. Is it because of the accident at the Lagoon? I told you, I'm really, really sorry. It won't ever happen again."

"Listen, son," says John. "Let's get real here for a minute. What you have to understand is that what happened up there was a freak occurrence. I've never seen that happen in the field before and I've been duck hunting since I was your age. In thirty-five years it's never happened. But it did happen, it happened to you. It's a bad shock, I know that. Jesus, it would have rattled any of the hunters out that day, me included. You're a brave man, we all think that, the way you've handled yourself."

"I messed up," says Rusty.

"You were very unlucky," says John. "It was rotten timing too, your first weekend out." John drops the blanket onto the ground between them. "That gelding I got for you, Cobber—"

"Cob."

"You're going to fall off that animal, like it or not. That's not me guessing," says John. "That's a fact. And when you do, if you have any intentions of being a good rider someday, you're going to fall off at least fifty times first. It's the same thing here. You tell me, what's the first thing you do when you fall off a horse?"

Rusty takes only a moment before he answers, "Give it a whack with your riding crop? That's what Mum used to do."

John frowns. "No, son. You get straight back on again. It's the only way."

"What if you're hurt?"

"If you're hurt?" John reaches out his free hand to help Rusty to his feet. "Then all the more reason to do what I just told you, get right back in the saddle. Now, there's a packet of balloons in the glove box, get them, will you?"

"Balloons? What for?"

"We're having a party."

In Rusty's momentary absence John closes his eyelids and stretches them by steeply raising his brows and crossing his eyeballs. This brings him quickly to the cusp of a sneeze. From the bush at the far end of the dam comes a bird call, a lone whistle, and he opens his eyes. Rusty returns with the plastic packet held at his solar plexus, elbows sticking out at his sides. Posture, that was another thing horse riding will sort out. You can't control a horse's mouth holding onto the reins the way he is holding onto those balloons.

"Blow one up while we walk," John tells him, then adds, "Not pink, pick another colour."

"Purple?"

"Or blue," suggests John. "Hell, pick whatever colour you want. It doesn't matter. As long as we can see it."

Two-thirds of the way around the dam are the first trees, trunks leaning slightly into the dam, branch tips reaching futilely out towards the centre.

"Let's set up here," says John. "I'm going to show you a ricochet shot. When it's your turn we'll start you in the prone position but that's not much use to you out on the water so I'm going to do this standing up." John takes the inflated balloon from Rusty. "This is going up there. Think you can climb up and tie it over the water? I'll pass it to you."

"Well yeah. Right now?"

"Giddy up."

In a flash Rusty is up in the tree swinging over the dam like a monkey before kicking his legs up and over the branch and pulling himself into an upright sitting position. You can't fault the boy for his youthful enthusiasm. John has the fleeting thought that if they weren't using live rounds, if the gun was loaded with bean bags or rubber bullets, this wouldn't be a bad game, Rusty sitting up there as the target. Like the carnival kind where someone sits above a tank of water and someone else throws balls at a trigger above their head to try and get them dunked.

"Rusty, tie up the balloon."

Before he jumps down, Rusty throws a punch at the red balloon suspended in the air below the branch. Not a bad right hook, John thinks. They'd make a man out of him yet.

They walk all the way back to the ute.

"Right, now that balloon is sixty metres away. So I'm going to try to ricochet a shot off the water using Dad's pump action and pop that target at sixty metres."

“Can you do it?” asks Rusty, following him back to the water’s edge.

“We shall soon see.”

While Rusty was at school John was out here practising the shot. It took him perhaps twenty minutes but he knows now it is indeed possible and he knows how. The trick is going to be making Rusty believe this time is his first attempt.

“Alright, here we go,” says John. “Sixty metre shot, well ricochet shot, with the 12 gauge. You ready?”

Rusty nods his head, his fingers already in his ears. John lines up his sight and breathes, allowing a few silent seconds to pass for dramatic effect and then pulls the trigger.

“No. Shot a little too high. Let me bring it down a bit,” he says.

The second time he fires the sound of his own shot missing the mark causes him to jump. “Damn! Brought it down a little too far. Try it again. Third time’s a charm.”

John shakes out his shoulders before raising the shotgun again, holding his breath, tensing his abdominal muscles.

Pop!

Red rubber is flung violently into the water.

“Third time was a charm,” says John. “That’s how you ricochet shot off water at sixty metres.”

Father and son step back to get a true impression of how far it really is.

Rusty pats his shoulder. “Good shooting, Dad.”

On Sunday, standing at the head of the dinner table, ready to carve the roast lamb, John is distracted by the wall closest to him, behind Ruth. Because it’s a thin interior wall, the effects of humidity have been felt more keenly and the paint failed to adhere properly. It has begun to deteriorate, is starting to flake, looks patchy and colourless compared with what he remembers of it, before Ruth left home. The advantage of thinner walls is more space within the house, which is the opposite of what John needs.

"Drinking," Ruth says to him. "That's a new thing for you?"

"Dad doesn't drink," says Rusty. "The only time I see him drink is when we're hunting. Isn't that right, Dad? You like a few beers then."

"That's right, these are just a few leftovers I'm taking care of," says John. "Pity there's no duck left, we prefer to eat wild game birds. Can't get better table fare. Go on, Rusty, tell your aunt how gratifying it was to shoot your first bird, and right after have a feed of it."

"How are you doing, Rusty?" asks Ruth. "Are you feeling OK about everything?"

John raises his voice. "After our weekend at Moulting Lagoon the boy is no more and in his place is a man."

As a sign of respect, John spins the knife on the table so that it does half a revolution and the blade points back to him, the handle to Rusty.

"Go on, son," he says. "Tonight you're the man."

At the same time, John notices that Rusty's hair is a tad long. Now that he is getting taller though, John has to admit it doesn't look so effeminate on him; he has the height and the budding of shoulders to get away with it—barely.

"I think you're ready to learn how to use a boning knife," says John. "Put that on the list."

John had only just begun to learn the skills of

butchery when his father died. Then they received a little money with which to buy their meat so John could focus on his schoolwork. In a pinch, a wallaby could be found after dark in the bush, shot and roasted like lamb. It became a risk with the new resident greenies who claimed everything was cruel. Early on he learned the best thing to say to these vegetarians was to ask them in his most serious voice, 'What about plants, don't they have feelings too?' For some reason that really got them going. Vegetables grew in their garden, eggs came from the chooks in the henhouse. Milk, cream and butter from the cows in the dairy. Their mother made jam from Stormlea blackberries. Fish came out of the saltwater of any one of the bays. Apples fell from trees in Highcroft's many orchards. If they needed something and didn't have it—a goat, a pig, tomatoes—they would barter with their neighbours.

The food on their table was a result of hard labour and the sacrifice of animals.

"What are you reading in English this term?" asks Ruth, apparently taking the hint.

"Um, *Middlemarch*?" says Rusty.

"What page are you on?" asks Ruth.

"I just finished chapter nine."

"Are you liking it?"

"What have they got you reading that for?" says John. "What I mean is, it's a bit advanced for grade ten, isn't it? A bit too advanced even for senior year. It's that new teacher," says John. "What's her name? Some double-barrel bullshit. What's she got you reading that for?"

The new English teacher has short spiky bleached blonde hair and the woman is rotund. They are always fat these feminists, like they have to prove a point.

"*Middlemarch* is actually a realist novel based on

historical events," says Ruth. "What's your problem with it?"

"I already said, *Middlemarch* is not appropriate for grade ten boys. It's a book they set on a university syllabus for English majors and feminists," says John. "Anyway, when's the test?"

"In three weeks," says Rusty. "It's an assignment, not a test."

"Right then, so to stay on schedule for the assignment you're going to have to be finished in two weeks, right? To give you time to actually write the thing?"

"What's the focus of your assignment?" asks Ruth. "Plenty of issues in that book, not just the status of women."

It is clear that Ruth is trying to use Rusty as a weapon against him and to control the situation. The incident at Moulting Lagoon has triggered her and her agenda and in her mind it has given her ammunition. The reality is she's shooting blanks.

"Like you said, he's a man now, not a boy," Ruth continues. "Rusty's old enough to form his own opinion on issues, like political and law reform. When a country and its politicians neglect issues for decades you end up with a situation like what happened in New Zealand. Yes they had a quick response, the new ban came just six days after their mass shooting but why'd it take that event to make a sweeping change when they already had an example of–"

John slams his empty beer bottle down and it rattles plates.

"That hair's getting a bit long, Rusty," says John. "Better ask your mum to give it a trim this weekend, eh?"

At half past nine John and Rusty set out on foot from the house armed with the pump action shotgun. John can barely separate the sensation of satiety as a result of the meal from his disgust with Ruth. The last suspicious scats he found were in the back eastern paddock so he heads in that direction.

"Has it killed anything?" asks Rusty.

"It hasn't yet had the opportunity."

"You've just seen it hanging around?"

John takes the rolled-up cigarette from his top pocket and sparks it with a flip top lighter, exhaling that first plume of smoke towards the stars. Then he knows he is drunk.

"Are you smoking now too?" says Rusty. "You should vape."

Even intoxicated John is attuned to the surrounding bush, could find in the pitch black his first cubby house, a burnt-out tree half a kilometre away.

"How many foxes do you think there are?" asks Rusty. "You reckon there's a den?"

Rusty trips on a rock, almost falls head over tit, the torch beam going berserk.

John spits a stray strand of tobacco off the tip of his tongue. "Did you hear about this Mayday caller hoax?"

Rusty sweeps the paddock with the spotlight. "Look Dad, I don't see anything out there. If it hasn't killed any chickens then maybe it was a feral cat you saw. They get really big."

John stamps the butt of his rollie out under his boot. "Since we're out here, how about firing off a few rounds? Take out a tree stump. Come on, it's just you and me."

"Dad, seriously ..."

"Hell, don't cry about it. Here, give us the torch."

John knows the safe ground and illuminates the way for Rusty who is quickstepping beside him. John's vision shudders with each step on the hard, uneven earth.

"So you've never used the dual band radio to make a prank call?" asks John. "You and your mates playing silly buggers?"

Out of the corner of his eye John can see the boy swinging his arms at his sides like a fool. John would like to shove a handful of ash into Rusty's clean mouth.

"Eh?"

Is he playing deaf now? "You heard me."

"Didn't you just say that they caught that guy? The mayday hoaxer?"

John ignores his deflective tactics, picks up the pace.

"I don't even use that thing unless I'm with you, it was a stupid present," says Rusty as they step into the yard and he walks off ahead towards the house. "Why couldn't you have thrown that into the dam instead of my PS4?"

"You running away 'cause you feel guilty about something, Rusty?" John calls after him, from beneath the empty Hills Hoist he has just spun. Then under his breath adds, "Welcome to the club."

Half an hour later, John is in the kill shed drinking a beer when they ambush him. Rusty stands partially behind Ruth, as if he is hiding from his father.

"I'm taking Rusty home," says Ruth. "I'm taking the car."

"So what's in your school bag?" asks John.

"Clothes and that," says Rusty. "I brought my toothbrush."

"No school books?"

"At home," says Rusty. "At Mum's."

"You understand what's in those school books, do you, Rusty?"

"More or less, yeah. Most of it. Some of it's hard."

"I'm surprised you understand any of it." John takes a swig of his beer and then begins rubbing thumb and forefinger around the open neck of the bottle, turning and turning as if he is tightening a nut that remains loose. "Just how behind are you at school?"

"That's enough, John!" shouts Ruth. "You shouldn't drink. It turns you into even more of an arsehole."

"Ruth, shut your damn mouth." With his free hand, John points a crooked finger at her. "I'm talking to my son right now."

Ruth reaches back to shield Rusty with one arm.

"So you got detention for bashing someone up with a baseball bat or something?" asks John.

"I never used a baseball bat," says Rusty.

"So you're just aggro in a useless kinda way then, huh?" John holds the bottle upright beneath his mouth like a microphone as he speaks. "But you're scared to stay here with me now? So you're a coward as well as a simpleton?" John laughs and catches Ruth's eye. "We knew another simpleton, didn't we, Aunty Ruth? He was aggro in a useless kinda way. Well, he was until he wasn't. Until he actually did something."

"I said stop it, John! You wouldn't be talking like this if his mother was here. You wouldn't dare."

"Just get out. Get out of my shed. Leave me in peace. Piss off, the pair of you."

"Come on, Rusty," says Ruth. "He's going to regret this. Wait and see."

"Rusty?" John calls after them. "Don't say anything

to your mother about our little chat. Are you a man, or not? Real men don't go crying to women to solve their problems".

"Oh she'll be hearing about it," says Ruth. "Every word."

John is done tiptoeing around them both, his son and his sister. Helen too if it comes to that. It is her fault, Rusty's failed attempt at husbandry. Something about the colour of the piglets' skin and the way they wriggled in his lap, is the excuse he gave his mother. That and their high-pitched squeals when he tried to cut their teeth. John is justifiably furious. It's not just the embarrassment, the feeling of shame that a son of his can't perform a simple, traditional farming procedure; it reflects badly on John as a parent and a farmer. If he'd have done the same thing the first time he docked the tail of a dairy cow his father would have beaten the living daylights out of him.

In John's memory, his father is faceless, features masked by the shadow that fell beneath the brim of his kangaroo leather Akubra, a hat which he often wore even indoors, and his voice is permanently raised. It seemed there was always something to be angry about. Of the two children, it was John who bore the brunt of their father's anger and in turn he probably took out his frustrations on Ruth. Lucky for her she was just a girl and so her father took little notice of her. When she did something to earn his attention, his response rarely altered. 'Pity your poor husband', he would say.

Chapter 13
Marina

When the first day of Moon's rehabilitation arrives, at the car he lifts his foot up onto the rear wheel tyre to do up his shoelace. Marina watches him. One end is looped around the index finger of his left hand while his right hand waits open like a crab's claw. It hovers over the taut lace for a moment as if he is uncertain of the next step in the process. Then his middle finger separates from the rest and hooks the loose lace, which wraps around the fingertip to form a loop, one half of a bow. Moon is her little brother, just a boy again, and she wants to tell him, 'You just have to tie it like this'. Marina must resist the urge to do it for him. Instead she asks, "Does it hurt, your hand?"

"No," he says. "It's just stiff. If it does hurt that's natural. It's supposed to hurt because I'm healing. The pain is there to show me what I should and shouldn't be doing."

Clearly he thinks she is again trying to get him to take his painkillers. Marina goes around the car to his side and takes his hand in hers.

"Don't put pressure on yourself," she says.

The wound on his wrist, as she turns it over, is shaped like a cross. A stigmata scar. She lets him go.

“You’ll do fine,” she tells him. “Tonight we’ll have sushi to celebrate. I found the bamboo mat and I bought short grain white rice.”

“There better be wasabi with that sushi,” he says, lowering his leg.

“Oh you’ll sweat plenty at the pool,” says Marina. “If you don’t sweat it’s not working. You remember what Mum used to say? That if you didn’t eat the wasabi you’d get haemorrhoids?”

It is true that wasabi contains some ingredient that is an anti-inflammatory, she can’t remember which now, and aids in pain relief. Moon is onto something with the wasabi craving.

“Yeah, I remember that. I think she just wanted to see our faces when the horseradish rush hit.”

“I remember when you were little and someone would ask you what you wanted to be when you grew up you used to say ‘a real man’.”

“I don’t believe that, Mari. Come on.”

“It’s true! That’s what you always said. There was one time, I can’t remember who it was that asked you what you wanted to be when you grew up, I think it was another kid, and you told them ‘a real man’ then they asked, ‘What is being a real man?’”

“Who would that have been?”

“‘When I grow up I want to be a real man like Mum’, you told them.”

“You’re making that up. I never said that.”

“I’m not, I swear! I was there because I remember telling you ‘You’re so unlucky you were born a boy’.” Marina laughs. “You know, while you’re rehabilitating you might want to think about a shave. You’re under my care now. *Casa del Marina. Mi casa* ... my rules.”

Moon flips down the sun visor.

"What do you think happened to her, the Venetian?" Marina clarifies, "The missing tourist."

Moon's brow furrows. "I honestly don't know."

"Well I realise you don't know, I'm asking you what you *think* happened."

"Maybe nothing."

"What do you mean? Something happened to her, that's obvious."

"Maybe she ran away. She might have met someone while she was travelling and left to be with them in their country."

"Yeah, OK, but why wouldn't she have contacted her parents, just to let them know she was OK, alive at least?"

"Everyone has their reasons, however bad the thing they do is. It always makes sense to them even if it doesn't to anyone else."

Marina clears her throat. "I think she's dead. I think she's been dead this whole time. I've seen a picture of her and she looked my size. The wind up on that cliff track almost knocked me off my feet a few times. She was probably standing too close to the edge looking at the view or taking a photo and it just snuck up on her and pushed her off."

"They would have found her body below the cliff."

"Not if a shark got her," she says, "or a rip."

"Do sharks even eat cadavers?" whispers Moon.

"Oh yeah! They do. I've seen great whites eating a whale carcass in Antarctica. They treated it like a smorgasbord ... just kept coming back for more."

"Can we stop talking about this please?" says Moon. "It's making me very uncomfortable."

"Oh, I didn't realise," she says. "We can stop talking about her, sure. The case will never be solved anyway. It's a mystery for the ages." Marina turns on the car radio. The music seems to calm her brother. As she drives, she steals glances at her passenger. The truth is she envies his imagination, the nature of it, which would choose a Romance over a Tragedy. It occurs to Marina for the very first time that she lost more than her faith at Port Arthur that Sunday: she lost her innocence.

It is a tiled rectangular pool and under sunlight the water appears natural, clear. Where air is jetted in at the sides it even bubbles, ripples the surface. The unmistakable smell of the chlorine makes Marina think about her work. Every Monday, Wednesday and Friday evening she swims laps at her local pool, arriving straight from the office. It is a cleansing scent for her, even pleasant, and she breathes it deep into her lungs. It was inevitable that her thoughts would return to work, she is only surprised that it has taken this long. That last week before she took leave to come here is one she'd prefer to put behind her, had made the decision to do just that as she boarded her plane at Sydney Airport. Once they reached cruising altitude she had ordered a gin and tonic from the air stewardess as a catalyst for this wilful forgetfulness. Marina believes that she is a kind person; it is a fact that she acts kindly in the workplace. That she can be a micromanager isn't necessarily a bad thing. Either is her personal policy of only being loyal to those subordinates who obey her without question. After all, that is the definition of loyalty, isn't it? To take orders and carry them out to the best of your ability without hating your boss in secret and saying unmentionable things about her behind her back? This whole business right before she went away, she blames that on the one girl, a temp no less, who went crying to her recruitment agency. No, it doesn't bear thinking about. By the time she gets back it will have blown over.

It is better to be feared than loved, if you cannot be both.

When it comes to survival in the professional jungle—in life in general—Marina has learned you always have to wear armour and carry a sword. Has she really become Machiavellian? That wasn't how she was raised.

The shiny steel bar at one end of the pool is the focus of Moon's rehabilitation. In his black swim shorts, Moon's upper body is completely exposed for all to see, his wound concealed behind a waterproof bandage. He is made to put weight on his wrist while his body is supported by the pool's volume, a flotation device at his lower back strapped securely around his hips. As Marina swims towards him, about to perform a soft tumble turn, his gaze is concentrated on the back of his hand gripping the bar. The way he moves, his lower body buoyed beneath him, it looks like he has no bones inside his skin, an invertebrate flopping about.

Just when she feels ready to leave the pool, Marina does one last lap, changing her stroke to butterfly. This is something she likes to do as a kind of encore. Marina would never, ever admit it to anyone, can barely admit it to herself, but the truth is that she's terrified of dismissal at the hands of a superior, of being terminated to the humiliation of nothingness. One of her comrades, another of the few females within the organisation at her level of management, had warned her after that last meeting with Human Resources that she could hear Marina's raised voice—shouting, she'd called it—through two closed doors.

Standing poolside, reaching for her towel with ghostly white wrinkled fingers, Marina shivers.

"OK, Moon, you can take the goggles off now," says the physiotherapist.

"So that's it, right?" Moon pushes them up onto his red swimming cap.

"How's the tingling? Do you still have it?"

"Well, yes. A bit in my arm but not much. I think it's stress related. I don't get sick so easily, not since I've been a vegan."

"I see. And can you do this easily?" One by one the physiotherapist touches each fingertip of his right hand to his thumb.

When Moon attempts to do this himself, he hesitates.

"There's no nerve damage, is there?"

"No," says Moon.

"The nerves are like bundles of electric cables. Your nervous system can malfunction due to physical trauma. The function of the nervous system is to control the body and as you just saw, that right hand isn't giving you an appropriate response. So it could be the muscle or it could be the nerves aren't sending out the signal to the muscle to activate the response. We have to take it step by step. If the doc has cleared you you're lucky. We don't have to retrain your brain."

Marina scoffs at his lecture. What a joke. Moon has probably studied more of Descartes's anatomy drawings than the physiotherapist had seen in textbooks during all his time at university. Descartes was notorious for his barbaric experiments on dogs. The man made some ridiculous statement about the animals being mere machines that squeaked and squealed when manipulated, that they didn't feel pain like we do, not even when they were nailed to a board to be cut open while fully conscious. It was Descartes's theory that only humans had souls which led him to this belief that animals did not feel pain, only acted as if they did: if animals were soulless then they were just machines, nothing more.

As they walk together to the car Moon says out of the blue, "I've been back to Port Arthur, once."

After a couple of steps Marina stops in her tracks. "What do you mean you've been *back*?"

Moon turns around, flicking the dry but flattened hair away from his face. "It was a long time ago, with Dad."

Marina looks over her shoulder to make sure they are not being followed by other swimmers. "Dad took you to the Historic Site?"

"Yes, he did."

"But why? Why would he take you there? For what?"

"I can't stand out in this wind," he replies.

"No," she agrees reluctantly. "Come on, you can tell me in the car."

Before she gets in Marina takes one last long look at her surroundings, inhaling a deep breath for whatever story Moon has to tell. A school oval like any other borders the road. Behind the oval there are tennis courts. At the front of the block is the Assembly Hall. The rest of the school spreads back to the left of her, mostly out of view.

After closing the driver's side door, Marina switches on the engine so she can turn the heating up high.

Almost immediately she feels the skin of her face dry out, tightening across her cheeks. Blinking, her eyes already irritated by chemicals, she puts her seat back. "So you were saying?"

"Around the time of the first anniversary there was a cricket match held at Port Arthur. It was between the Australian One Day side and a local team. A charity event to benefit the community. I was ten, I think. Dad took me to it. All I remember is that Steve Waugh hit a six and the ball landed in the water near the Broad Arrow Café and everybody cheered."

The Clark Cliffs Cemetery protest is the opposite action of the duck rescue, the protestors gathering in the twilight to await nightfall, rather than in the pre-dawn to await first light. While a candlelight vigil outside the cemetery has been organised for 8:00 pm, when the five-hour spotlight cull commences, a splinter group including Marina and Moon will stay on the edges of the grounds until cover of darkness and then, each with a recording device, collect footage of the killing to distribute to media.

To date, the death toll is forty-five pademelons and thirty-four wallabies.

For some reason, Marina keeps thinking about the legendary story of the Port Arthur convict who dressed himself in kangaroo skins and attempted to hop inconspicuously across the infamous dog line at Eaglehawk Neck only to indeed be mistaken for a kangaroo and shot by hungry guards.

The trio begin their uphill hike at the base of low cliffs in the car park looking out onto Norfolk Bay. Marina and Moon create a harmonious balance with Mike, the team leader from the duck rescue, now an equal in no position of authority over the siblings, in between them in an uneasy orbit. Marina ensures she keeps a safe amount of distance between herself and Mike.

A wolf in sheep's clothing is what Marina feels like as she acts in a congenial and humble manner, displaying maturity as she admits her error at Moulting Lagoon. All the while she finds excuses to check her phone.

"I don't agree with their characterisation of you," says Mike. "But I think it's irrelevant."

"Nothing my sister did rises to the level of ... Did they say she *bit* a shooter? Is that what they're claiming? I was there and I saw everything. That's a complete lie."

"The Department of Primary Industries, Parks, Water and Environment is entitled to prohibit any action that creates interference or constitutes harassment of legitimate shooters," says Mike. "Do they have any evidence of interference or harassment?"

Moon redirects the conversation. "Marina, how did you feel on the duck rescue?"

"Disrespected and unsafe," she says. "At times, under attack."

"Here's what I don't understand, Marina," says Mike. "You're a seasoned activist, have crewed with Sea Shepherd, how was Moulting Lagoon different to all the other actions?"

"It's never gotten physical before," says Marina. "A hunter had a bird, it was still alive and—"

"A swamp harrier," Moon interjects. "Completely prohibited species."

"Moon, no," she says. "Moon you warned me to stay ten metres away from the hunters but in the heat of the moment—"

"OK, got it," Mike cuts her off.

It's not until Marina has spoken, that she realises this is the truth; it silences her.

"What you need to say is that it wasn't your intent to disrupt the shooters' activities," says Mike, turning his head to add, "At any cost."

Marina looks at her brother, his wrist still in a sling. Pressing his eyeglasses against the bridge of his nose with the forefinger of his good hand, he offers her a staunch nod.

The two men begin to argue about the Animal Liberation Front. Moon claims the actions of the ALF are non-violent because they do no harm to human or non-human life, his justification for their destruction of property being that violence can only take place against sentient life forms. As her brother compares the destruction of animal laboratories and other facilities to slavery abolitionists burning down quarters and tearing down the auction block, or resistance fighters blowing up gas chambers in Nazi Germany, Marina wonders if Mike knows that until recently Moon was a Quaker.

For Marina, the landscape itself is deafening. Visible in the eroded, collapsed sections of the cliff is a dark, ashy band with layers of concentrated shell, bone, charcoal and botanical remains, the result of repeated use by Aboriginal hunters and gatherers over thousands of years. This brushing of the past against the present reminds her that humans leave imprints on the landscape over time.

"I think one of the first real vegans was an eighteenth-century abolitionist called Benjamin Lay. He's a personal hero of mine, an anti-slavery campaigner. The Society of Friends thought he was insane because he lived in a cave and refused to eat meat or wear the skin or wool of any animal," says Moon. "Anyway, as soon as I began to think about animal rights in terms of the human slavery analogy it was the only approach that made sense. I'd grown up hearing stories about the early abolitionists, not just Lay and Woolman but others like the women who used leaves to dye their bedspreads and refused to use silver before the abolition of slavery."

At the top of the cliffs the group stops to catch their collective breath, standing amidst the scattering of aboriginal shell middens. These sites of deeply layered deposits spanning millennia emitted a strange power, an ancient magic.

As they enter the cemetery, Mike takes a phone call and then announces abruptly, "It's off. They're not going to shoot tonight."

For a moment the activists look around at one another in slight disbelief.

"Because of us?" asks Marina.

"Too many phone calls and emails from the public after the story in yesterday's paper about the Port Arthur victims' graves being here. The candlelight vigil is still going ahead as planned."

"What if they just do the cull another night?" says Moon. "And don't tell anyone this time?"

"They've agreed to meet with residents to discuss other options," says Mike. "We've won the battle but we haven't won the war."

"Not yet," Marina says and turns away.

Although they stand in a burial ground with nothing but death and decay beneath their feet a great weight is lifted. As Marina looks about her she sees that everything points skyward. The arched wings of the angel statue nearby, the fingertips of its praying hands and the curved headstones of the surrounding graves.

Chapter 14

Ruth

Being parted, Seamus begins to consume Ruth's head like the incapacitating, recurrent throb of a migraine. Lying on her bed in the lamplit room she can hardly bear to open her eyes for if she does she finds she cannot focus on anything, her gaze skidding off surfaces like car tyres on an icy road.

To help her family she must set her love for Seamus aside, at least temporarily. The way her mother would, when they were children and Stormlea was still prone to power outages, seal water in mason jars and place them high up on a shelf beside boxes of household candles, always prepared to survive a few days without electricity or running water.

The feelings for Seamus that course through her are overwhelming. In vain she has tried to find the words to name them, in an effort to seize control, tame or ground them like a current of electricity. The more she tries—the faster she chases thoughts around her head—the sicker she becomes. It is as if she has been bitten by a venomous snake and the only way to slow the poison is to be completely still.

Even in her sickness she senses Seamus as if he

were merely in the next room and if she were to call out from her bed, or knock on the wall between them, he would respond. Ruth picks up her phone to check for a message from him but the battery is dead. Reaching to the floor for the cable, she plugs it in and leaves it on the bedside table to recharge.

Dizzy, her vision blurred, she rises and stumbles to the bedroom door, walks down the hallway using the wall to steady herself. In the dining room she collides head-on with the afternoon sunlight streaming through the front windows.

Returning to her room from the kitchen with a glass of water, Ruth hears her phone chime with delayed messages. A couple of text messages she deletes without reply. Then a message from Seamus:

Get on the Gransha Road. Go straight up it till you reach the roundabout. You'll see the yellow house on the right, the Orange Hall and the Ballygrainey Presbyterian church on your left. Drive past the yellow house and keep going over the old railway bridge. There you'll find the six road ends. I'm working in the old stone byre.

Ruth opens her eyes. Directly above her the bedroom ceiling has floated down while she slept, like a stratus cloud developing overnight as the earth cooled, ready to be burned off with the rising sun. Lying flat on her back beneath the covers she realises her shoulders are pinned as if someone, or something, is kneeling on top of her. When she tries to call out the words are handfuls of sand in her throat. Her old friend, sleep paralysis. Not some succubus terrorising her, it is a phenomenon she began to experience the year before she left home.

To her dismay it followed her across Bass Strait to the mainland. The more you fought it the longer it persisted and so she wills herself to relax, to remain calm, despite the primitive instinct within urging her to scream for help and struggle to get up. Sleep paralysis is like quicksand, the more you struggle in it the faster you will sink.

A cow bellows in agony in the pre-dawn. The sound is what woke Ruth, such a dreadful sound, it travels not only through the window pane but down the drainpipes as well, which amplify the agony before spitting it out into the room. It is a different sound than the one she became accustomed to as a child, the frantic bellows of the mother cows during the first 24 hours after calving, as they were separated from their offspring permanently. Coming down the drainpipes the noise is truly horrifying, like a victim trapped inside the hollow Brazen Bull of Ancient Greece, a fire lit below its bronze belly, the prisoner slowly roasting, their screams transformed into those of a bull through the sadistically engineered acoustic apparatus.

Once Ruth is freed from her nightmare state she rolls across the bed with the sheets wrapped around her torso like a straitjacket. With her nightdress soaked in cold sweat she pants into the flattened pillow. The fearsome bellowing does not end with the release from the paralysis. The beast is right here in the room with her. Kicking her legs beneath the covers she finds her voice at last.

"John!" she shouts through a dry throat.

If only she could reach the light switch over on the wall. Ruth elbows her way out to sit on the edge of the bed. It seems she has awoken into one of the seven circles of hell, the sensation of burning brought about by biting cold, a devilish irony not lost on her. Finally, after what has seemed like an eternity, Ruth gets off the bed and escapes the room, slamming the door shut behind her.

Where is her brother?

In the kitchen she turns on a light and checks the time on the clock on the wall above the bench. The minute hand is a third of the way around the face, the hour hand on the numeral five. Out gathering the herd, that is where her brother is, no doubt. The stove fire is unlit though. Perhaps he woke late after a sleep disturbed by the down cow and thus was in a rush to get ready for work. No matter. Ruth takes her duffle coat from the hook on the back of the front door and goes outside.

The atmosphere is so frigid you could drag your hand down through it. Ruth's breath appears as an apparition before her eyes. On the top step she withdraws into her anorak as her bare feet hop into her gumboots. In a few minutes she will be numb. It is no use fighting it, just let it happen, she tells herself. It is just light enough to see where she is walking, her boots snapping the grass, stiff with dew, underfoot. The heifer, sensing her approach, falls silent. A small mercy. Ruth finds the animal where her brother left it days before. John has dropped handfuls of hay down but it is spread sparse as yellow pick-up sticks across the concrete floor caked with piles of semi-frozen manure, which thankfully let off little odour. When the heifer spots her out of the corner of its vision the large head swings around and its wide eyes fix on her. Even from a distance it is plain to see the animal has had enough. The snot pouring from its nostrils down its lips, its tongue lashing out at nothing but air and those desperate black eyes tell the whole story. Anger flares up in Ruth, quickly engulfing her pity for the animal. Seized by the emotion Ruth turns on her heel and marches to the kill shed.

Rare Bird Farm is her home, where she was raised the daughter of a dairy farmer, and she has just as much say in what goes on here as John does. Right now her brother is useless. An impotent middle-aged man who gets no vote.

Inside, the shed is in a shambles. John is drinking, that much is clear. Ruth pushes open both doors to let in the growing daylight. The rope handled ammunition chest is where she last saw it, her father's old shotgun balanced on the lid. Ruth takes a deep breath of determination and goes to it. An inner voice reassures her that this is just like riding a bike—you never forget. How long has it been, really, since she held a gun in her hands? The calculations are too much for her given the state she has gotten herself in. It doesn't matter. You never forget. The name is the first thing she recalls. This is a Remington 870. It is the model used by the forces, her father was in the habit of telling them that. Loading it could be confusing. Fear strikes at Ruth's heart. There is nothing to do but pick it up, which she does. It is still heavy even held in the hands of an adult. Not as heavy as a troubled conscience. Ruth soldiers on. First she checks the safety is on, then turns the weapon sideways and lodges the stock inside her armpit with the trigger facing away from her body. Ruth can just fit five shells in one hand, the fingertips bent to hold them side by side across the palm. With her thumb pressed firmly behind the gold toned cap she pushes the first one straight up into the loading flap until she hears the strident *click* of the shell rim passing the magazine catch. The shotgun only takes three shells in total before it will take no more. Ruth bends at the knee to place the remaining two shells back in their box. Standing tall once more, she holds in the action release button and pumps the slide back and forth.

Cha-chunk.

That was it; as easy as that.

Only then does she question whether a birdshot was going to penetrate the skull of a cow. Was it the semi-automatic rifle she needed? Ruth lays the shotgun back down on the ammunition chest and picks up the rifle. With no trouble she finds the rod feed. She hasn't fired it since she was about twelve but it used to be John's favourite toy. Ruth has never loaded a .22 but she has watched her brother do it often enough. The rod under the barrel holds the rounds. Does the end unscrew? She pulls out the guide rod just under the barrel, unscrewing it, and pulls out that rod until she can load the bullets, the rounds fit in only one direction, rear first, into the magazine tube. One bullet at a time, fifteen in total, until it is full.

Close and twist.

Ruth remembers learning to use this firearm, John standing behind her steadying her elbow.

Fire!

Afterwards she turned her face and smiled, the scent of propellant drifting between them with the gun smoke.

This is going to get worse, what she has to do next. It is no use kidding herself that she has a choice. The present moment is already being stowed away like all else she experiences, for posterity.

When it is over, having abandoned the rifle beside the dead cow, Ruth returns to the kill shed to collect the other weapon.

Ruth drags the shotgun by the barrel behind her through the slick grass all the way down alongside the front drive.

Wherever the sun shines great sheets of steam rise off the icy paddocks that flank her. So unsteady are her legs, so heavy her feet, that she might as well be trudging through snow. Before the loggers came, their father took her and her brother into the bush beyond Cripps Creek to hunt wallaby. Unless he had no choice, he only went at night. In the daytime it was too easy to hit them, he said.

Ruth stops walking and lifts the shotgun, tosses it in the air so she can catch the butt, remembering what she told her father when he offered her this weapon for the first time.

"Here, take it," he said. "It's a rare bird isn't it?"

"Yeah very," said John.

"No, I'm not here to hunt," she replied. "I only came because you asked me to."

"And what will you have for dinner tonight?" her father asked.

"I prefer not to," she insisted, her mother's polite rehearsed words, coming out of her mouth.

"Let me see," said John, stepping up to take the shotgun from their father. "Is it hard?"

"The first time," he said. "Then it's like everything else."

Purposefully, their father walked away from them, further into the bush.

"Come on," whispered John. "We have to go with him."

Standing over Cripps Creek, the farm's old water source, Ruth is aware that it springs from the base of Mount Raoul, is born in its shadow. According to John, until the recent storms the creek was just a dry bed full of fallen branches and pine needles surrounded by rotten brown tree trunks, no sunlight able to penetrate the canopy above. Now the creek has intent, a strong will, desires to return to the Tasman Sea and be at one with the Southern Ocean.

When Ruth scoops up its water in cupped hands and drinks, the cold is like the shock from an electric fence and she realises that with chilled lips she is tasting her own childhood upon her tongue.

Wiping her hands off on her jeans before picking the shotgun back up from a pine needle pillow, she says, "Let's see if it flies."

Chapter 15
John

At the dairy, John sticks his head into the birthing stall to check on the down cow. Today is its last day on the farm. Its number is 163 and John has already circled it in red pen in the ledger, which means an animal's number is up. The calf 163 bore was a male so its number had also been circled in red at birth. By now it is veal. Farming is a revolving door. They come in, they go out. One way or another. Simple.

John's first thought, upon finding the heifer dead where it sits, is of Rusty. At the moment there is not much blood, just enough sprayed on the hay below its head to let him know the animal has been shot. When it is pulled out of here though, tipped on its side, that is going to be a real mess. John can see it now, him standing between the open door of the birthing stall and the teeth on the backhoe, the chain wound through them, with a stubbie held in one hand. 'Let's hope we don't screw up' he'll say, taking a swig. The heifer's carcass convulses with the motion of the tractor's engine. As it is lifted off the ground a tide of dark blood runs from its nostrils.

This is going to make one hell of a mess. It's a two-man operation, even with the tractor doing most of the work.

John's next thought is *why*? Why would the PVN start killing his cattle? John has been farming on his own for more than two decades now, since he inherited Rare Bird in 1998 when he was 25 years of age. He's grown and raised everything. His cows are direct descendants of his father's herd, at one time the largest on the Peninsula. Cows that he first began milking when he was ten years old. What is it with these nosey idiots? Some people simply don't know what they're talking about and it's none of their business in the first place. The question 'why?' leaves his mind as he concludes that not one of these vegans would own a firearm, let alone possess the know-how or the gumption to fire one at point blank range into the head of a fully conscious animal. That would have been hard, even for him.

It was Helen, she is the culprit.

Rusty has told her about the calving paralysis and she has come around with something to prove. What exactly? That she may only be a woman, just the mother, but she is the better farmer? Did she bring Rusty with her to showboat? John turns and looks around the yard for any sign of them. Then he remembers, he is not alone on the farm any longer. Perhaps his sister knows something.

Before he returns to the house he finds a tarpaulin and covers the dead heifer up. Moving it and burying it will have to wait until after milking and not before Rusty has finished school. It won't do to have the other animals see this. It's not just the death of one of their own, it's the manner of death. If they set eyes upon the scene they will know their sister met a violent end.

Unsettled, or worse yet, distressed, cows is the last thing he needs.

While John waits for Rusty at the church bus stop it occurs to him that this is the very spot he first laid eyes on Helen. In those days it was only the Kettles and the Whiteleys who had school-age children living in Stormlea and their parents took turns to drop off or pick up all four kids. John didn't like Helen when they were children. They never got on. Later, when he began courting her, he apologised and told her that it was only because he liked her so much that he'd been so mean to her. At the time he said it he probably had even convinced himself that it was the truth. Anyway, she bought it, hook line and sinker. In hindsight, that was a catch he should have thrown back. If Helen hadn't have had blonde hair, been a natural blonde, it never would have happened. John liked blonde women. It wasn't just the blonde hair, Helen rode horses too. Always he had tried to find a girlfriend who was like his first love.

John is relieved when in the distance the bus appears to save him from the keen pain of regret. For John, the past was always better than the present is. If his memory shows bias, well then, it is what it is. There is nothing he can do about it.

"Have you heard from your aunt?" John asks Rusty as he gets into the car.

"Aunt who?"

"Ruth," says John. "Has she contacted you?"

"No," says Rusty. "Why, did she say something?"

"About what?"

"Nothing."

"I s'pose it was expecting too much that she would say goodbye to her own nephew. She's taken off, got your grandfather's shotgun with her. That would have been yours, you know?"

"Aunt Ruth stole grandpa's gun? But why?"

"Not before she killed one of the dairy cows. Should have known she had her eye on Dad's gun when she made a big deal about how I didn't sell it in the buyback."

"Wait! What do you mean she killed a cow? You mean like, slaughtered it?"

"Who knows with her." John refocuses his attention on the road ahead. "Anyway, she's up and left, your aunt, without saying goodbye to anyone. Robbed you of your inheritance. I'd report it stolen but she knows it's unregistered. Probably why she took it. I wanted to give it to you. I thought you should have it to remember me by."

"It's Grandpa's though."

"Yeah. My father, me, you," says John. "Where you come from, that'll mean something to you one day."

"Ok."

"Alright then."

A minute of silence passes between them and then Rusty asks, "Why did she go? Did she leave a note or anything?"

"No, no note. A while back she said something about having problems with the Irishman. He buggered off home to do some new arts project. I got the feeling they didn't have a very good holiday together down here. Maybe he saw the real her for the first time, who knows. She's left us in it though. We have to dig a hole this afternoon for the beast she shot. You can thank your aunt when she rings you at Christmas time."

Firewood is stacked neat inside the tank, the round ends like a packet of tailor-made cigarettes. The cows are still in the yard outside the dairy. They are always working. They're just like convicts. They study the guards. They study the gates. They study the locks. They study the keys. They study the patterns, the habits. They have nothing but time on their hands. Escapes could occur through a door, a window, the ventilation system or by breaking down the walls. John knows more than enough about the convict history of the area, about Port Arthur, to understand how it must feel.

"Can't we do it on the weekend?" asks Rusty.

"Good Lord! Anyone would think you'd grown up in the concrete jungle. The earth will be softest now. If we wait until the morning it will have turned rock hard overnight. We have to do it now. Ever heard of decomposition, Rusty?"

Like a full stop to end his declarative sentence as well as illustrate his point, a single march fly is already buzzing inside the stall, landing on the tarpaulin.

"See that?" says John. "By the weekend we'll have maggots."

"Gross."

"Gross is right."

The grass here comes into its own this time of year. During the summer months when it gets hot the grass is quite bitter but in autumn when the cold weather comes the grass becomes sweet and the cows relish it. John leads them back up to the paddock with his practised call, "Come onnn! Come onnn!"

They prefer to travel in single file along the path they

have worn through the grass. With the afternoon sun at his back, John casts a long shadow and the first animal to reach him at the gate stops and refuses to cross it. Cattle with calves are much harder to move because the calves don't understand how to be herded, they're like little children who can't speak, don't yet understand language. They learn it very quickly because its built into their genetic makeup but when they're young they don't herd out very well so it's difficult to drive the mothers who are sentinels watching closely over them. All around him the bellows of cows are blaring like big rig air horns.

As John is dragging the gate across the grass, out of the corner of his eye he glimpses movement in the back paddock opposite him. Turning and standing tall, he at first cannot believe his eyes.

Could it be?

But it is.

The elusive creature has got itself stuck in his fence. In that instant John is Captain Ahab, face to face with the white whale. Even at this distance John notes that it is strangely large for a fox. Still, it's a fox, no question.

John reacts quickly, doesn't waste a moment to secure the gate. Straight down the lane he runs, his arms pumping at his sides. By the time he reaches the dairy he is making a mental note to cut back on the smoking, his lungs burning with breathlessness.

Rusty is still in the shed when John blasts in to grab his rifle and wire cutters.

"Bring your shotgun," he shouts. "We've got it. It's alive and kicking."

The fox is suspended sideways in the barbed wire fence. Only its eyelids move, blinking slowly, until John cuts the first wire and its head bobs up and then down as if it was a puppet on strings. Frustratingly, he cannot see where the wires are connected but when he snips a second time the body spins around so that the fox is facing him. The head is bowed, eyes now staring at the ground. John reaches behind it, tapping a wire with the cutters trying to figure the puzzle out. Getting down on one knee, he cuts another wire. It snaps back like an elastic band but the fox doesn't move. Then he grabs a loose, high wire and threads it back through the fence before yanking on it. He yanks again, even harder.

Finally freed, the fox falls backwards onto the ground, rolls.

"Let it get out there a little bit," he tells Rusty. "Don't shoot it that close."

Things move fast. Someone hit the warp drive and John is trying to navigate through the blur. It's moment to moment. John jumps over the collapsed fence, the rifle held across his body, his finger behind the trigger. The grey clouds are right before his eyes like the smoke from a rollie when the wind is blowing into your face. With the light passing through it, the cloud smoke is a toxic blue. His throat burns, a lump the size of an apple cheek lodged there.

"Come on, you got it," yells John. "Go, go, fire!" John lowers his gaze to the ground and rushes without breaking into a run. "In the head!" he blurts out.

Quick steps.

Then John's eyes meet Rusty's and he swings up his rifle. Rusty stands with the school bag still slung across his body, the shotgun barrel pointed at a 45-degree angle at the ground. As John steps towards him, Rusty retreats. Toe to heel, step for step. Until he trips backwards, falling down. Quickly Rusty rises back up onto his knees, as if he'd just taken a boot to the chest. All John can hear is the wind like a sylph witness in the stand of trees at his back. John raises the rifle and takes aim. With a grunt he lunges at Rusty, his face so taut he can see his own nose as a sharp beak and the creased, sunburned bags under his eyes. Rusty's eyes are squeezed half shut and with his mouth closed he is snorting and then inflating and deflating his cheeks, blowing the air out over chapped lips. John recognises the patterned breathing of contractions from when Helen gave birth. Pant, pant, blow: *hee hee puh.* John bares his teeth and swings the rifle to his right.

Fires!

Rusty falls sideways onto his hands, putting his head to the ground. A moment after the gunshot John hears him whimper. Rusty's shotgun is in the grass perpendicular to his knees. Shunning John's gaze, Rusty rights himself. His blue eyes are glazed over, filled with tears. No fear or sadness shows on his face. Those eyes are held by steel cables; he has turned them in, as if to send his brain a different picture than the one right in front of him. A single tear, fat as a drop of blood, falls onto his cheekbone. John notices the fine moustache above his son's top lip quiver before his arms fall out at his sides and he topples over.

Across the paddock all John sees is the fox's tail like a chimney flue brush before it disappears into the sanctuary of the bush. The smoke clouds have turned to falling ash all around him and the sunshine is like cameras flashing in his face. To block the blinding light,

John puts his gun down and raises his hands in the air, like an innocent man.

John wakes flat on his back on the laundry floor. Shocked upright by the chilled concrete slab beneath him, he experiences tremors down to the bone. Shirtless, he stands bent over the concrete tub splashing warm water up into his face, rubbing it over his chest and down his arms. On the back of his right hand a few eyelashes are stuck like the short strokes made by a ballpoint pen left unlidded on a page.

John lifts his unwashed gingham shirt from the top of the washing machine, expecting to find his rifle. It's gone or it was never there. Looking out through the window John could swear he sees a silver gull flying almost camouflaged against the nimbus clouds. Then it is confirmed by the squawking as if the gull was fighting over the spine of a gutted fish. Occasionally you do see them at the farm. It is only a twenty-minute walk to water. Next a pair of parrots followed by a forest raven. The birds are flying fast. In the space of two minutes John notes six different species overhead. This happens in big swells but there is no sign of wind, only the faintest falling rain. Footsteps on the porch. John holds his breath and waits for knocking at the door. The landline starts ringing. While this could be a neighbour, somehow John knows it is the police. Helen has set them on him. John tiptoes to the door, puts his ear to it and breathes silently as he listens.

Morning. He's not answering his phone.

A pause.

Well you better tell her to meet us there.

Sure thing.

I'll see you in a few.

John can see the police uniform in his mind's eye. A shakedown to get full custody, that's what this will be. Like it matters. He can't deal with this bullshit now. He'll get back onto Rusty's firearms instruction when he gets his feet under him. Maybe he has been going about it the wrong way.

Before John casts out into the sunset he pulls his wallet from his back pocket and takes out the old polaroid of the bay mare. With a simple flick of his wrist he does himself a favour and lets it go. This notion of a change of life baby, a new start with the love of his life, it was only ever pie in the sky stuff, he can see that now. His own son, yes it's his responsibility but you don't take on somebody else's grief. Not that a child is grief exactly, but at least with your own offspring it is your sins. No member of his family has ever gone to jail, not since convict times, which can't be judged the same way. Blood spilled is history but blood is still blood and blood is thicker than water. Anyway, he's got to get back to work. If he doesn't come up with a new play against the PVN these other matters, including matters of the heart, are going to be what they call moot points.

John stands below the ridge, a third of the way down the slope, with a fish on the line.

"It's a big one," he says.

The image of the striped trumpeter decimated the day of the fog is still fresh in his mind and there is no way he is going to pull this one across the rocks and risk the same thing happening again. The fish and the ocean current are pulling him closer to the water and he scurries back and forth trying to find safe footing. Finally he jumps further down. With the rod straight once again, having narrowed the distance and relieved the tension on the line, he turns his head to survey the sets further out, gripping the rod handle between his clenched thighs. Holding the rod in his left hand he raises his right to shield his eyes from the glare. Across this plateau shallow pools of seawater have formed in the hollows—not a good sign. Beyond the tapered end of the rock the sea is reasonably flat so John turns his attention back to his reel. Taking one cautious step back he leans into the rod.

Reel, reel, reel, reel!

Then three quick small steps forward. It is the sound at his back from over the ridge that alerts John to a sudden surge and he responds as if someone had called out his name to warn him. Keeping hold of the rod one-handed, he pulls it behind him like a child flying a kite as he runs at an angle back up the slope. Away to the right-hand side a wave is broken by the top of the ridge and cascades down to meet a lesser wave thrown up directly in front.

"Shit," he says, taking his rod in both hands and bracing his feet in line with his shoulders, opening his stance. While his back is turned a second wave crashes over the ridge and inundates his position. The blue tackle box is swept away. "Shit!"

John lowers his centre of gravity, going into a shallow standing squat, as the water rushes around his ankles. It proves not to be a problem. The force of the water does not move him from the spot.

Come up, come up, come up, come up.

This time he runs parallel to the ridge towards the shore. The tackle box floats, bobbing in the whitewater a metre out.

No, forget about it! Forget about it!

John manoeuvres the rod around behind his head like the arm of a dance partner. Facing the seaward end head-on, the rod is now in his left hand with his arm stretched out while his right struggles for balance, unable to reach down to anything for support. The moment the water dissipates he swings the rod over his head as he turns into the ridge, switching it into his right hand, which is stretched straight, the elbow locking. With his gaze fixed on his feet he pounces from raised rock to raised rock, a safe distance from the slippery slope. The back of his shorts are soaked right up to the top of the pockets and at the front up into his crotch.

Let it go!

John ignores the inner voice, placing his right hand on his hip nonchalantly as his back muscles scream at him. It feels like he has definitely pulled something. John breathes through the pain as the sea settles back down below the outcrop. Holding his rod above the reel he strums at the taut line with his forefinger, plucks it with his fingernail.

Dead man walking.

John turns his head over his shoulder to check the ridge but there is no sign of spray.

"Lost the fish," he mutters.

One moment John is standing watching the setting sun, the next moment he is hit from behind, his legs give way under him and he feels his tailbone crack on rock. Then he can only see his feet in front of him, dragged fast by strong invisible hands out into the sea. Out of the blue, his survival instinct kicks in and with nothing else solid to catch hold of, John's fingers shoot up for his ears, beneath the brim of the beanie on his head, as if they were grab handles on a moving bus.

Chapter 16
Marina

Marina is bringing in washing from the clothesline when Moon tells her about the blue whale sighting by rock climbers nearby at The Paradiso.

While the news instantly lifts her spirits it does not surprise her. At this time of year the animals travel from feeding grounds in Antarctica to warmer waters. Tasmanian sightings are consistently made during late autumn and early winter as the whales move through these waters in search of late-blooming zooplankton, during their annual migration.

"Such amazing animals that don't impact our lives at all, yet they have to put up with our greed and pollution," says Moon. "Remember what happened to the last whale that came here?"

Marina remembers only too well. The sighting of a blue whale at the mouth of Pirates Bay was spoiled by the actions of a fishing group holding a bluefin tuna competition in the area. Even after being made aware and told to stay clear they trolled lures over it.

The largest animal on Earth, this individual would likely not be as big as the blue whales in Antarctica, which grow to over 30 metres. Still, it could be close to twice the size of a humpback. The colour of the animal alone is amazing and definitely worth seeing. If she is lucky enough to spot this animal it will be only the fourth time she has seen a blue whale in the area in all her years coming to the Peninsula.

Taking the washing basket inside and setting it down on a kitchen stool, it is with a shard of trepidation that Marina makes her way across the newly vacant stillness of the lounge room to study the framed Tasman Peninsula climbing and abseiling map on the wall. This was her father's possession, not one of the many rolled-up maps her mother had hoarded at their house in the Huon Valley. Marina had argued with Moon about whether or not it should be taken out of the frame to pack it, in case the glass broke during transit and damaged the print. Marina thought it a fruitless waste of time.

As she stands in front of the map and starts to look at it in detail she notices first the lowest points of the Peninsula, the tips of Cape Raoul on the left and Cape Pillar on the right. Almost directly between the two capes, straight upward, is Port Arthur. All of her concentration now focuses on the promontory from where the whale has been spotted. At first glance, it resembles a Tasmanian Devil's oversized head, complete with its iconic yawning gape—the angle Crescent Bay forms with its high dunes and rough waters opens powerfully to a bone crushing 80 degrees. Above the open jaw are the distinctive, sharp features of the face blackened by dolerite—the Hidden Face and the Mount Brown Main Face. Over this is the small, rounded ear, engorged with blood, of an agitated devil, aptly named The Furnace. On the back of the ear, like a tick burrowed in, a parasite, is

The Paradiso. In a fully confrontational pose, the devil faces the entrance to Port Arthur, at the ready.

From behind her comes the malignant squeal of the broken-locked screen door. Marina turns. "Come and tell me what this looks like to you," she says.

"Huh?" replies Moon as Marina takes the map off the wall and holds it face up, balanced on her pelvic bone.

As he looks at the map beneath the glass Moon says, "Can you be more specific?"

"Where the rock climbers saw the whale," she says, pointing with her nose. "That right there, what does that look like to you? Does it remind you of anything?"

"Why, is it important?" Moon continues to study the map, squinting behind his eyeglasses.

"Not in the least."

Then he puts his hands in his pockets and looks instead into her face, unnerving her.

"You're giving up?" she says, tilting the frame back towards herself protectively.

"You said it's not important."

"It's not."

"But it obviously is to you," says Moon. "Is it important as a location on a map, or as something else?"

"I'm sorry but I'm going to have to leave you alone for a little while," she responds. "I'll be back in an hour, maybe only half."

"I'll come with you," he says. "I'd like to see it too."

"Not to be rude, but I think I'd rather go alone."

"I understand, cetaceans are important to you," says Moon.

"I'll try to get a picture of the whale for you. Don't worry, I'm only going down to the beach. There's no chance of me falling off a cliff taking a selfie."

"That's not funny," he replies.

Moon reaches to take the map from her but she is reluctant to relinquish it.

"Are you ever going to tell me what really happened to the hens?" says Moon, peering over his eyeglasses at her. "I saw the damage to the coup where something bit right through the metal wire. I know Yoko and Ono didn't just escape because you left the gate open."

Marina weighs her options while looking at her brother. Is it fear, uncertainty, stress or aggression she is feeling?

"Mari," says Moon, putting a reassuring hand on her shoulder. "It's OK. You can talk to me, you know."

Marina sets the map down on the floor, facing it against the wall.

As she is leaving she turns back and finds Moon has picked it up, turned it over on his bent knee and begun to meticulously remove it from the frame with his one good hand.

As the sun sets over Eaglehawk Bay, rows of golden stripes span the blue water. 'Christ's bruises', is how her mother referred to the startling light effect. Her mother's voice comes to life quoting scripture in her ear:

But he was wounded for our transgressions, he was bruised for our iniquities: the chastisement of our peace was upon him; and with his stripes we are healed.

It is because of the whale, perhaps, that for the very first time, this familiar sight reminds Marina of the southern lights in Antarctica—one night, in particular. Lying in her bunk, almost asleep, she was roused by a fellow crewmember who told her that an aurora was visible from the deck, not a good display, probably not worth getting up for. Despite this dismissal of the phenomenon, something urged her to act. All day she had observed only the ice flows cartwheeling by the ship. What Marina discovered outside was that the solar wind and magnetic fields had produced a thicket of tiny shooting stars, a vertically striped curtain of brilliant white stretching across most of the southern sky. Marina was at once enraptured. In an awed whisper, she uttered, 'Wow', over and over again. Ever since, she has been an avid southern lights chaser.

Beneath a cloud-packed and layered realm Marina stands alone on the isthmus and sees the ashes of her mother's body shed on the sea, on the combers far out. This is it, the spot to tip the amphora urn.

In the distance the flat wet rocks of the tessellated pavement are mirrored tiles reflecting sublime shades of pink whilst beside them the sea is superficially fiery orange.

A pair of jet skis race across Pirates Bay, on the opposite side of the isthmus, turning out their rear ends, sending up spray.

Accelerate—break!—accelerate.

Each rider stands up in his seat, gripping handle bars like the horns of a bucking bull. The jet skis are as dissonant as a pair of dirt bikes tearing up the beach. No lifeguards patrol Eaglehawk Neck and so the hooligans get away with it.

Strolling down onto the beach, Marina turns her attention to a couple of men running towards the water. They wear identical black knee-length swimming shorts. One's body is more bronzed until his feet kick up fine clouds of sand in his wake to reveal soles white as the undersides of pipi shells. As soon as the water is deep enough, despite the intimidating temperature, they dive in and begin swimming shoulder to shoulder straight out towards the horizon.

In the rising wind, Marina's polyester blouse flaps like a sail at her back. A beach wind farm here would reap a good harvest. Although they ate a late lunch, she is already planning a dinner of potato and sauerkraut salad. More nutritious food is just what Moon needs. She recalls Captain Cook had kept the crew of the First Fleet from succumbing to scurvy with tins of sauerkraut, tricking them by offering it to the officers first so that it was mistaken for a delicacy.

Back on the street behind her there is a sudden explosion. Marina throws her hands over her head and crouches to the sand. A pacific black duck lifts off the water. Its dark form in flight takes Marina back to Moulting Lagoon. Immediately her heart-rate escalates and she flinches at the sound, the smell, of phantom gunshots. Marina closes her eyes against the sight of wounded birds snatched up by the hunters only to have their necks wrung. When she stands and turns to face the street she finds the culprit: a biker with long grey hair and a matching beard, wearing red gloves, a black leather jacket and dungarees, simply starting his motorcycle engine. Shaken, Marina hastens away from the Blowhole end of the beach, following the shoreline of Pirates Bay. Ahead of her, a pair of Red-capped Dotterels sprint and fly around each other like magnets attracting then repelling. Over at the outcrop there is someone rock fishing without a life jacket. The ocean here is treacherous and people think they are impervious to danger. Marina wonders if the Venetian's body will ever be recovered. It is madness. They globe trot and then come to die on Tasman Peninsula. The bodies generally reappeared on the beach within a few days. She wonders too if the family of the Venetian woman has questions. 'I'm very sorry' she would tell them, 'Tasman Peninsula is a very dangerous place. I know.' And then, would she strip naked and unpack her own memory baggage, like the personal belongings of a dead person returned to their loved ones, for them to sort through? Or, would she excuse herself?

The sound of the weather helicopter overhead shifts Marina's thoughts. After Moon was wounded, in the corridor of the hospital she had walked a moment with one of the paramedics from the scene. 'Do you have a cigarette?' the paramedic asked her. Marina gave her a sideways glance, surprised that a health professional was a smoker. 'No'. A trail of tiny star tattoos adorned the paramedic's neck. 'You have amazingly gorgeous eyes' the paramedic said. A compliment Marina had heard so many times it had lost meaning. 'They remind me of a dog' the paramedic said and then quickly added 'a husky, I mean. Siberian blue, that's what colour they are, your eyes'. This had made Marina relent, even smile. 'Your stars are pretty too'.

Gazing out to sea, Marina wishes she could have inherited *Imago* from her mother's estate. The sound of the harbour still haunts her. In the wind, the masts of docked yachts created incessant noise like the banging of prisoners' empty tin cups against cell bars. She is restless. Even a dinghy would do, just to get a little way off the coast. Never seasick—perhaps this is one of her superpowers—she longs for the bounce of the waves beneath her seat.

The propeller blades of that phantom wind farm are going into overdrive. Squalls are heading inland from the east. The bronzed swimmers exit the water from a spot much further down the beach, the current having dragged them quicker than she expected. On the wet sand an adult play-fights a child, each of them making sound effects as they exchange blows that don't connect.

"You lost!" the boy shouts at the man who spins him around by one arm before lifting him up onto his shoulders.

The high-pitched voice of a female draws Marina's attention. "We must always leave shells on the beach."

Dutifully a little girl bends to set her small treasure back down on the sand.

As the grey sky is closing in on Marina, like an oversized itchy sweater, she spots something fifty metres out to sea.

A frolicking seal?

The next moment she sees a pair of arms rise up above the black bobbing head and begin waving frantically at the beach. The beanie is torn off by a crashing wave. Marina realises what has happened even before she glances over at the outcrop to see that the rock fisherman is gone.

By the time her eyes return to the drowning man he is punching down at the surface, jabbing his fists into the churning water. This bout isn't going to last long.

Marina bends over to rip off her shoes and socks, never taking her eyes from the fisherman losing his fight with the sea. With the back of her right hand she wipes off her lipstick. Inhaling and holding her breath she presses a full set of fingertips into the squeaky clean sand. As if she has heard the sound and seen the smoke of the starting pistol, she exhales and takes off in a sprint for the shoreline.

Underwater, Marina pays close attention to the light that surrounds her, but what was she focused on only a moment ago? Right now, she sees photons, plentiful and dense, below the surface. The light has momentum, beams so intense she can feel them. Marina does not understand where it is coming from for the sun has just set and the moon not yet risen. Thick blades of white, undulating light, flexible as javelins, are anchored to the seafloor. From each blade, fronds grow like the beckoning fingers of countless hands.

In complete control of the moment, Marina chooses one stimulus to the exclusion of all others.

The light is of a clear, easy brightness, and near its centre the most radiant.

First, her body becomes silent. And then, she is nothing more than her clothing. Slowly sinking, sleeves extend above the neck hole of her shirt, maintaining a gently curved line, shoulders stay down, collar turns up and the legs of her slacks bow beneath a canvas belt.

When finally Marina breathes, all of the light is sucked out of the sea.

Chapter 17
Ruth

The automated glass doors of the Melbourne International Airport slide open. Ruth enters the concourse and takes a deep breath of the temperately controlled air. Although this is *Departures* she feels overwhelming relief, like she has at last arrived.

Beyond security, on the way to the gate—dwarfed by an enormous window overlooking the tarmac—Ruth passes a newsagent and for a moment considers buying a book to read on her long journey but the trashy paperback novels are as unappealing as the recycled air and artificial lighting of the terminal. Instead she relaxes into a waiting chair and pulls out her phone, brings up her itinerary to scan the string of flights: Melbourne to Singapore; Singapore to London; and, London to Belfast. In all, just under twenty-six hours travel time.

Then, checking the news, Ruth frowns in consternation. She opens the full story and reads it closely.

The search has resumed for missing Tasmanian swimmer Marina Aquilina, who is feared drowned off Tasmania's south-east coast.

Two police boats and a dive team are scouring waters around Eaglehawk Neck after Ms Aquilina, 37, vanished while swimming on Sunday. The swimmer is understood to have become caught in large and powerful surf conditions south of the Blowhole.

A second person, a rock fisherman, was caught in the same swell but managed to get himself to shore.

"The scenario appears to be that a female swimmer tried to assist the rock fisherman but was unable to pull him from the surf," Tasmanian Police Inspector Ken Gideon said.

Short of breath, Ruth immediately brings up her contacts list and calls John's mobile, with only one thought in her head:

Billy Barkers.

The call goes straight to voicemail.

For a brief moment, Ruth flashes back to the feeling of helplessness, the sense of drowning in distance, the broad but shallow Bass Strait like the cold glass television screen separating her from the news the night of the massacre. Ruth was in her first semester of university on the mainland and what would turn out to be her only semester studying law. Two weeks after the Easter break she had just handed in her first assignment. The ridiculous contract law scenario is something she will never forget. A painter and a pianist and a daughter's wedding. It ended with a scene of devastation, a house strewn with the shattered wreckage of a grand piano. *Did a conversation support a contract? Was there sufficient consideration?* Ruth heard the news of the shootings and watched the aftermath unfold from the suffocating safety of her residential college. On the small, fuzzy screen, with its poor reception like foul weather, the events appeared squally and seemed completely removed from reality. The police had no names at that stage, or at least were giving none away. On the Peninsula, though, telephones rang, relaying the news from individual to individual, hours before the official list of the dead, and wounded, was made public. As each person picked up the receiver it was like black dominoes falling.

Ruth takes a long, slow breath in through her nose. First her lower lungs fill, then her upper lungs. She holds this breath to the count of three. Exhales slowly through pursed lips. By taking control of her breathing, Ruth relaxes enough to be able to tune back into the story and search for further information there.

Police are now treating the search as a body recovery mission and hold little hope Ms Aquilina is alive.

Her devastated family, as well as members of the Sea Shepherd Conservation Society, joined authorities in the extensive sea and air search on Tasman Peninsula.

Ms Aquilina, from Sydney, was last seen on Sunday afternoon when she set off from Doo Town, located 80km south of Hobart.

Now it hits Ruth. Doo Town. *Doo-No-Harm.* It's the Quaker family, the *Old Quacker* John called the veteran duck rescuer. It was the *Old Quacker's* son who was wounded during the accident at Moulting Lagoon. Aquilina, it's the surname. This missing swimmer—Ruth searches back up for her name—Ms Aquilina, Marina, Marina Aquilina, 37 years old—is the sister?

Authorities widened the search area yesterday after examining drift patterns. Police believe the Executive Senior Manager drowned in freezing Pirates Bay waters.

Divers are focused on body recovery today.

"You can't say it's completely impossible, but as far as I'm concerned the likelihood is she has drowned and her body has submerged," Inspector Gideon said. "We're looking at the recovery of a body."

Relatives were briefed by police. "They are coping reasonably well considering the circumstances," the officer said.

"In the meantime we urge people to take care along the coast. We are imploring people to swim only at patrolled locations, in between the red and yellow flags," he said. "And if you are going to fish off rocks in spite of the warnings at least wear a life jacket."

Large swell and king tides continue to batter the Tasman Peninsula coastline.

Speaking on behalf of her devastated family, her brother and fellow animal rights activist, Moon Aquilina, said, "If she wasn't such a strong swimmer then she wouldn't have gone in but she is a very strong swimmer and she has been trained how to survive in cold water. My sister risked her life for a complete stranger because she didn't have a choice. Compassion."

More relatives flew to Tasmania last night.

Friends have described Ms Aquilina as having "a great deal of conviction".

Before trying John's landline, Ruth leans back in her chair and takes a minute to let it all sink in.

This woman, Marina, had a great deal of conviction—this much is clear. The brother is wrong, though. Marina didn't risk her life for a complete stranger; she has most likely drowned risking her life for someone who would not have gone into the water for her. Ruth knows that for a fact.

Imagine it, facing a life-threatening situation, where

one's courage is being tested to the full, one's capability for compassion towards a fellow human being. Marina not only entered the water, she remained and fought for John, fought with John, against the sea. What a cruel irony that the saviour should perish while the undeserving survives.

Ruth calls Rare Bird Farm but it rings out. She continues to try both numbers until the moment she hears her final boarding call and must switch off her phone.

On the flight to Singapore, Ruth is seated beside a young couple who cannot stop touching one another. New love. The woman has an Australian accent while the man is a Scot. When they order sparkling wine, they toast and sip in unison, as if celebrating. Eager to bask in their glow, nearby passengers strike up conversations with them and the couple is happy to engage.

Ruth has never felt so alone.

I wandered lonely as a cloud.

Unexpectedly, she finds herself thinking about the Port Arthur gunman. It came out, after the shootings, that he used to book long distant flights, using the fortune he inherited from the Tattersalls heiress, just for the company. On an international flight the stranger who happened to be seated beside him was literally a captive audience. A trick he must have learned at some point. A simple trick really, a child's trick. After criss-crossing the world many times over, the Public Trustee that managed his money put an end to the trips. Would he really have kept flying until the money ran out, she wonders? Did companionship become an addiction for him?

This thought is the cue for a sudden, involuntary memory recall:

It was Summer holidays and whenever he wasn't doing chores around the farm John would ride his bike to Carnarvon Bay. Some days their mother made it a condition that he take Ruth with him.

While the shackies played with their row boats, spearguns and surfboards, the locals knew how to make their own fun like stealing waxed cardboard real estate signs from the fences of different properties and taking the Dog Bark Road shortcut to Crescent Beach. They would run up the tall sand dunes and from the top, standing between the coast-clinging sheoaks, get a view of The Blade of Cape Pillar in the distance. They used the signs as toboggans to ride down the golden dunes. They could go weeks without seeing another living soul at Crescent Beach. It was their secret place.

At Carnarvon Bay on the school holidays there were loads of other kids around all the time, thirty sometimes and at least a dozen regulars.

Staring at the horizon from the beach was like peering into an unlit window—sea to sky glass. Lightning flickering, a switch turned on, filament catching but not taking and then blown out. An unstable, inconsistent stream of electricity flowing through the filament. Perhaps a loose socket.

Flicker, flash then blink.

Darkness.

A moment later, thunder!

While they roasted marshmallows around the usual dusk bonfire, John sat polishing a piece of driftwood until it shone like a pistol and he had split open the worn elbows of his thrift store denim jacket.

"Hey, are you playing a game?"

Ruth recognised the much older boy carrying a

speargun, wearing a head to toe black wetsuit.

"Erm ... I don't think so," said Ruth.

It was easy to forget that the girl John liked was Rubber Lips's sister. She was normal. Just another one of the shackies whose families owned holiday homes at Carnarvon Bay.

"Oh," he said. "If you were, I would join you, or, I don't know. It's a bit smelly after a while, this beach."

"Now can you see what I need the firewood for?" said Robin Whiteley.

"Yeah, man," said John. "It's a great bonfire. You nailed it."

Silver gulls fed on flying insects in the dying light. At a distance it appeared as iron filings flung into the sky, sporadically attracting or repelling each other as if the air currents produced a magnetic field.

"I don't think they like you," said Ruth finally.

"I've got friends under the water," he said.

"Your friends are in the water?"

"Sea," he said. "They're my friends ... mmm ... we scuba dive. Dad is taking me out. We're gonna start the little seagull engine up in a minute."

Ruth rubs the heels of her palms in her sore, prematurely dried out eyes. Closing them, she forces the past from her mind, for the moment at least, until she is reunited with Seamus. She invites in only the dull whine of the engines.

When the plane lands in Singapore and begins to taxi to the gate, Ruth pulls out her phone in anticipation.

Ding.

The bell tells all on board that it's safe to unbuckle and stand up. Ruth holds the phone beneath her chin as she springs up out of her seat and opens the overhead locker.

Inside the Singapore Changi Airport, with other passengers Ruth reaches a point on the way that forks: connecting flights go left while; baggage collections go right. At this crossroads Ruth pauses to call John's landline. After only two rings she hears what she thinks is her nephew's voice at the other end of the line.

"Rusty?"

There is no reply.

"Rusty?"

Again, silence at the other end of the line. About to tell him 'It's your Aunt Ruth' she finally gets a response.

Dad's gonna be alright. They're keeping him in one more night ... for observation. Mum's gone back up there to take him some clothes.

The line goes dead.

Has he hung up? Is it the connection?

So it was John, she knew it. But he's OK, John is going to be OK.

By the flight to London it feels as though Ruth has gone into another dimension outside of normal space and time. While other passengers move freely about the cabin, some carrying crying babies, others sucking on nicotine inhalers or waiting for the toilets, she huddles beneath a blanket wearing her headphones, ever watchful for the flight attendant who will bring her next meal. As she sits and watches movie after movie, the scenes like waves rolling onto shore, she tries not to check the time or bring the flight path up on the screen in the headrest in front of her. When finally she does and finds they are flying over Poland it is a sickening sensation to know that in the darkness below is a real place, the physical sites of evil and suffering, not just the scenes in films or the stuff of nightmares. Ruth's fingertips reach to touch the inside of the cold, frosted window; her hand jumps back, as if from a live electric fence.

When sleep takes her, she is plagued by terrible visions of giant sea monsters.

The way to the departure gate for the trip to Belfast feels like a path in a labyrinth. As it goes on and on, and Ruth further and further in, she begins to fear that she will miss the flight. As she hurries she does her best to read the news updates on the shuddering screen of her phone.

Divers find dead body in SS Nord near Fortescue Bay

Police are investigating whether a body found by search and rescue divers inside the wreck of SS Nord may be a woman missing since February.

Police spokesman Sergeant Don Livingstone said that due to predation and tissue loss, which could be the result of boat strike or shark attack, it was unclear how long the deceased female had been in the water.

"The body will be taken to the coroners office to establish the female's identity," Sgt Livingstone said.

Police said DNA tests would need to be completed to help identify the woman.

Police are believed to be examining whether it is the body of Venice woman Pietra Toniolo, 27, who disappeared on February 9 while on a Three Capes Walk hiking tour.

Last month, Miss Toniolo's father told the Bayside Leader he believed his daughter was the victim of a tragic accident.

Ruth finds herself torn, hoping that it is the body of Pietra that has been found. The missing tourist's family have already come to a place of acceptance. This other woman, the good Samaritan, her family is still living in hope, have only just received the news. It is a disconcerting feeling, to say the least, hoping for the life of one person when it means dooming another.

Ruth spares a thought for the family of *Pi-et-ra*, overseas.

Ruth knows a little about The Nord. It struck on the same uncharted rocks that sank the steamship Tasman before it. It's the same spot where the fishermen drowned during the tuna fishing competition in 2006 and the site of the miracle rescue of the young men from their capsized boat while she and Seamus were staying at Fortescue Bay. What a place for the woman's body—whether it turned out to be the missing Italian tourist or, this good Samaritan, Marina, who went to her brother's rescue—to be discovered. These tragedies deposit fresh layers of trauma on Tasman Peninsula.

Once on board the plane, Ruth is seated in 1A as if fate has conspired with the airline to get her to the ground again as quickly as possible. From her window seat at the front of the cabin she can see reflected in the glass of the jet bridge door the profiles of the first officer and pilot in the cockpit. The Irish accents of the cabin crew are a comfort, making her feel immediately closer to Seamus.

Almost there.

When the plane reaches its cruising altitude over the Irish Sea, the turbines of an offshore wind farm appear far below, like the uniform white crosses of a war grave cemetery.

Mercifully, it is a short flight.

As the plane descends and circles over Belfast Harbour, with a thrill Ruth recognises the giant yellow gantry cranes. Seamus has often spoken about the twins, Samson and Goliath, which dominate the city skyline. Ruth's pupils, where the colour enters, are camera-like lenses and inside her eyeballs the yellow is translated into images. Intermingled with the flower heads of Highcroft's daffodils and a canopy of Stormlea's blossoming blackwoods. Ruth sees the fluorescence visible in a spirit level and the Sunlight in stockpiled bars of soap.

A major motorway forms a distinct U-bend around one end of the port. The water of the circuit board-like harbour flows into the wide expanse of Belfast Lough and then east back into the Irish Sea.

The pilot's voice comes over the loudspeaker.

It's a warm and sunny sixteen degrees in Belfast this morning.

Ruth raises an eyebrow. Sixteen degrees is supposed to be warm for mid-summer? Fortunately, she is coming off the back of a winter in the Tasmanian wilderness.

For those passengers seated on the left-hand side of the aircraft if you look out of your window now you'll see below us the Titanic Quarter. Harland and Wolff have been building ships on the dry dock since 1791, most famously it's the birthplace of the RMS Titanic. The quarter's undergone major development in recent years, all starting with the lead up to the Centennial of Titanic back in 2012. I'll repeat what the locals will tell you, 'She was alright when she left here!'

A murmur of laughter floats through the cabin.

When the airliner's landing gear deploys, reminding passengers that their own vessel has not yet arrived safely at its final destination, in the seats beside her a mother takes a child's hand then begins to hum softly to him. Alone, Ruth takes her own personal talisman, the Western Union telegram, from her handbag beneath the seat in front. With the little yellow piece of paper pressed between her palms, she stares out of her window.

Now something interferes with the view of the city below: a tiny hole in the innermost pane near the bottom corner, a hollowed-out snowflake of frost formed near it. As she focuses on the breather hole Ruth tries to recall the name of the famous tune the band played as Titanic sank. The title, it's right there on the tip of her tongue.

About the Author

Amy Barker holds degrees in English Literature and Creative Writing. Her debut novel ***Omega Park*** won the 2008 Queensland Premier's Literary Award for Best Emerging Author, was shortlisted for the 2010 FAW (Fellowship of Australian Writers) Christina Stead Award for fiction and was Winner of the 2012 IBBY (International Board on Books for Young People) Ena Noël Award.

Paradise Earth is Amy's second novel. It won the 2013 DJ 'Dinny' O'Hearn Memorial Fellowship and for six months she was writer in residence at the Australian Centre, University of Melbourne, where she mentored undergraduate and postgraduate creative writing students. Amy has undertaken residencies at Varuna The National Writers' House, the Tyrone Guthrie Centre for professional artists in Ireland, and most recently, she had a three-month writing stint in a cell at Old Melbourne Gaol, which like Port Arthur, is a Pentonville model prison.

Amy lives in Melbourne.

Amy Barker is uniquely poised to write about the terrible events from Port Arthur 1996. While not at Port Arthur itself on the day of the massacre, she spent her formative years on the Tasman Peninsula, in close association with both victims and members of the gunman's family. Barker and Stormbird Press offer our deepest condolences to everyone who lost someone on that tragic day. While the backdrop of the gunman and the event are real, the depiction of characters in Paradise Earth are fictional, and not intended to mirror anyone living or passed. It is our hope that this work may help to find the words to commemorate an unspeakable tragedy.

An Invitation from Stormbird Press

Stories about our world, and our relationship with nature, have been told by people for thousands of years. It is how we share our moral tales, empower ourselves with knowledge, and pass wisdom to the future.

Our titles all passionately communicate people's reverence, wisdom, and inspiration about the places, plants and animals, habitats and ecosystems, of our shared home—*Earth*. They whisper where we've been and foretell where we are going.

Around campfires and hearths, beside streams, across tundras, under the shadow of mountains or the wide branches of mighty trees, and in the pages of Stormbird's books, people's stories and wisdom carry like feathers in the wind.

Join us and become part of our community of eco-book-lovers.

We will keep you up to date with our latest catalogue, give you access to new releases before they arrive in bookstores, give you chances to win signed editions, and much more.

www.StormbirdPress.com